채명희 그림에세이

살며 생각하며 그리며

Living, Thinking, Painting
Painting Essays by Myonghi Chai

살며 생각하며 그리며

발행일   2025년 12월 10일

지은이   채명희
펴낸이   손형국
펴낸곳   (주)북랩

출판등록   2004. 12. 1(제2012-000051호)
주소   서울특별시 금천구 가산디지털 1로 168, 우림라이온스밸리 B동 B111호, B113~115호
홈페이지   www.book.co.kr
전화번호   (02)2026-5777   팩스   (02)3159-9637

ISBN   979-11-7224-973-1 03810 (종이책)   979-11-7224-974-8 05810 (전자책)

작가 연락처 문의 ▸ ask.book.co.kr

전용 게시판에 문의를 남기시면 저자에게 직접 전달됩니다.

(주)북랩 성공출판의 파트너

북랩 홈페이지와 SNS에서 다양한 출판 솔루션을 만나 보세요!

홈페이지 book.co.kr   •   **블로그** blog.naver.com/essaybook   •   **출판문의** text@book.co.kr
카톡채널 북랩

채명희 그림에세이

Living 살며
Thinking 생각하며
Painting 그리며

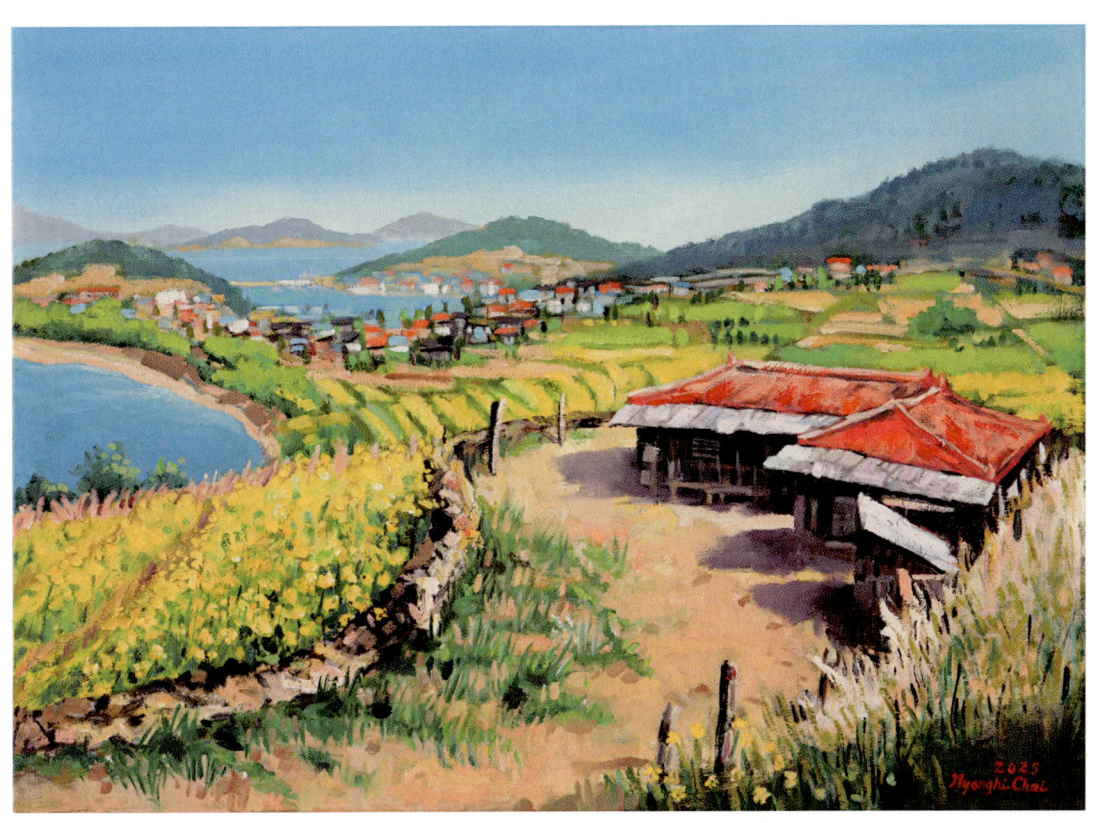

북랩

_____ 님께

당신의 오늘이 어제보다 낫기를 기원합니다.

저자 채명희

To _____

May your today be better than yesterday.

Myonghi Chai

나의 어머니 고(故) 정영자(1942-1993)님과
시어머니 고(故) 이길님(1941-2014)님께 바칩니다

In loving memory of my mother, Yongja Jung (1942–1993),

and my mother-in-law, Gilnim Lee (1941–2014)

여행의 서정과 삶의 빛

채명희의 회화는 일상과 여행의 기록을 감각의 회복으로 담아낸다. 그의 작업은 장소에서 느낀 공기의 온도와 빛의 결을 포착해, 그것을 시간의 한 단면으로 재구성한다. 정지된 듯한 풍경들은 아름답게 시각화되어 우리네 일상 속 쉼표처럼 다가오며, 그 기억들이 화면 전체에 부드럽게 스며든다.

그는 명확한 형태보다 빛의 흔적에 집중한다. 그 색채들은 현실보다 한층 더 서정적인 세계를 만들고, 그녀만의 감성으로 확장된 현실 속에는 기억과 감정이 뒤섞인 풍경이 가득하다.

관람자는 작품 속에서 마치 어디론가 다녀온 듯한 감정에 잠기고, 이내 삶의 여백을 느낀다. 그의 회화는 존재에 따뜻함을 비추는 빛의 상징으로서, 어둠이 아닌 빛을 가슴으로 받아들이게 하는 휴식의 공간이 된다.

그녀의 작업은 단순한 머무름의 예술이 아니라, 온몸으로 받아들인 낯선 아름다움과 평온함을 고요히 쌓아 올린 시간의 흔적이다.

오랜 세월 후학을 길러온 시간을 뒤로 하고, 그간의 작품과 따뜻한 글을 한 권에 엮은 이번 출판을 진심으로 축하드린다.

강남구
서양화가

The Lyric of Journey and the Light of Life

Myonghi Chai's paintings embody the recovery of the senses—a poetic rendering of everyday life and her journeys. In her work, she captures the subtle temperature of the air and the delicate texture of light within each place, recomposing them into a single moment in time.

The landscapes, seemingly still, are beautifully visualized, approaching us like gentle pauses in daily life, as memories softly pervade the canvas.

Rather than focusing on distinct forms, she traces the lingering movement of light. Her colors create a world more lyrical than reality itself—a world expanded by her own sensibility, where memory and emotion intertwine.

Her paintings evoke in the viewer a sense of having journeyed somewhere far, returning with a renewed awareness of life's quiet margins. Each canvas becomes a space of rest—a symbol of light embracing existence, not the darkness.

Her art is not one of mere stillness, but a serene accumulation of time, of unfamiliar beauty and tranquility absorbed fully through body and soul.

Now, setting aside her long years of teaching, she gathers her paintings and warm essays into this volume. I offer my heartfelt congratulations on its publication.

Nam-gu Kang

Oil Painter

(Translated by Myonghi Chai)

연구실 문 하나를 사이에 두고 23년을 함께 지냈습니다. 처음에는 "좋은 분이 오셨구나" 생각했지만, 세월이 흐를수록 "참 대단한 분이구나" 하는 생각이 들 때가 한두 번이 아니었습니다.

그와 나눈 많은 대화를 통해 그의 생각의 깊이와 삶의 방향을 자연스레 엿볼 수 있었지요. 그는 분명 고운 품성과 곧은 인격을 지닌 사람입니다. 자신의 자리를 묵묵히 지키며, 스스로의 가치를 조용히 높여가는 이입니다.

무엇보다 그는 편안한 침묵보다는 불편한 진실을 택할 줄 아는 용기를 지녔습니다. 세상이 때로는 허망한 열정으로 우리를 몰아세워도, 그는 자신이 가야 할 길을 끝내 잃지 않았습니다.

언젠가부터 그는 붓을 잡고 그림을 그리기 시작했고, 그의 열정은 빛나는 불꽃처럼 타올랐죠. 그때 깨달았습니다. 그가 진도 출신이라는 것을—문인들의 유배지이자, 시와 서화의 향기로 물든 그 땅의 기운이 그의 안에도 흐르고 있음을.

그림을 그린다는 것은 자신의 내면으로 깊이 들어가 영혼과 대화하는 일입니다. 그의 그림과 글에는 그러한 영혼의 숨결이 깃들어 있습니다. 그의 맑은 마음은, 그의 예술을 통해 누구나 느낄 수 있을 것입니다.

파울로 코엘료는 말했습니다. "우리는 필요한 순간, 언제든 길을 바꿀 능력이 있다"고. 그는 그 말의 살아 있는 증언자입니다. 삶을 예술로 빚어내는 사람, 그가 앞으로도 많은 이들의 삶을 예술로 물들이리라 믿습니다.

문학박사 김성식
칼럼니스트·조선이공대학교 명예교수

We worked in neighboring offices for twenty-three years. At first, I thought, "*What a kind person she is.*" But as time passed, I often found myself thinking, "*What an extraordinary person she truly is.*"

Through our many conversations, I came to glimpse the depth of her thought and the direction of her life. She is a person of gentle virtue and upright character—one who keeps her place with quiet strength, and steadily lifts her own worth without pretense.

Above all, she has the courage to choose uncomfortable truth over easy silence. Even when the world urged us hollow passions, she never lost sight of her path.

When she began to paint, her passion flared like a bright flame. Then I understood—she was from Jindo, a land once known as a place of exile for poets and scholars, steeped in the fragrance of poetry, painting, and calligraphy. That same spirit lives in her still.

To paint is to journey inward and commune with the soul. In her paintings and writings, the breath of that soul is unmistakable. Her pure heart can be felt by anyone who meets her art.

Paulo Coelho once wrote, "At every moment of our lives, we have the power to choose the road we take." She is living proof of that truth—one who shapes life itself into art. I believe she will continue to color many lives with her art.

Ph.D. *Sungsik Kim*

Columnist and Professor Emeritus

Chosun College of Science & Technology

(Translated by Myonghi Chai)

친구를 떠올리면 먼저 아름다운 미소와 따뜻한 마음이 떠오릅니다. 대학을 졸업하고 긴 시간이 흘렀어도, 만나면 우리는 금세 그때로 돌아갑니다. 마음 놓고 웃고, 스스럼없이 이야기할 수 있는 친구가 있음이 늘 감사합니다.

언젠가 추억을 품은 친구들과 알바스텔라를 찾았습니다. 따로 꾸민 방에 그림이 가득했고, 수상작도 여럿 있었습니다. 그 앞에 서니, 제 마음에도 알 수 없는 뿌듯함이 차올랐습니다. 처음엔 '취미'라 여겼습니다. 그러나 어느새 십여 년. 작품은 해가 갈수록 깊어졌고, 저는 놀라움을 감출 수 없었습니다. 은퇴 이후 더 빛나는 전성기를 맞아, 친구가, 멋진 화가, 참된 예술가로 살아갈 모습을 저는 선하게 봅니다.

그림 옆에 제목이 놓이면 관람자는 상상의 날개를 펴지요. 그러나 이 그림 에세이집은 시(詩)가 곁들여 있어, 작가와의 소통이 더 쉽고, 더 깊습니다. 명희는 순수한 영혼으로 자연을 바라봅니다. 창조 질서 안에서 피조물로서의 자리를 분명히 알고, 유한한 생을 아름답게 완주하고자 하는 소망을 작품에 담습니다. 친구는 시대의 양심을 품고, 책임을 외면하지 않고 있습니다.

바라기는, 명희의 소망처럼—두 그루 나무가 한 뿌리로 이어진 대 흥사 연리근처럼, 부군과 함께 영원한 사랑의 약속을 이루며 인생 의 아름다운 잔치를 계속 펼쳐가길 축복합니다.

이 책이 많은 이들의 하루에 평안과 위로가 되기를 기도합니다.

박혜원
캐나다 리빙스톤교회 협력목사
난민 선교사

When I think of my friend Myonghi, I first recall her beautiful smile and warm heart. Though many years have passed since college, whenever we meet, we slip back as if we were right back there—free to laugh and talk with ease. I'm always grateful for such a friend.

I remember visiting Alba Stella with friends who shared a bundle of memories. In a room carefully arranged, her paintings filled the walls—some even prize-winning pieces, which drew me closer. Standing before them, I felt a quiet pride rise up within me. At first, I had thought painting was merely her hobby. But now, more than a decade later, her work continues to deepen and mature. I can easily imagine her entering an even brighter season after retirement— continuing to flourish as a fine painter, a true artist.

Usually, a painting's title invites the viewer's imagination to unfurl. Yet this art book feels different: each work is accompanied by words—poems that open a deeper dialogue with the artist, more easily. Myonghi sees nature with a pure and contemplative heart.

Within the Creator's order, she understands her place as a created being, and she hopes to complete her finite journey with beauty and grace. She also carries the conscience of her time and a keen sense of responsibility.

My hope and blessing is that—as in her own wish, like the intertwined-rooted trees at Daeheungsa Temple—she and her husband may fulfill their promise of enduring love and continue to celebrate the beautiful feast of life together.

May this book bring peace and quiet comfort to many hearts.

Grace Hyewon Park

Assistant Pastor, New Livingstones Christian Fellowship, Canada

Refugee Missionary

가을은 모든 잎이 꽃이 되는 두 번째 봄이다
-알베르 카뮈

이 책에 실린 내 작업은 두 물줄기로 흐른다.

하나는 나무와 꽃, 작은 풀들이 빚어낸 서정 가득한 대자연의 섭리이고, 또 하나는 사랑하는 이들과의 추억이 깃든 장소다. 이 생명의 순환 속에서 나 역시 자연의 일부임을 깨닫고 안도하게 된다.

어린 시절부터 이름 모를 작은 꽃들로 가득한 들판을 동경했다. 도시에서 자란 나는 몇몇 꽃의 이름밖에 알지 못했지만, 문학작품이나 영화 속 장면들을 통해 상상의 들판을 그려보곤 했다. 계절 따라 온갖 종류의 풀과 꽃이 피어나는 낮은 언덕, 세찬 바람이 불기도 하고 햇살이 쏟아지기도 하는 그곳을 뛰어다니거나, 이끼 낀 숲속을 헤매는 상상 말이다.

내가 가장 사랑하는 계절은 가을이다.

한 해의 수고가 마침내 결실로 맺히는 시간. 봄날의 분주함과 여름날의 치열함을 견뎌낸 끝에 맺은 열매는 풍요롭든 그렇지 않든 그 자체로 훈장처럼 자랑스럽다.

그 열매마저 떨어진 후, 빛바랜 잎들이 꽃처럼 다시 피어나는 순간의 숭고함. 차가운 겨울바람 속에서도 마지막 잎새와 담담히 이별하는 의연함. 카뮈가 가을을 "두 번째 봄"이라고 찬미한 까닭일 것이다.

겨울은 결코 끝이 아니다. 영원한 이별처럼 보이지만, 혹독한 시간을 견뎌내는 동안 땅속에서는 생명이 분주히 움직인다. 봄이 오면 나무는 제 살을 찢어 새순을 틔우고, 온 세상은 햇빛과 바람, 비, 새와 벌의 힘을 합쳐 다시 살아난다. 여름을 지나온 잎들은 또 다음 봄을 기약하며 떠날 채비를 한다. 체코의 작가이자 정원가인 카렐 차페크는 말했다.

"11월의 땅속에서 다음 봄을 위한 설계도가 이미 완성된다."

가을에 잎이 지는 까닭은 어쩌면 이미 봄이 시작되어 새로운 싹이 움트고 있기 때문일지 모른다. 가을은 끝이 아니라 시작, 생명의 시작이자 미래의 시작이다.

그리고 또다시 가을.

자연의 순환 속에 나의 시선과 마음이 머물고, 그것은 다양한 모습으로 캔버스에 담긴다. 나는 시간의 흐름 속에서 사라지지 않고 성장할 수 있는 존재임을 깨닫는다.

그래서 나는 늘 감사하다.

Autumn Is a Second Spring When Every Leaf Is a Flower

—Albert Camus

The works in this book flow through two streams.

One follows the great rhythm of nature—revealed lyrically in trees, flowers, and grasses. The other leads to places imbued with memories of loved ones. Within this cycle of life, I find solace in knowing I am part of nature itself.

Since childhood, I have been drawn to nameless blossoms in imagined meadows. Growing up in a city, I knew only a few familiar flowers, yet scenes from literature and film let me imagine: running across low hills carpeted with seasonal grasses and blossoms, sometimes windswept, sometimes bright with the sun; or wandering through moss-covered forests.

My favorite season is autumn—

the time when the year's labors finally bear fruit. After the bustle of spring and the fervor of summer, every fruit, whether plentiful or few, stands proud like a medal.

Even as the fruit falls, fading leaves bloom again like flowers. I love that sublime moment. In autumn's quiet farewell to the last leaf, I see dignity. Perhaps this is why Albert Camus praised autumn as "a second spring."

Winter is not the end. What seems an eternal farewell hides life stirrings beneath the soil. When spring comes, trees split their bark to unfurl tender buds, and the world revives through sunlight, wind, rain, and the tireless labor of birds and bees alike. The leaves of summer, too, prepare to leave—already promising the next spring. The Czech writer and gardener Karel Čapek wrote, "By November, the soil already holds the blueprint for the coming spring."

Perhaps leaves fall in autumn because spring has already begun— new life quietly forming within. Autumn is not an ending, but a beginning—the beginning of life, the beginning of the future.

And once again, autumn.

In nature's eternal cycle, my eyes and heart linger, and I capture it on canvas in many forms. In the flow of time, I do not vanish—I grow.

And for this, I am grateful.

목차
Contents

Part 2   삶—함께 걷는 여정
Life—A Shared Journey

제목		Title of the Artwork

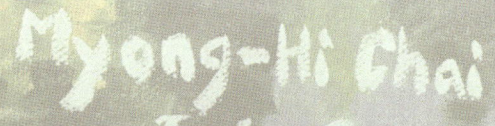

Part 1

다시, 가을—

생명 순환과 존재의 안도

가을은—
끝이 아니라
새로운 시작을 품은 계절

Part 1

And Again, Autumn—
The Cycle of Life and the Peace of Being

Autumn—

not an end,

but a season cradling new beginnings

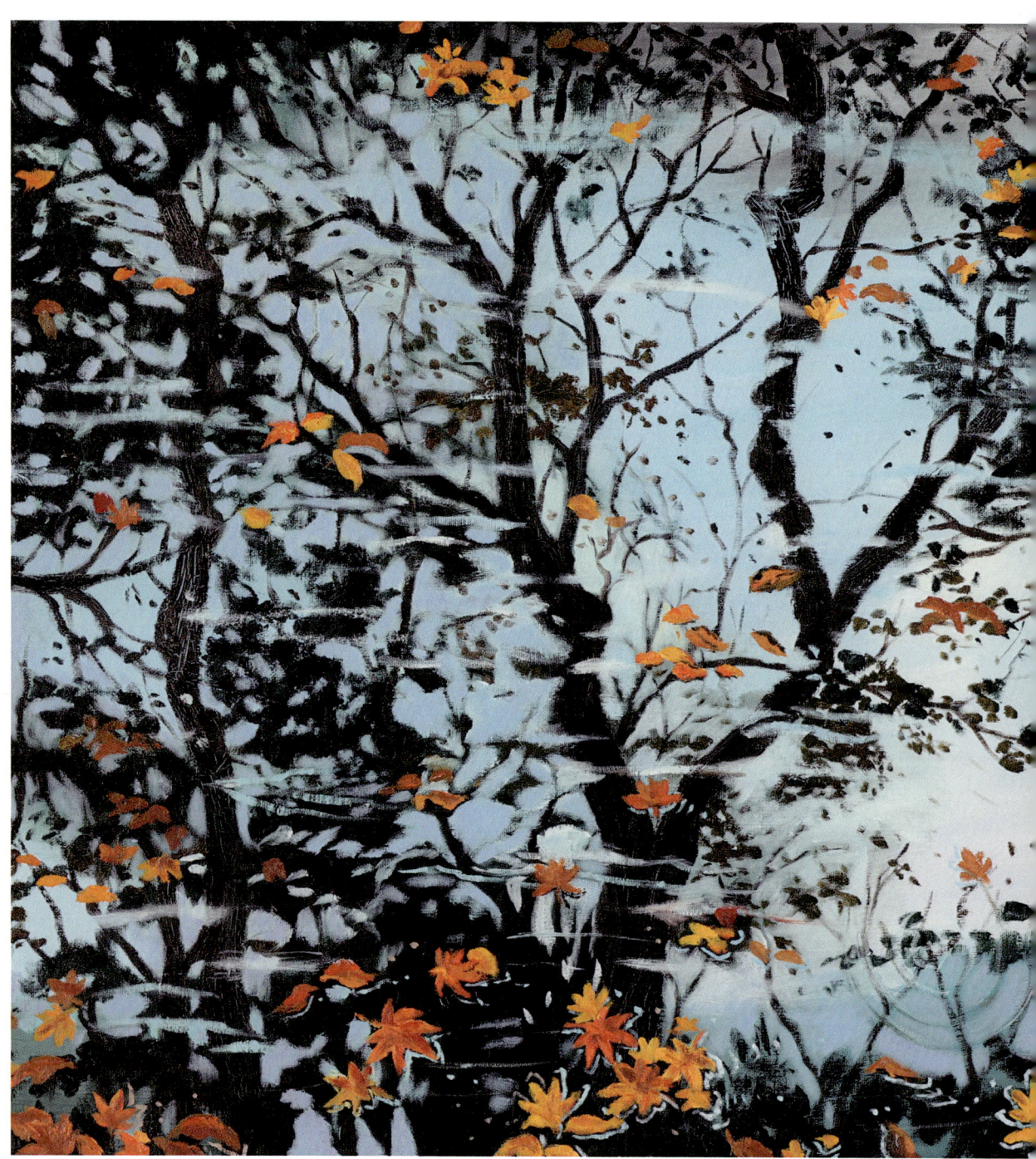

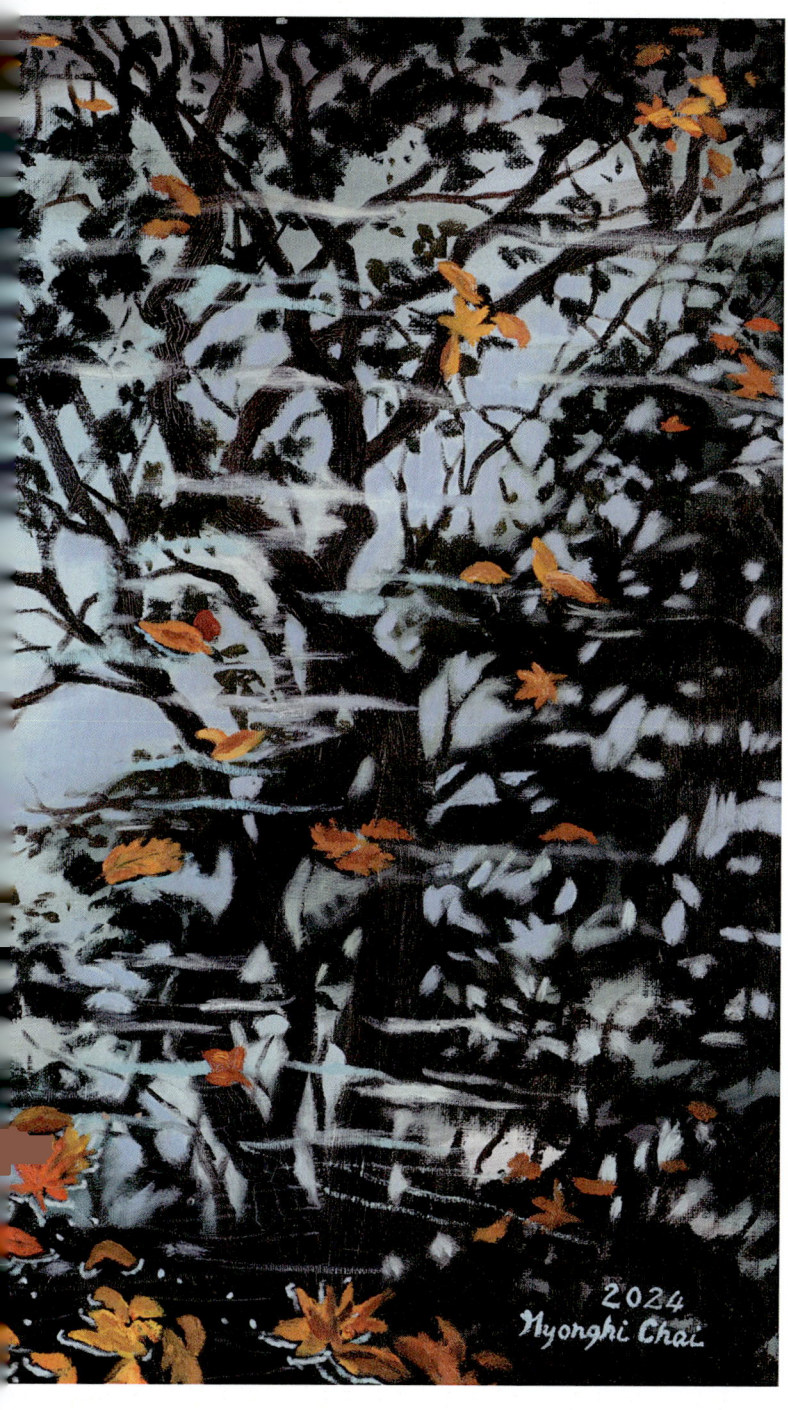

《잎이 지는 이유》 *When Leaves Leave*
Oil on canvas, M30(60.6 × 90.9㎝), 2024

아, 가을이다!
쌀쌀한 바람이
치맛자락을 춤추게 할 때
당신의 마음은 어디로 향하는가?

나무들은
화려한 단풍잎을 하나둘 떨구며
기나긴, 고독한 여행을 준비한다.

그대는 아는가,
잎이 지는 이유를.

Ah, it is autumn!
When the chilly wind
lifts the hem of your skirt,
where does your heart turn?

The trees begin to shed, one by one,
their brilliant autumn leaves,
preparing for a long, solitary journey.

Do you know
why leaves fall—
the secret of their leaving?

《감나무집의 겨울》
The Persimmon House in Winter
Oil on canvas, P10(40.9 × 53cm), 2016

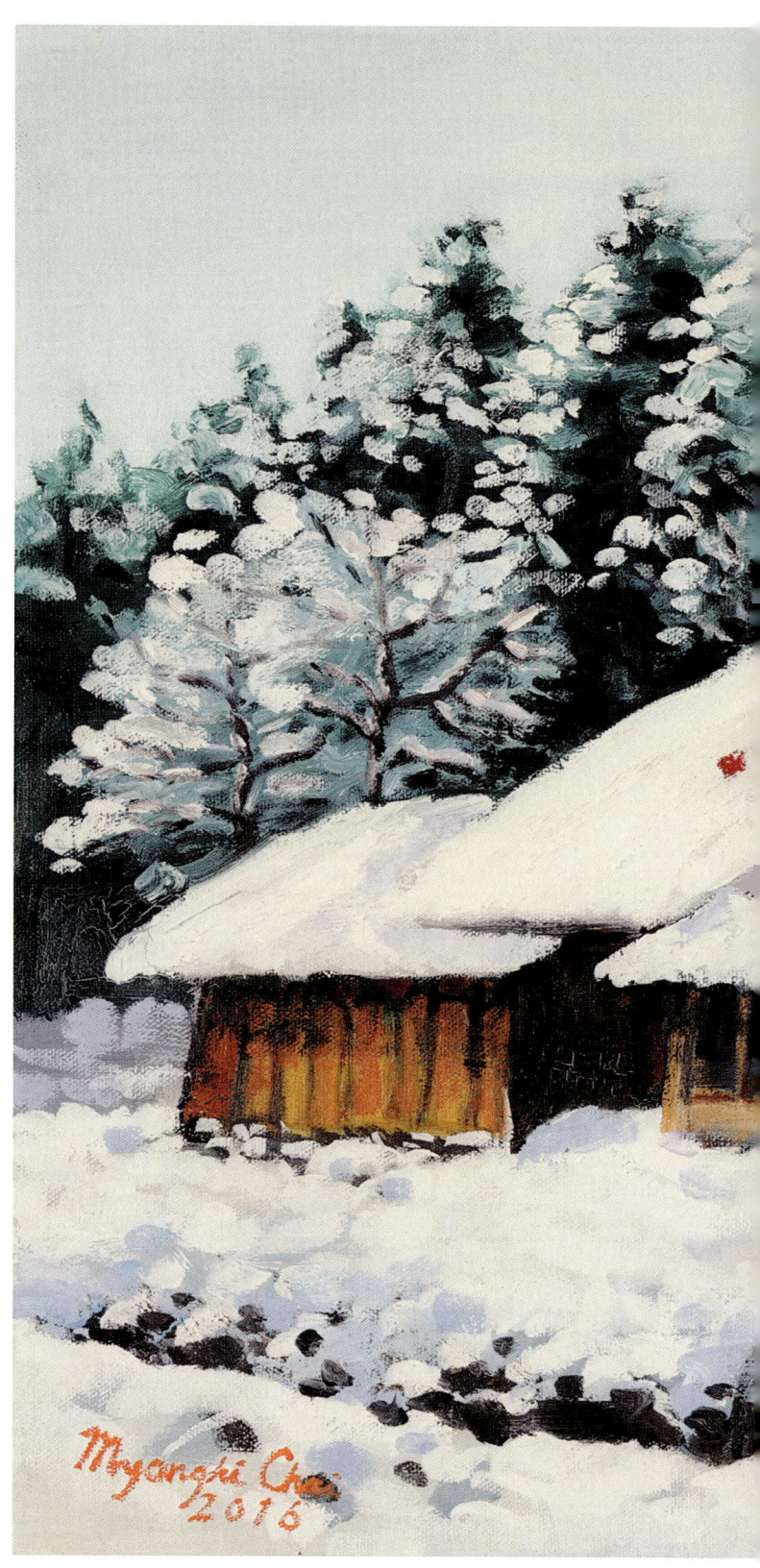

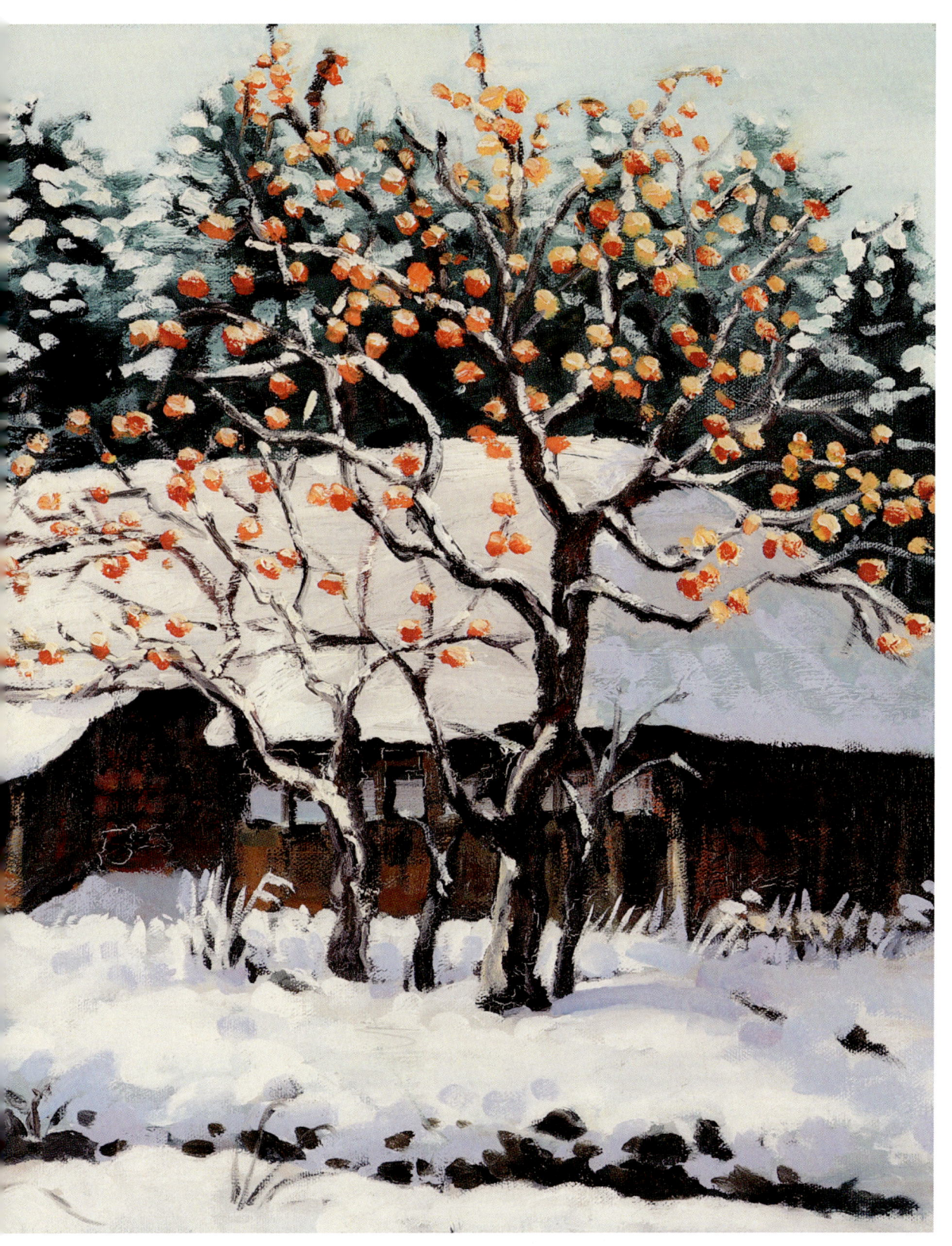

잎이 모두 지고 나면
어느새
세상을 하얗게 덮으며
겨울이 다시 온다.

매서운 바람에도
우리가 의연히 견딜 수 있는 까닭은
이 겨울이 끝이 아님을
알고 있기 때문이다.

When the last leaves have fallen,

winter arrives again,

quietly blanketing the world in white.

Even in the harsh winds

we stand steadfast,

for we know

this winter is not the end.

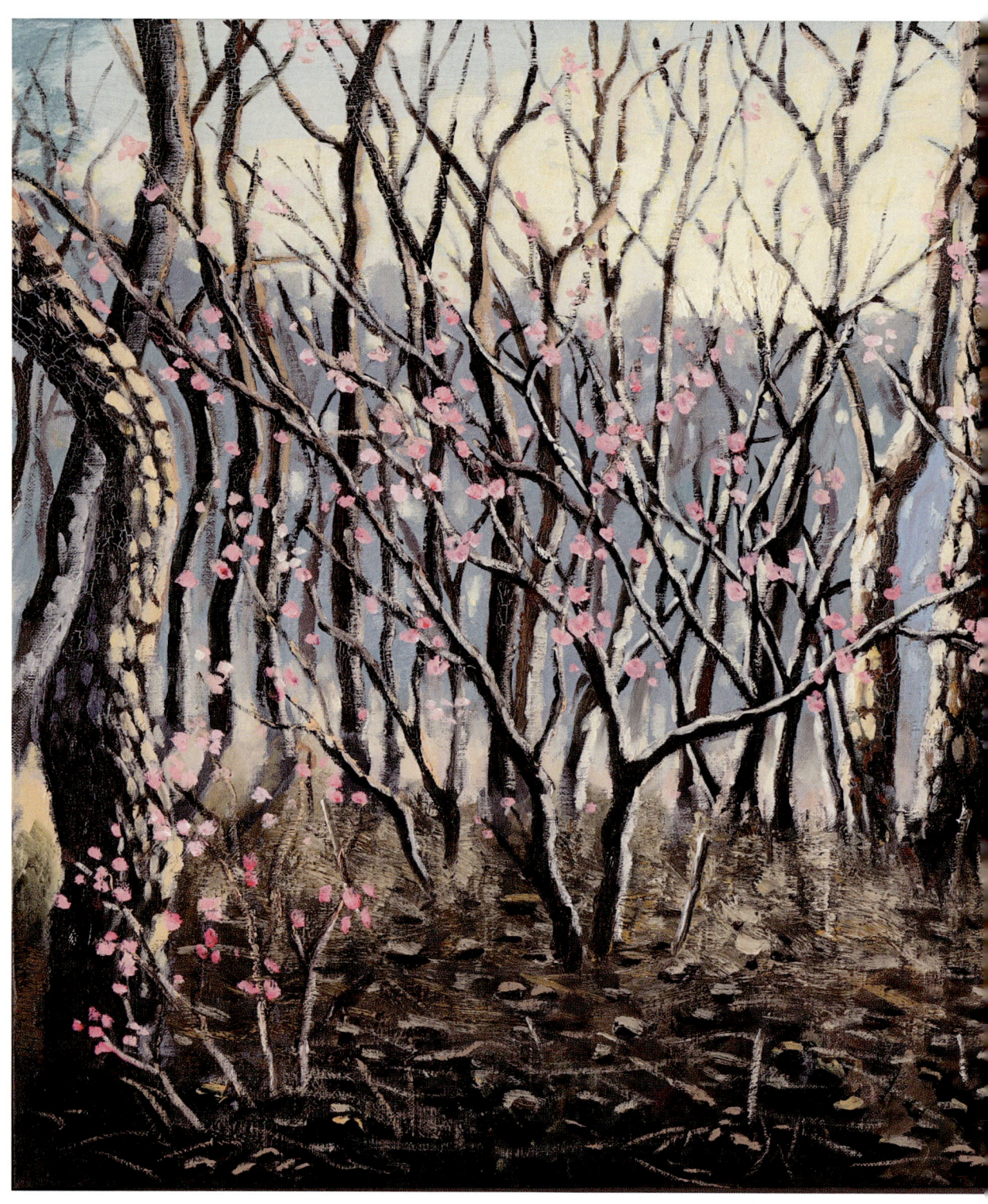

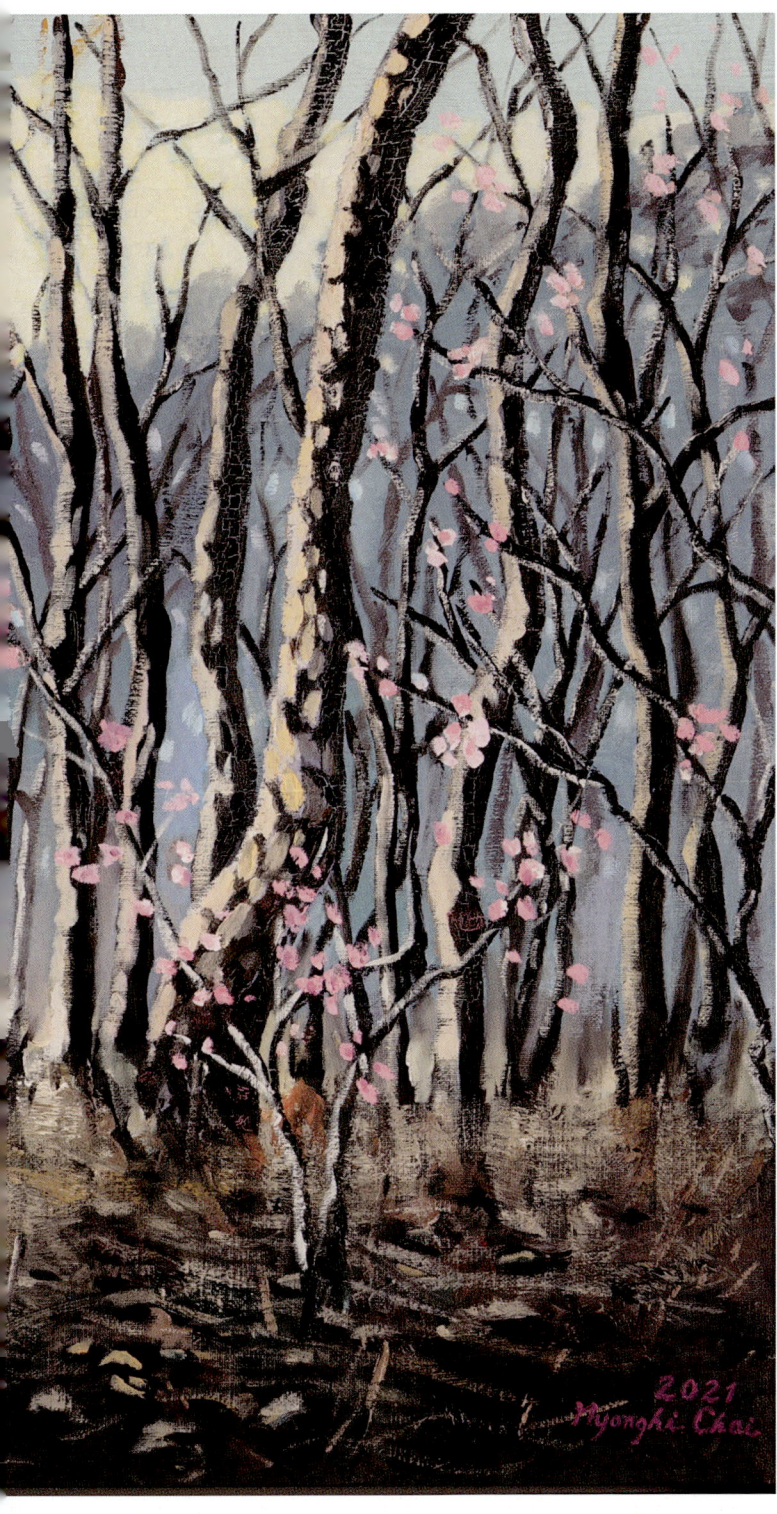

《소생》 *Back to Life*
Oil on canvas, P30(65.1 × 90.9㎝), 2021

얼어붙은 땅속 깊은 곳에서는
이미
이듬해의 새싹을 예비하는
미세한 움직임이 꿈틀거린다.

그리고 우리는 알고 있다―
마침내
따스한 봄을
기필코 잉태한다는 것을!

Deep beneath the frozen ground,
a quiet stirring begins,
already preparing
next year's shoots.

And we know—
winter surely
bears within itself
the promise of spring.

《소생 II》 *Back to Life II*
Oil on canvas, M50(72.7 × 116.8㎝), 2023

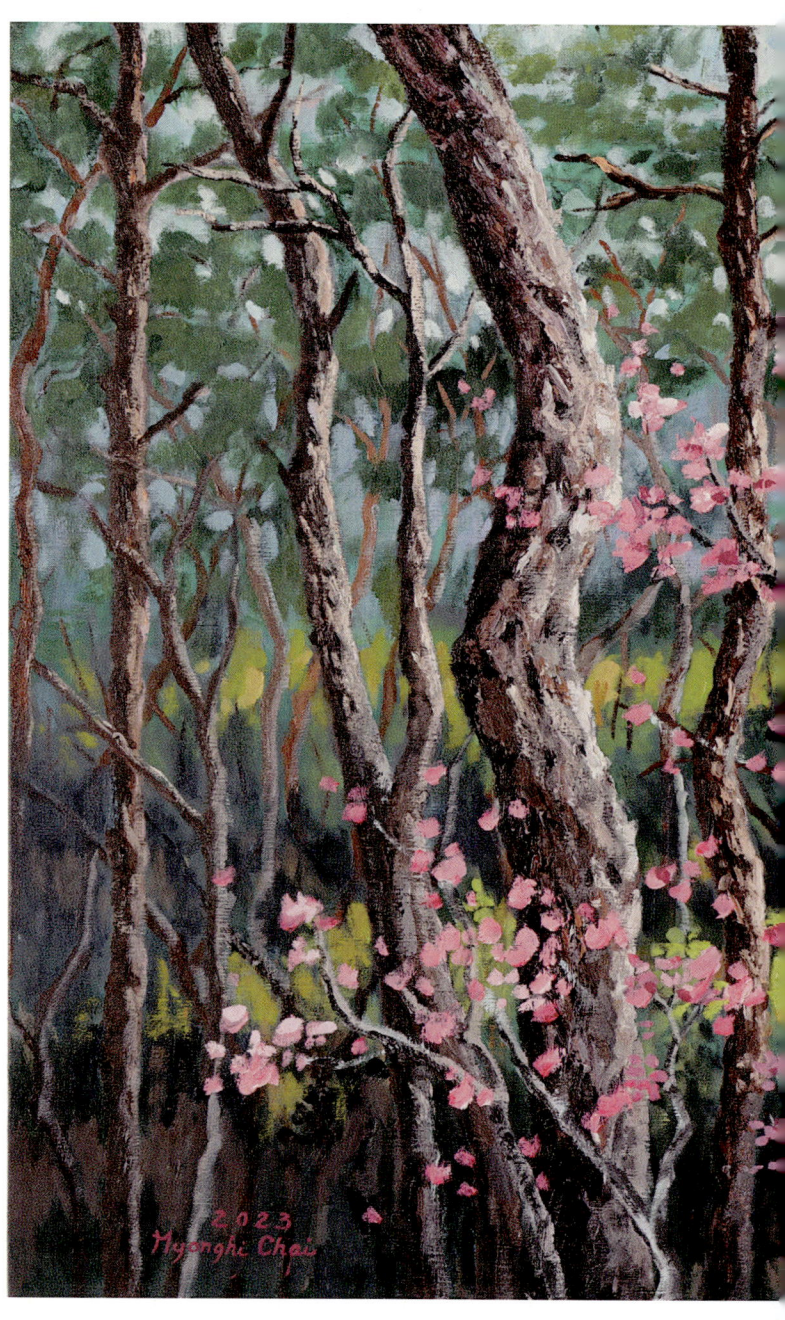

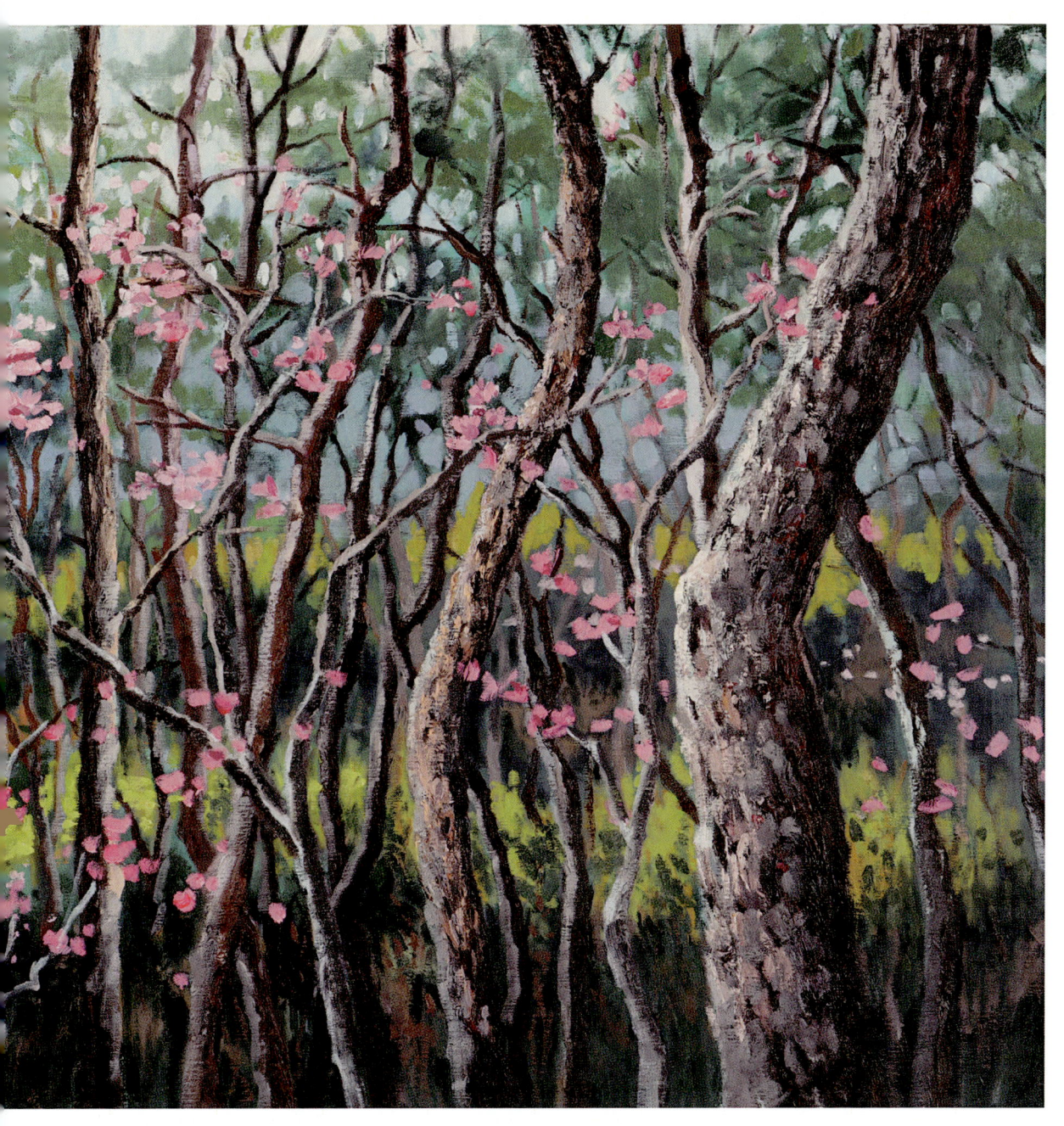

겨우내
메마른 몸으로 버티던 나무들 위로
봄 햇살이 수줍게 내려앉으면,
숲속 진달래가
연인을 맞이하듯 버선발로 달려 나와
이파리보다 먼저 꽃망울을 터뜨린다.

그 모습은
온 세상이 다시 살아나고 있음을 알리는
봄의 노래 같다.

그래, 생명이 깨어난다.
다시, 봄이다!

As spring sunlight shyly settles
on the dry branches
that endured the long winter,
azaleas in the forest—
as if a lover rushing barefoot
to greet her beloved—
leap into bloom
before their leaves appear.

It is a song
proclaiming the world's return to life.

Yes,
life is awakening!
Spring again.

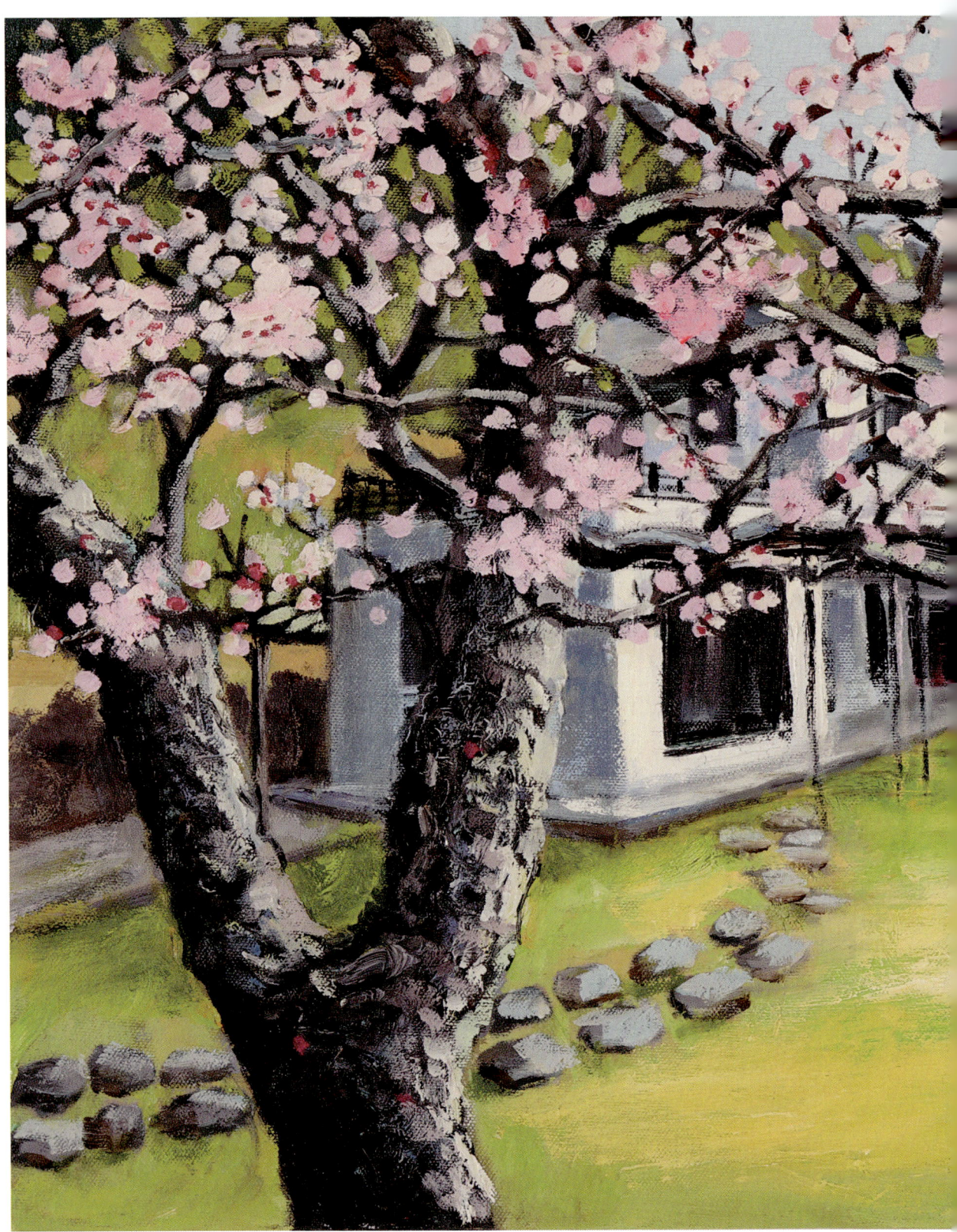

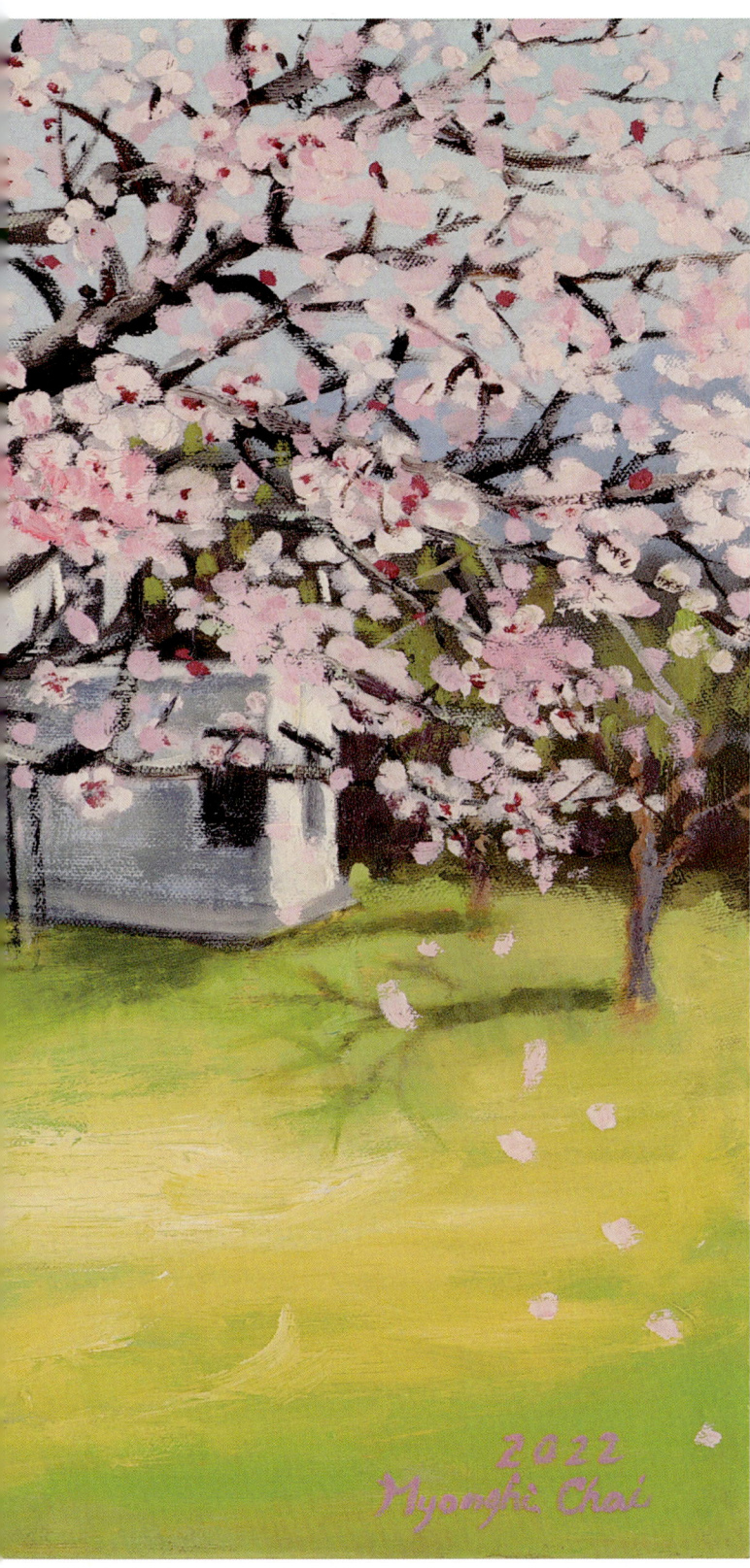

《살구꽃이 핀 알바스텔라》
Apricot Blossoms in Alba Stella
Oil on canvas, P10(40.9 × 53cm), 2022[1, 2]

---

1 알바스텔라는 전남 담양에 자리한 작가의
   작업실 이름이다. 그곳 마당에는 오래된 살
   구나무 한 그루가 고요히 서 있다.

2 Alba Stella is the name of the artist's
   atelier, located in Damyang, Jeollanam-
   do, Republic of Korea. There, an old
   apricot tree still stands in the yard.

그리고
숲속 진달래의 노랫소리를 가장 먼저 듣는 이는
마당 한켠에 고요히 서 있는
늙은 살구나무다.

다정한 할머니처럼
이파리보다 먼저
연분홍 미소로 화답하며 속삭인다.
"아, 또 왔구나? 봄이로구나!"

수십 번 맞이한 봄이지만
단 한 번도
당연하다고 여긴 적은 없었다.

해마다 이 순간은
늘 경이롭고,
또 은혜롭다.

And the first

to catch the song

of azaleas blooming in the forest

is the old apricot tree,

standing quietly at the edge of the yard.

Like a tender old grandma,

she answers with a soft pink smile,

even before her leaves appear:

"Oh, you've come again? You must be Spring."

Though she has welcomed spring

countless times,

never once

has it felt ordinary.

Each year, this moment returns—

as wonder,

as grace.

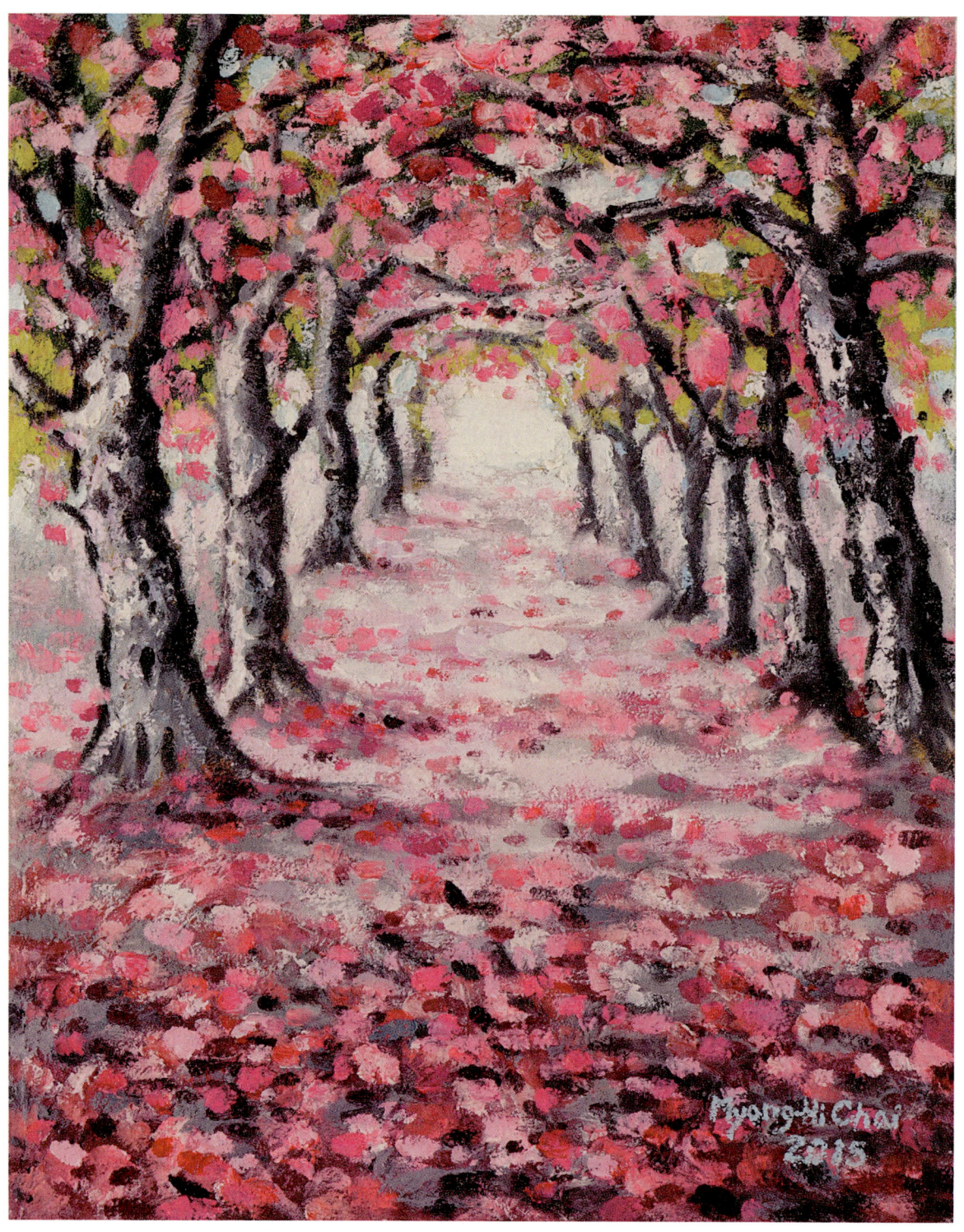

《봄의 설레임》 *Spring's Flutter*
Oil on canvas, P10(53 × 40.9㎝), 2015

"준비된 자 먼저!"

이제 무대는 벚꽃의 차례.
연둣빛 잎새가 채 나오기도 전에
발그레 상기된 얼굴로 달려 나와 봄을 끌어안는다.

그 생동하는 분홍빛 왈츠가
우리 가슴을 얼마나 설레게 하는지!

"Those who are ready, go first!"

Now it's the cherry blossoms' turn.
Before the tender green leaves can even appear,
they rush forward—
cheeks blushed pink—
to embrace spring.

Their pink waltz, so alive,
fills the air with delight
and stirs our hearts
with anticipation.

《다시, 봄!》 *Spring, Again!*
Oil on canvas, P10(40.9 × 53㎝), 2024

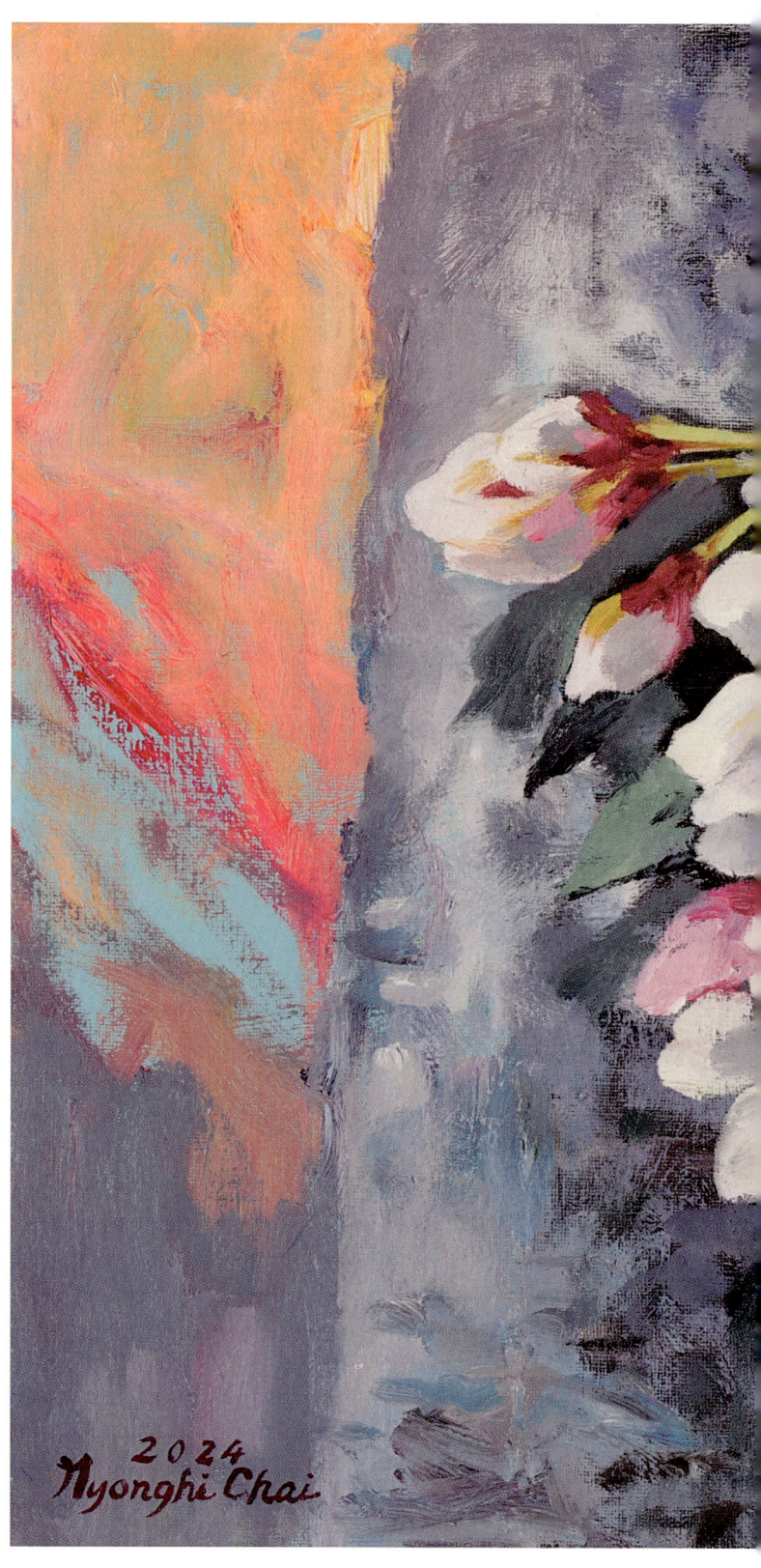

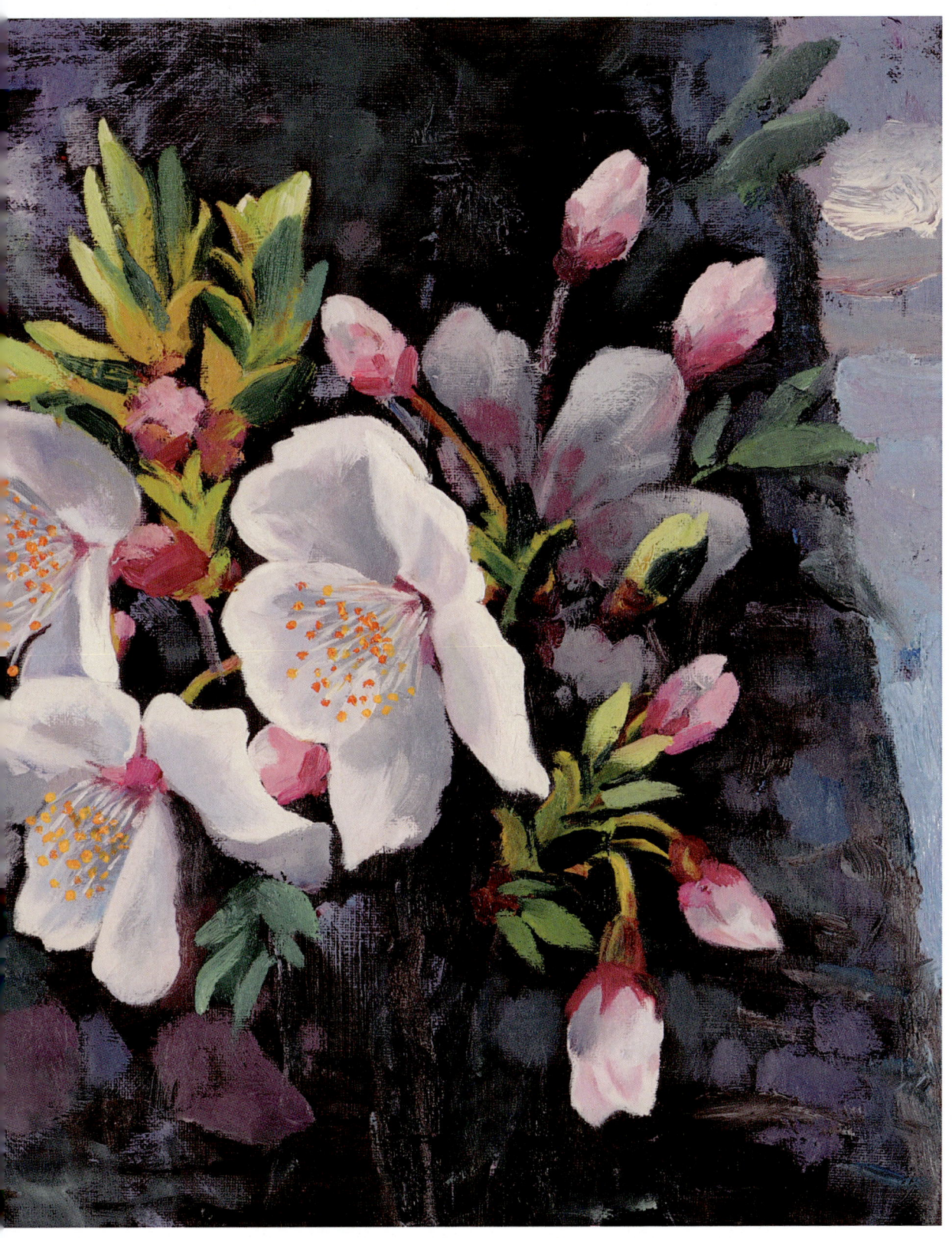

바람 끝에
봄기운이 대롱대롱 매달려 있음을 느낄 때쯤,
공원 산책길에서
벚나무 고목의 갈라진 틈새로 피어난
여린 벚꽃을 마주쳤다.

너무 반가워
눈물이 날 뻔했다.

아! 다시 봄이다.

Just as I began to feel

the breath of spring

hanging on the edge of the wind,

I came upon tender cherry blossoms

blooming from the cracked bark

of an old tree along the park path.

So moved,

I almost wept.

Ah—

spring again.

겨우내 마른 가지 끝에서
처절히 꽃봉오리를 준비한 동백,

붉은 미소를 살짝 보이더니,
툭—
봉우리째 떨어져
땅 위에서 다시 한번 피어난다.

그렇게 쉽게 떠나기엔
너는 아직도
보여 줄 것이
너무나 많다.

All winter long,
at the tip of a bare branch,
the camellia endures,
shaping its desperate bud.

Then at last—
a hint of crimson,
a fleeting smile—
and plop!
the blossom drops whole,
only to bloom again upon the earth.

You still have
too much yet to show,
too much
to leave so soon.

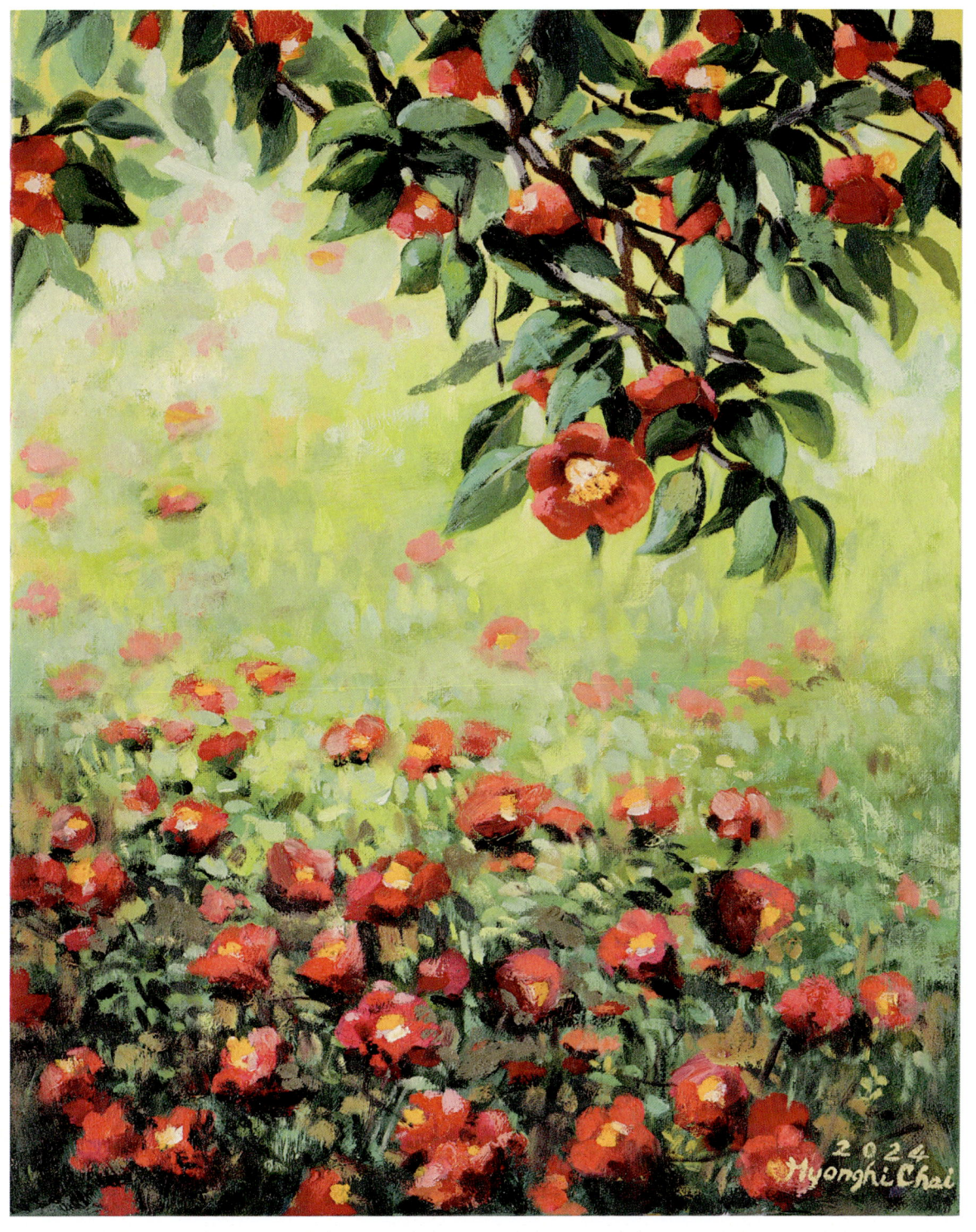

《동백, 당신의 마음속에서 세 번째로 피어나다》 *Camellia: Third Blooming Within You*
Oil on canvas, P10(53 × 40.9㎝), 2024

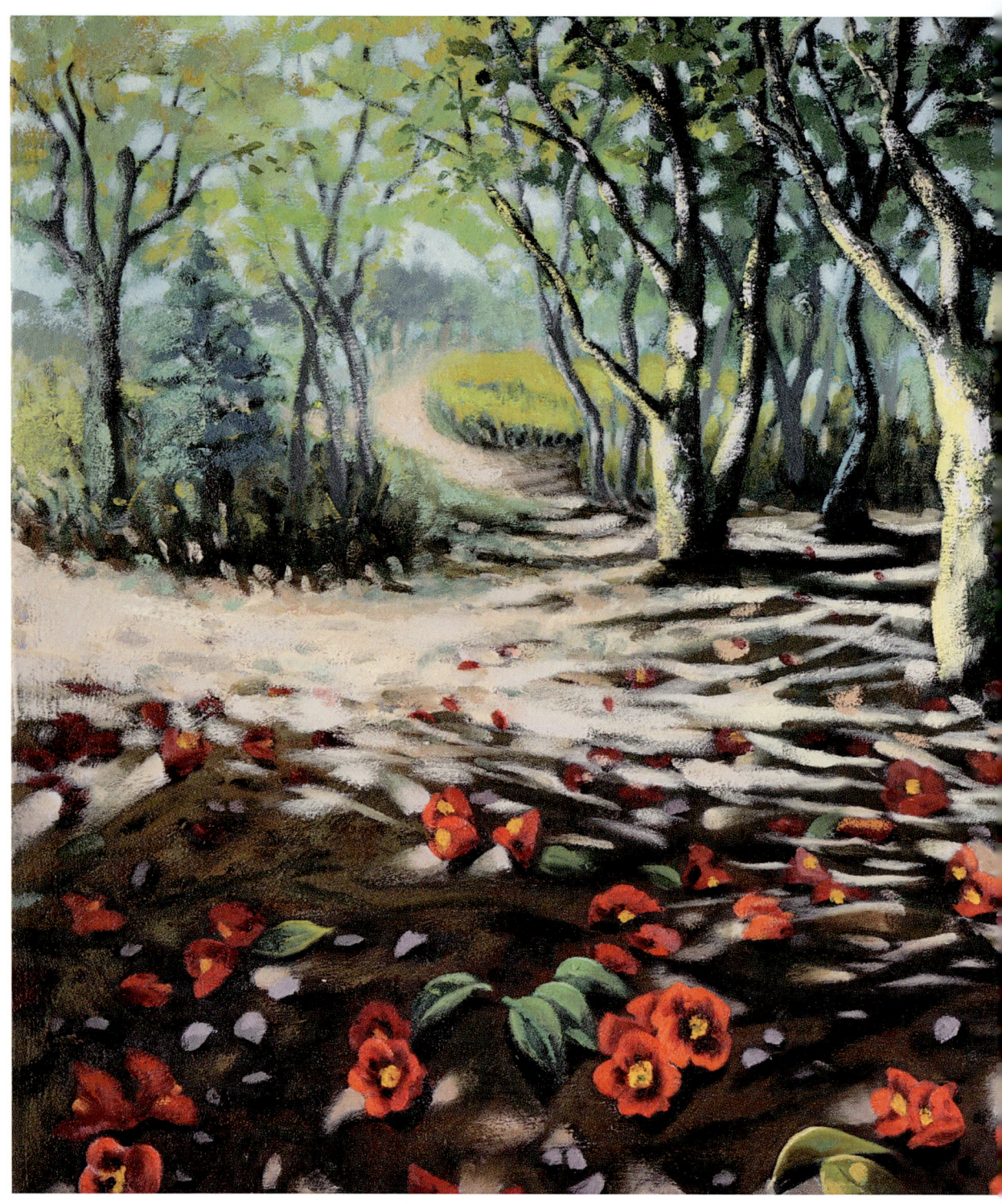

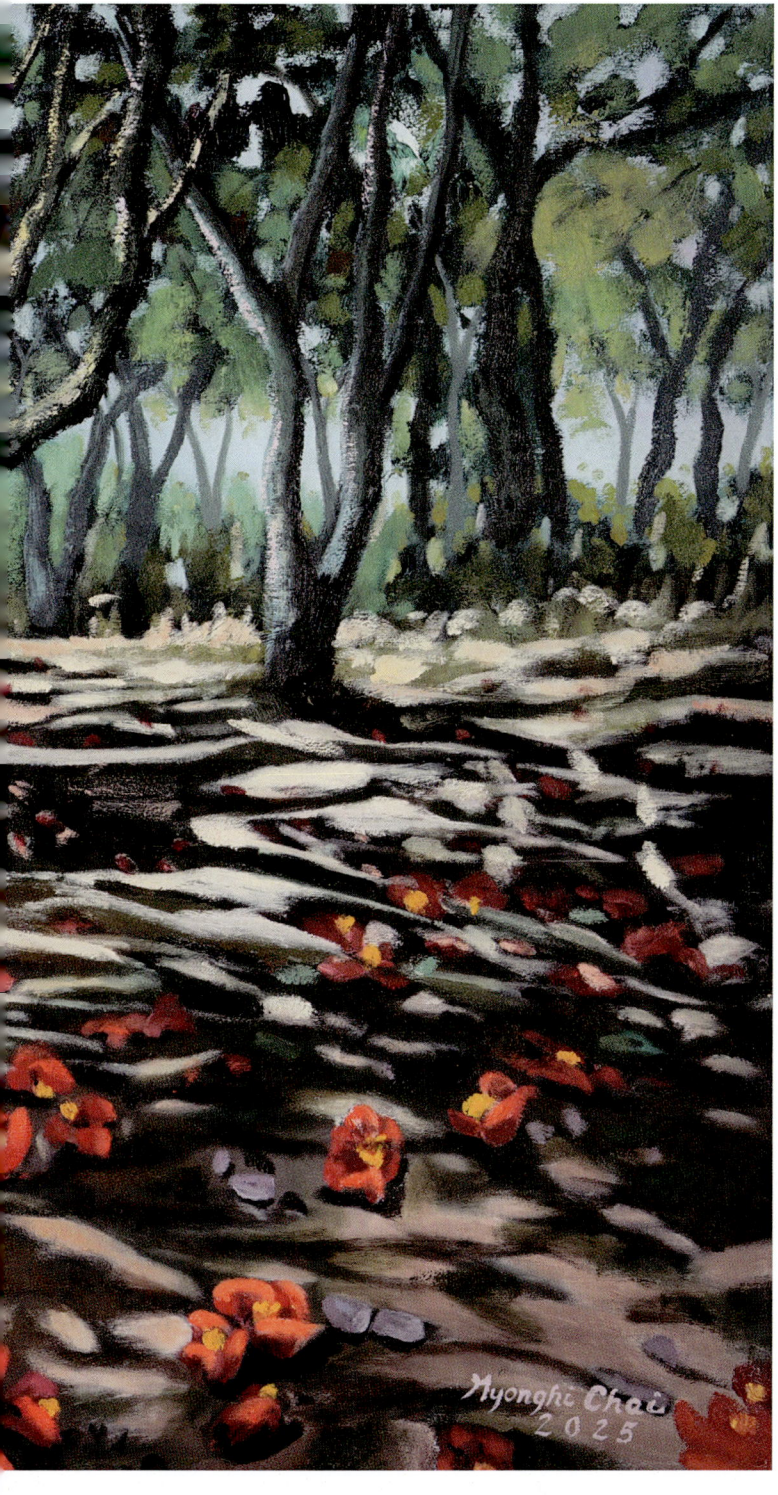

《동백, 당신의 마음속에서 세 번째로 피어나다 II》
Camellia: Third Blooming Within You II
Oil on canvas, P30(65.1 × 90.9㎝), 2025

땅에 누운 채
다시 피어난 너를 바라보노라면,
내 마음 깊은 곳에서
너는 세 번째로 다시 피어난다.

그것은 네가
떠나길 망설이기 때문일까,
아니면 내가
끝내 너를 보내지 못해서일까.

As I gaze at you—

fallen, yet blooming again on the ground—

you blossom once more,

for the third time,

within my heart.

Is it because you hesitate to leave,

or because I cannot bear

to let go of you, after all?

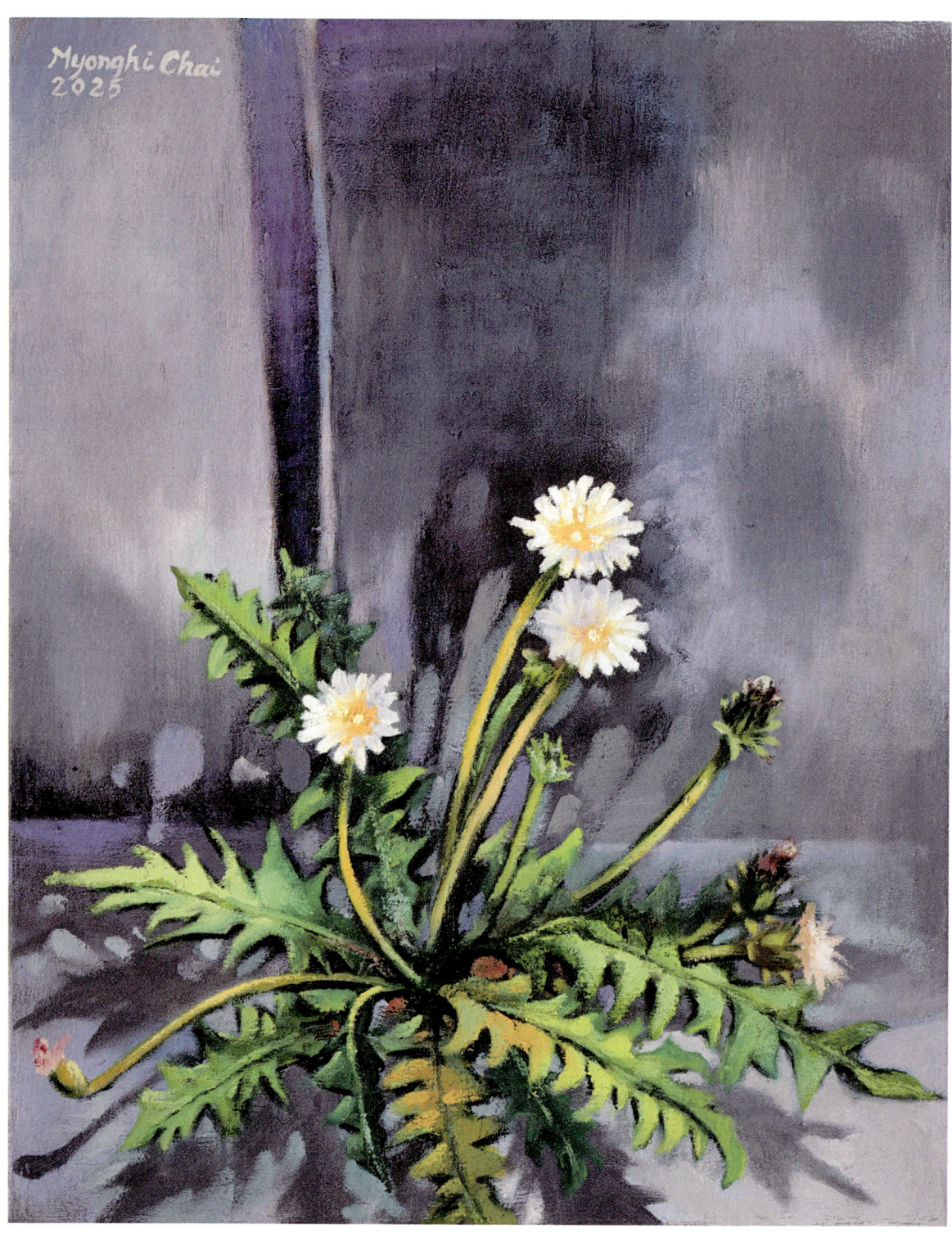

《생명력》 *Vitality*
Oil on canvas, P10(53 × 40.9㎝), 2025

천천히 길을 걷다가,
전봇대 아래 구석진 틈에서
하얗거나 노란 작은 얼굴을
수줍게 들어 올린 채
제 시간을 살아가는 민들레를
문득 발견한 적 있는가?

바야흐로, 온 대지에
생명력이 가득 차오르고 있다.
봄이, 무르익는다!

Walking slowly,
have you ever felt the quiet, serendipitous joy
of finding a dandelion—
lifting its shy white or yellow face
from a hidden corner
beneath a telephone pole,
living its own brief moment in time?

Now the earth brims with life.
Spring ripens.

《알바스텔라의 여름》
Alba Stella in Summer
Oil on canvas, P10(40.9 × 53cm), 2021

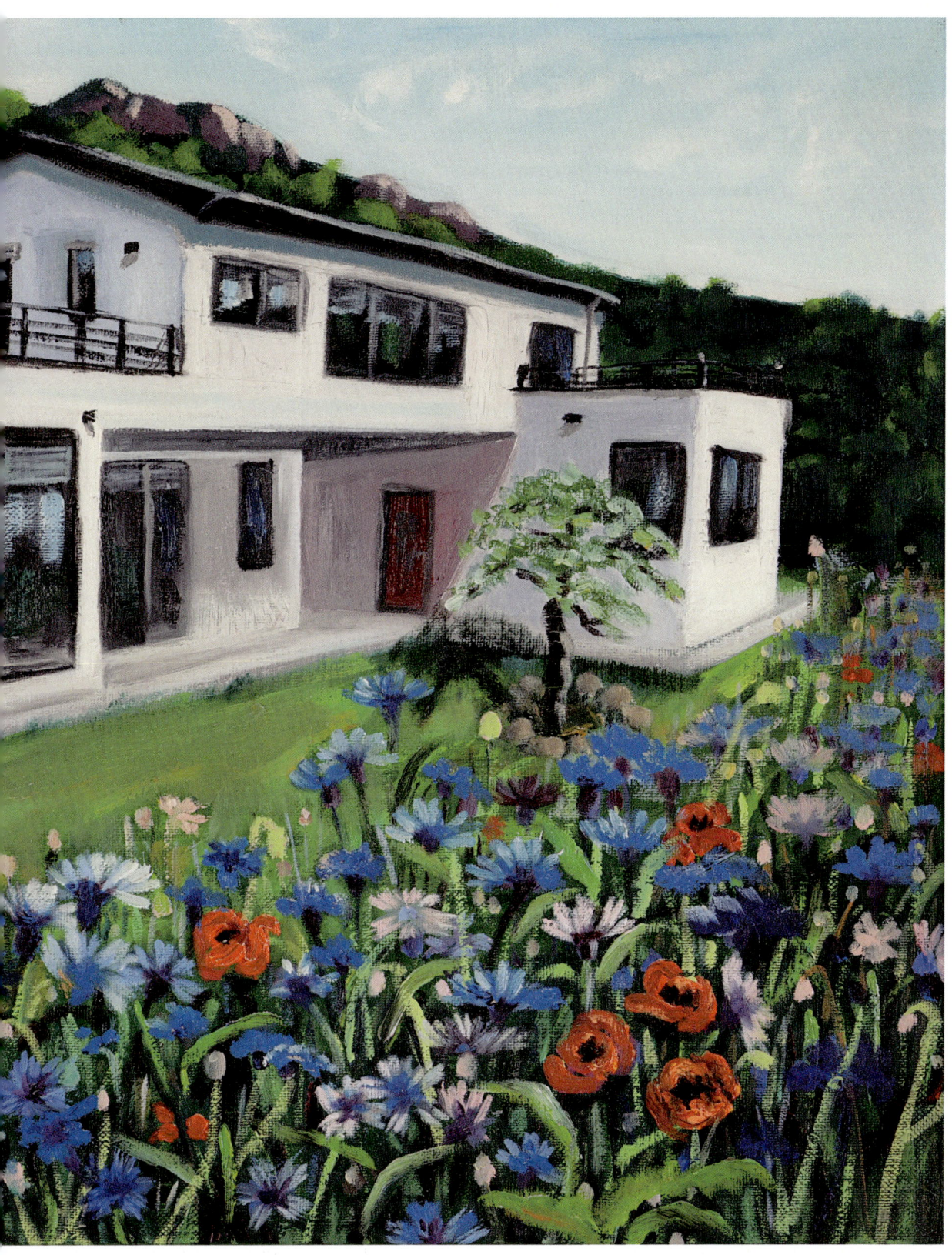

살랑살랑 봄바람이 불고
온 세상이 생명의 기운과 따스함으로 가득 차면,
뒷산의 늦장꾸러기 이파리들도
하나둘 얼굴을 내민다.

앞마당 꽃밭에서는
수선화, 수레국화, 개양귀비, 붓꽃 무리가
서로 앞서거니 뒤서거니
꽃피우는 경주를 벌인다.

알바스텔라의 여름은
그렇게 피어난 생명들로 가득하다.

When soft spring breezes blow
and the world is filled with warmth and vitality,
the late, sleepy leaves on the back hill
stretch and peek out one by one.

In the front garden,
daffodils, cornflowers, poppies, and irises
take turns in a joyful race—
each eager to bloom before the others.

Alba Stella's summer
is teeming with life,
in full bloom.

5월은 내게 노스탤지어의 계절.
대학 시절, 인문대 벤치 위에 초롱처럼 매달려
연보랏빛 미소로 우리를 와락 안아주던
등꽃이 떠오른다.

그 향기로운 그늘 아래서
우리들은 초록, 핑크, 보랏빛으로 빛나던
저마다의 꿈을 얘기했었다.

그 친구들은 지금 어디서, 무엇을 하고 있을까.
그 꿈들은… 모두 이루어졌을까.

May is, for me, a season of nostalgia—
a time of college days
when wisteria hung like lanterns
above the bench by the Humanities Building,
embracing us in their soft violet smiles.

Under that fragrant shade,
we spoke of our dreams—
green, pink, and violet—
each shining in our own color.

Where are those friends now?
And have their dreams—
every one of them—come true?

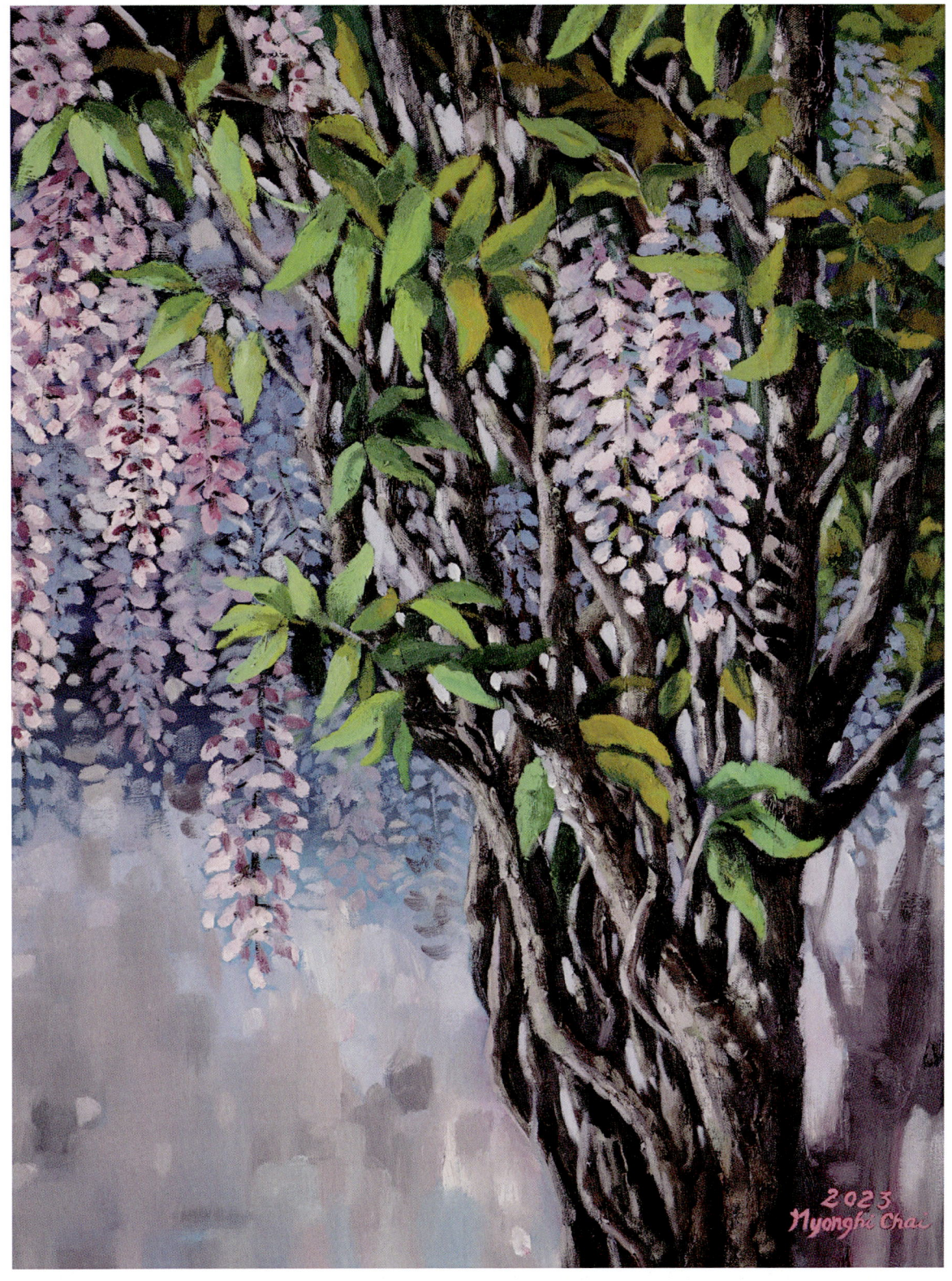

《어서 와!》 *Welcome!*
Oil on canvas, P20(72.7 × 53㎝), 2023

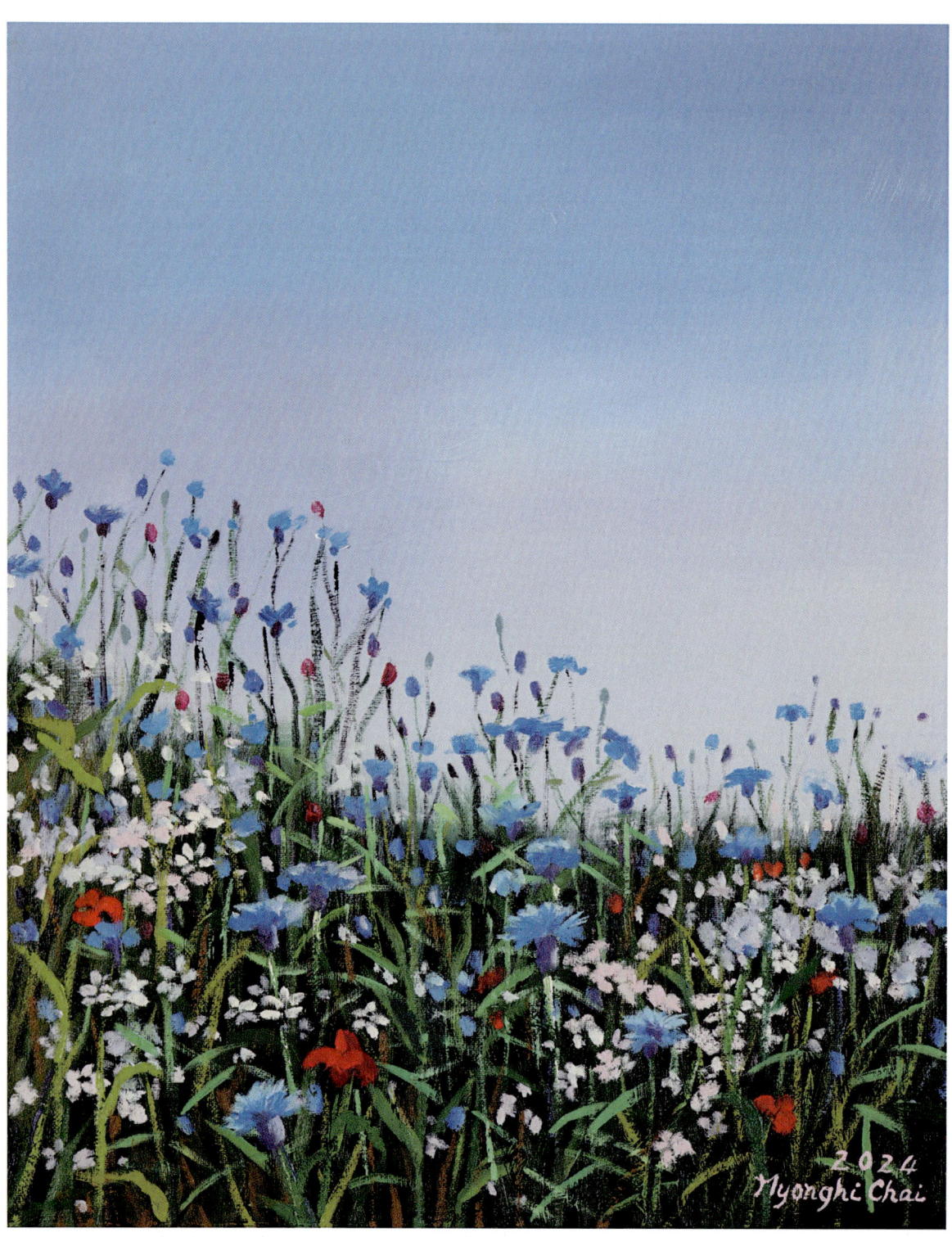

《바람 살랑 불어》 *Breezy*
Oil on canvas, P10(53 × 40.9㎝), 2024

살랑이는 봄바람에 기대어,
뒷산 언덕에도
파란 수레국화가
하나둘
피어나기 시작한다.

On the gentle spring breeze,
blue cornflowers
begin to bloom,
one by one,
across the back hill.

하나둘 피어나던 수레국화가
어느새
장성 황룡강 주변을
온통 푸른 물결로 물들인다.

The cornflowers,
once blooming one by one,
now paint the banks of the Hwangryong River in Jangseong
with waves of radiant blue.

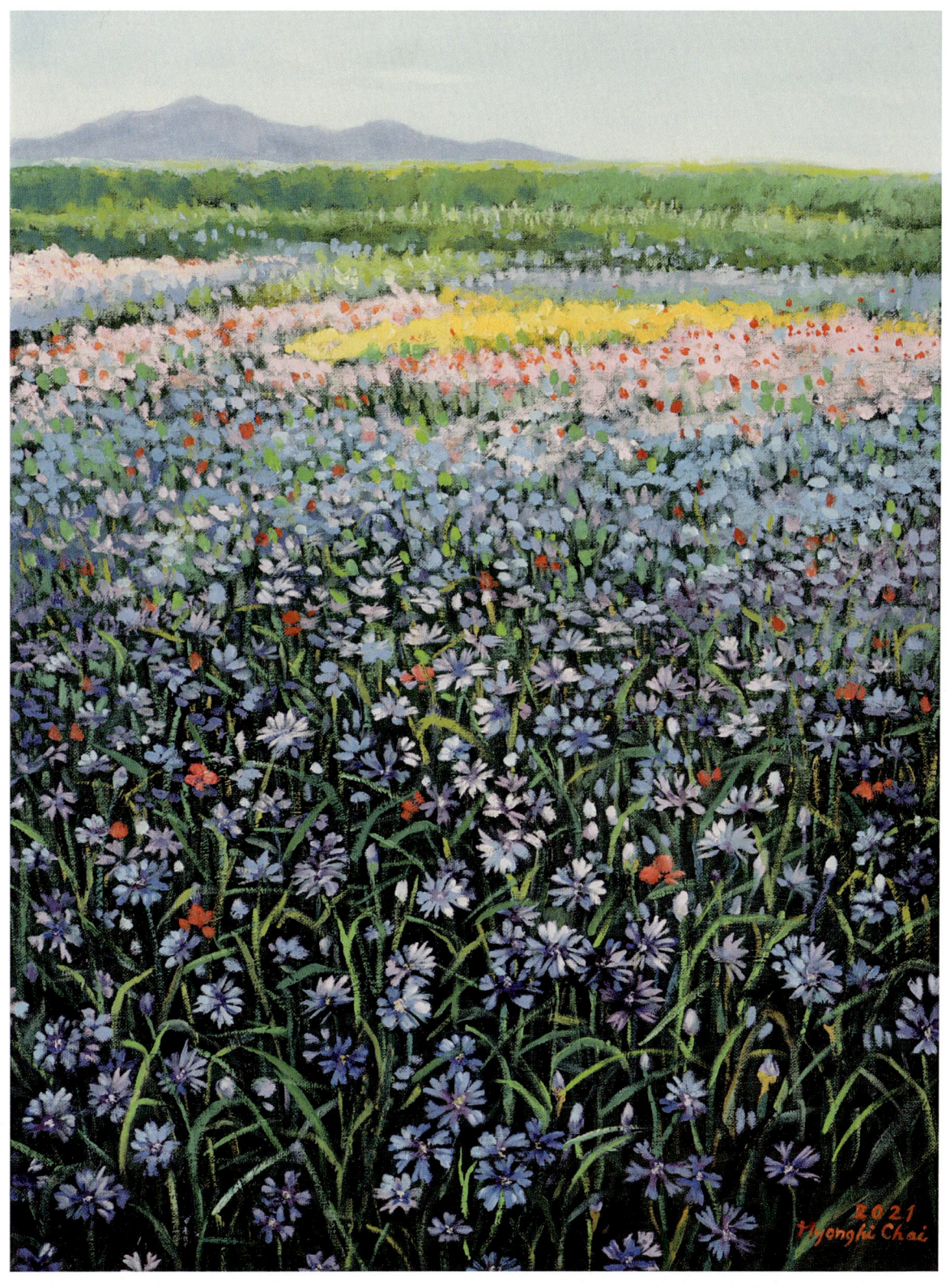

《화양연화—수레국화》 *The Bloom of Life—Cornflowers*
Oil on canvas, P20(72.7 × 53㎝), 2021

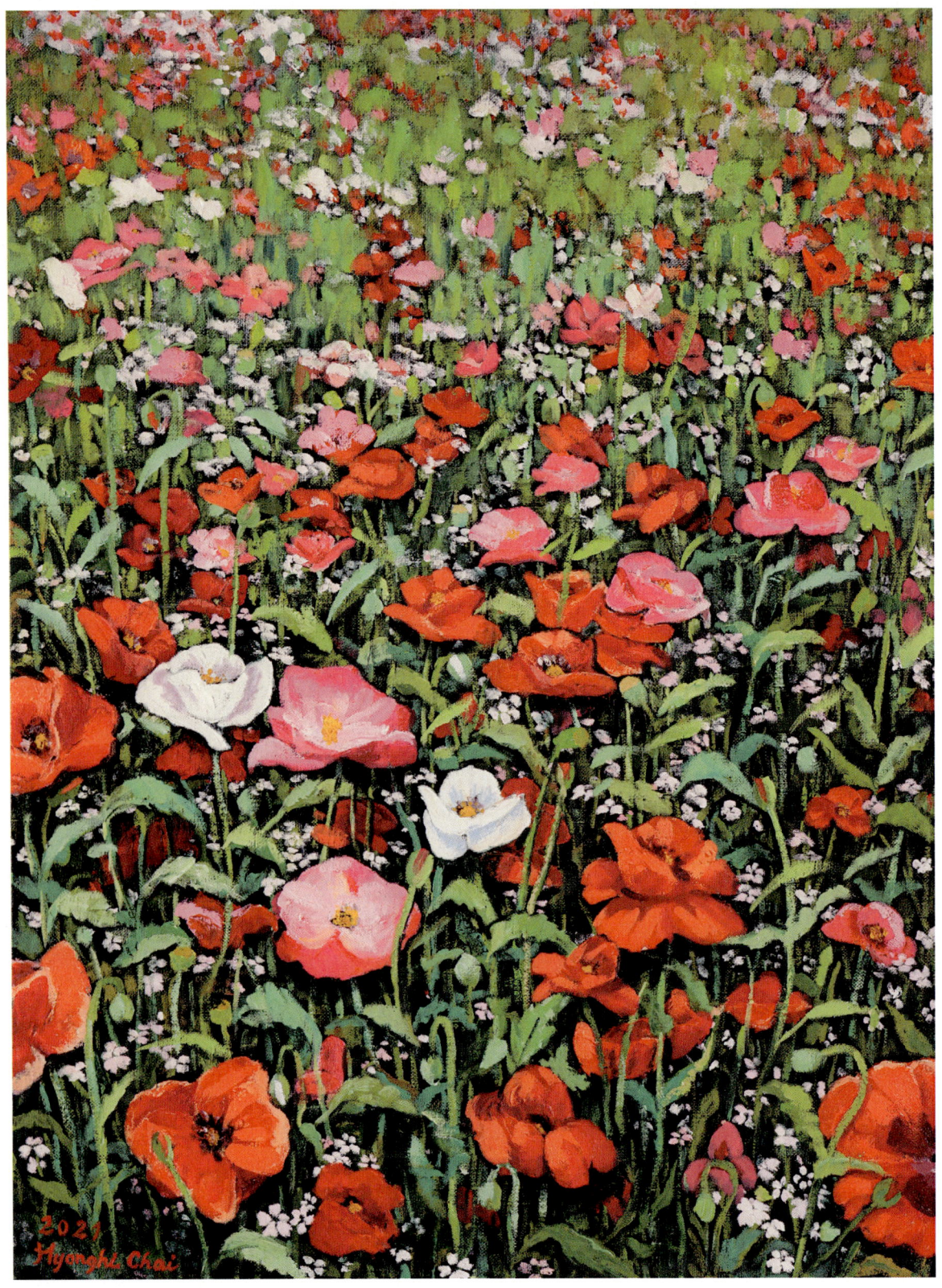

《화양연화―개양귀비》 *The Bloom of Life—Poppies*
Oil on canvas, P20(72.7 × 53㎝), 2021

수레국화의 푸른 물결 곁에는
어김없이
붉은 개양귀비가
더욱 눈부시게 피어난다.

이즈음에는 어디에서든
누구나
삶의 가장 아름다운 순간을 목격할 수 있다.

과연, 나의 화양연화는 언제였을까.
혹시… 바로 지금이 아닐까?

And beside the blue sea of cornflowers,
as always,
scarlet poppies bloom,
ever dazzling.

Around this time of year,
wherever you go,
you can glimpse
life's most beautiful moment.

Then, I wonder—
when was mine?
Or… could it be now?

누구에게나
꽃처럼 빛나는 화양연화의 순간은 있다.
굳이 크고 화려하지 않아도 괜찮다.

여름 햇살이 뜨거워질 무렵,
고요한 들판이나 도로 가장자리에서
보송보송한 강아지풀이
서서히 황금빛으로 물들어 간다.

어떤 시선도 기대하지 않은 채,
그저 자기만의 계절을
담담히 살아내는 그 순간—
정말이지,
작은 것이 아름답다.

Everyone has
a moment in life that blooms like a flower.
It need not be grand
or dazzling.

When the summer sun grows fierce,
along quiet fields and roadsides,
fluffy foxtails
slowly turn to gold.

Expecting no one's gaze,
they simply live their season,
in humble dignity.
Truly—
small is beautiful.

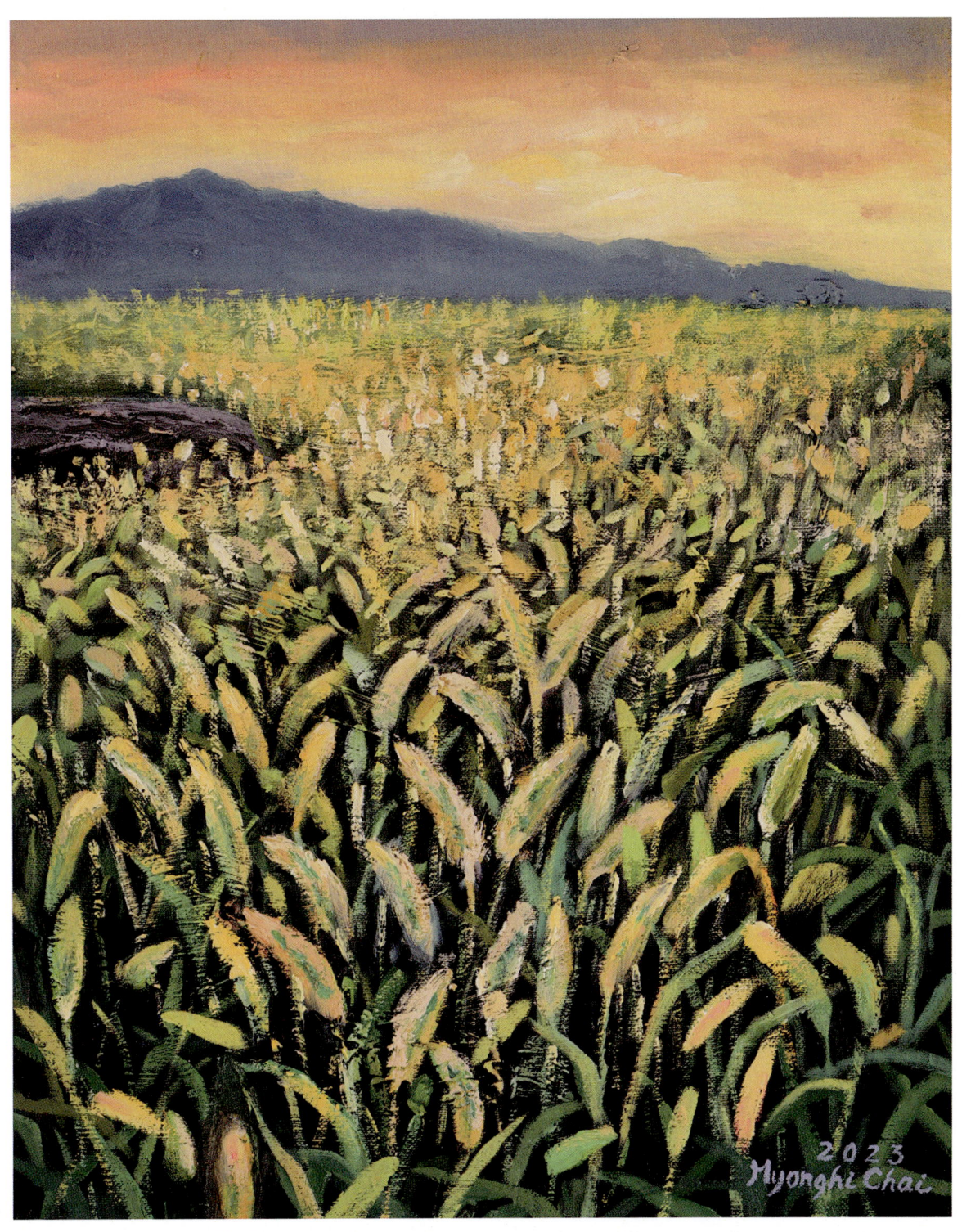

《작은 것이 아름답다—강아지풀》 *Small Is Beautiful—Foxtails*
Oil on canvas, P10(53 × 40.9㎝), 2023

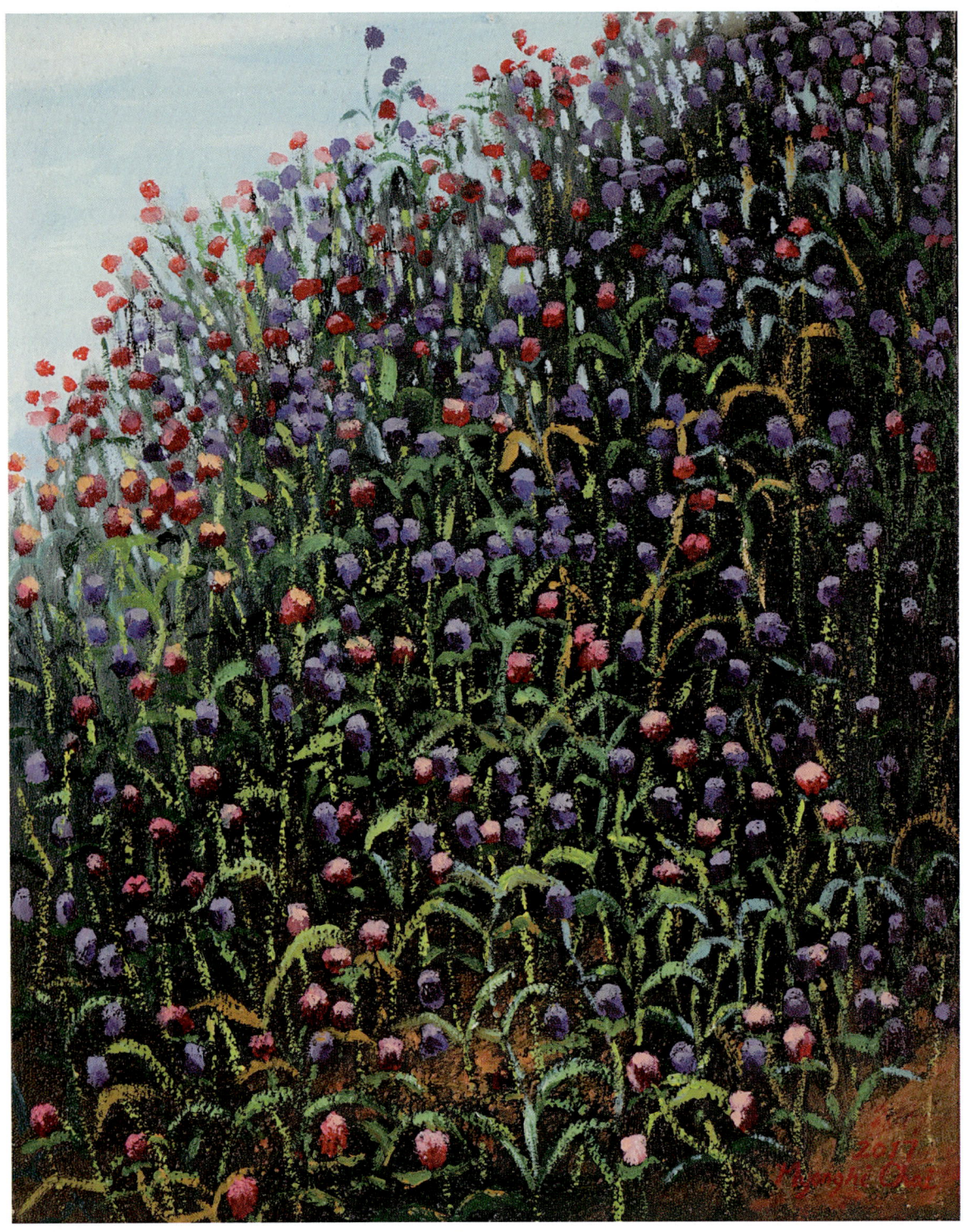

《천일홍, 천일 동안》 *A Thousand Days of Amaranth*

Oil on canvas, P10(53 × 40.9㎝), 2017

천일홍,
'시들지 않는 꽃'.
빨간, 보라, 노란, 하얀 작은 동그라미로
여름 화단을 수놓는다.

천 번의 종이학을 접어본 사람은 안다.
피고 지고 다시 피며 견뎌내는,
그 한결같은 마음을.

Amaranth—
the "flower that never withers"—
stitches a summer garden
in dots of crimson, violet, yellow, and white.

Those who have folded a thousand paper cranes
know well the spirit of amaranth—
to bloom, to fade, to bloom again,
enduring the summer heat
with a steadfast heart.

여름—
해바라기의 계절.

햇살이 뜨거워질수록
태양을 더욱 열렬히 사랑하는
해-바라기.

다가갈 수는 없지만
나는 늘
당신을 좇아 바라본다.

Summer—

the season of sunflowers.

The hotter the sun,

the more ardently

the sun-flower loves it.

Though I cannot draw nearer,

still—

my heart turns toward you.

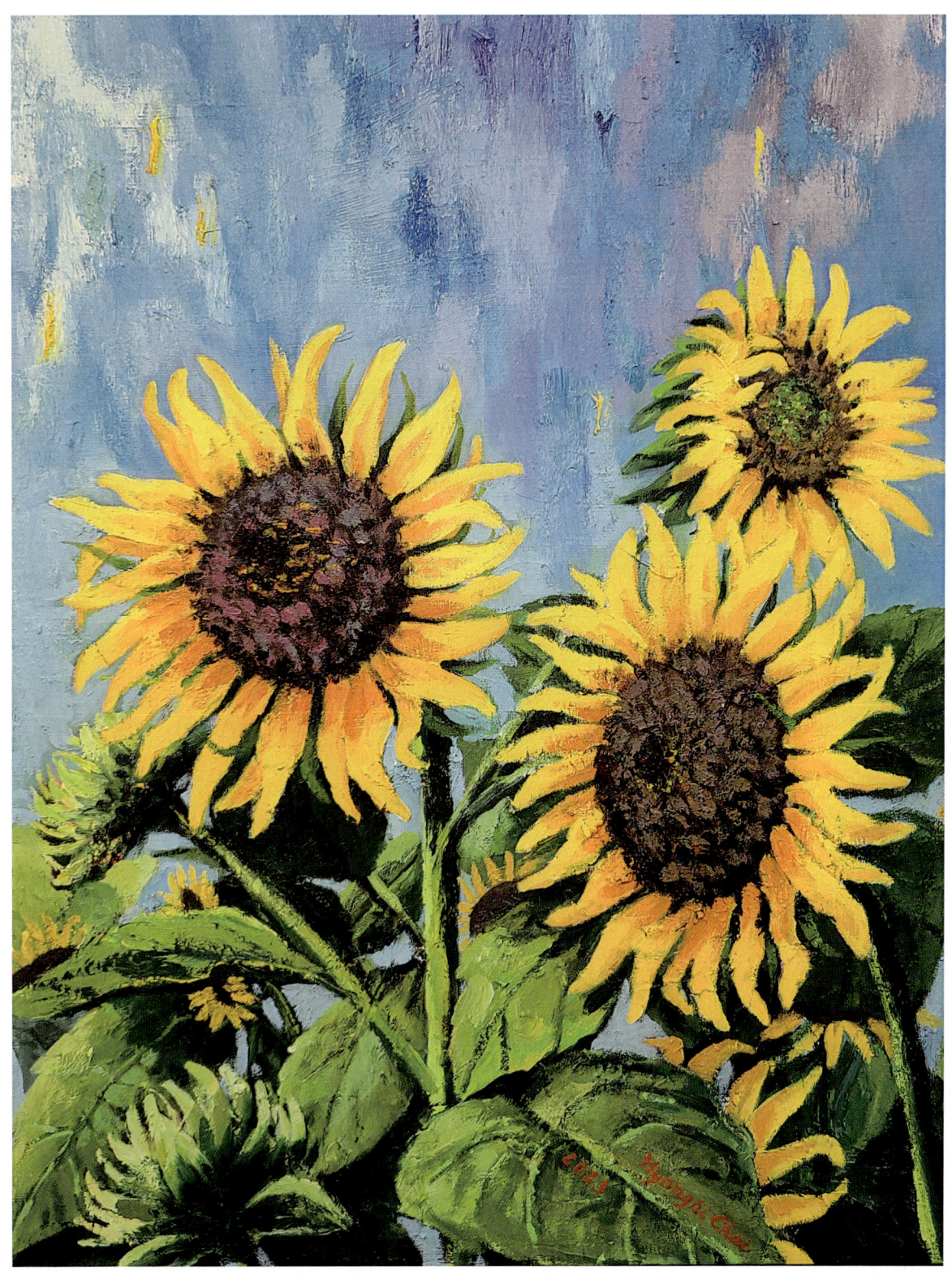

《나마스테 II》 *Namaste II*
Oil on canvas, P20(72.7 × 53㎝), 2023

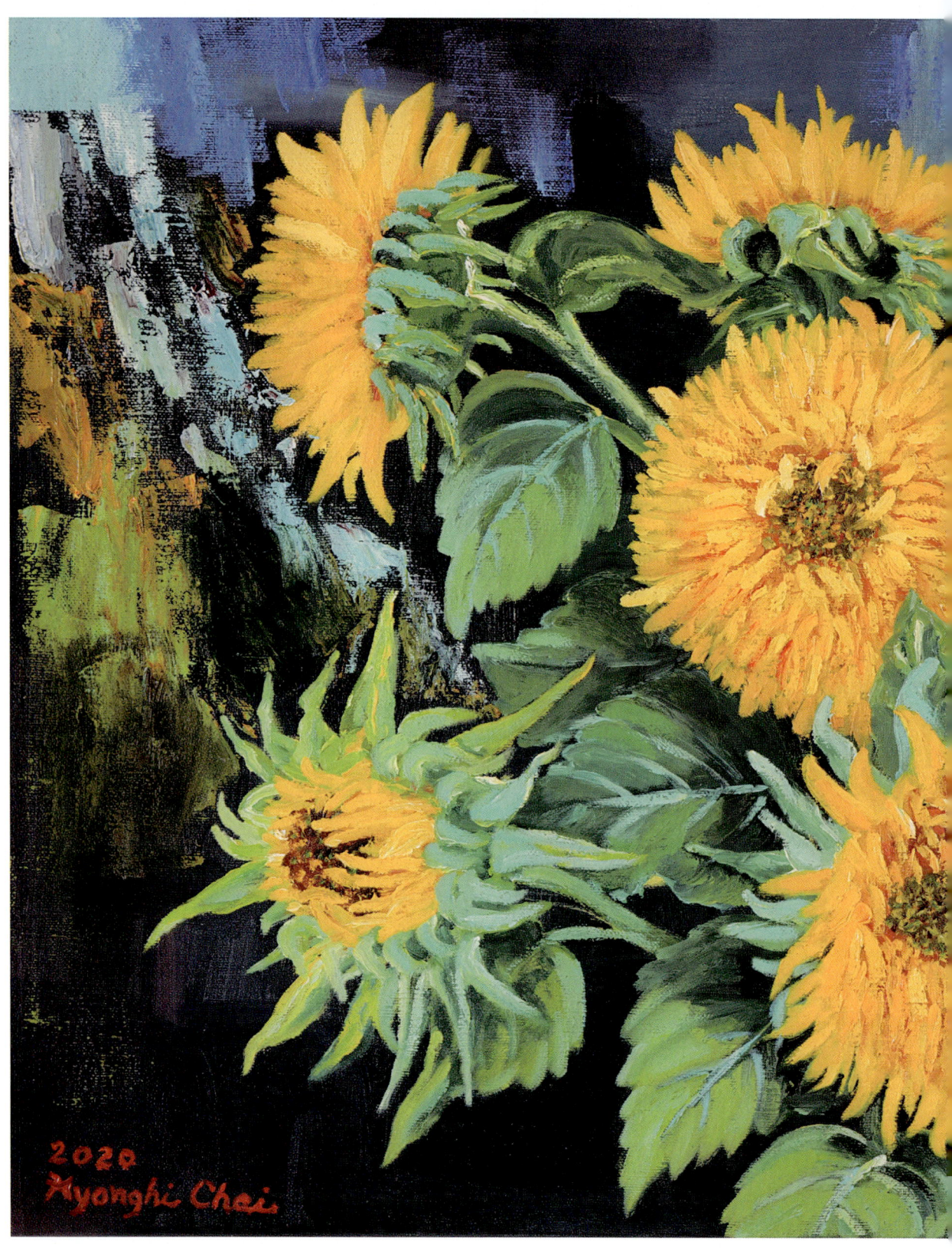
2020
Myonghi Chai

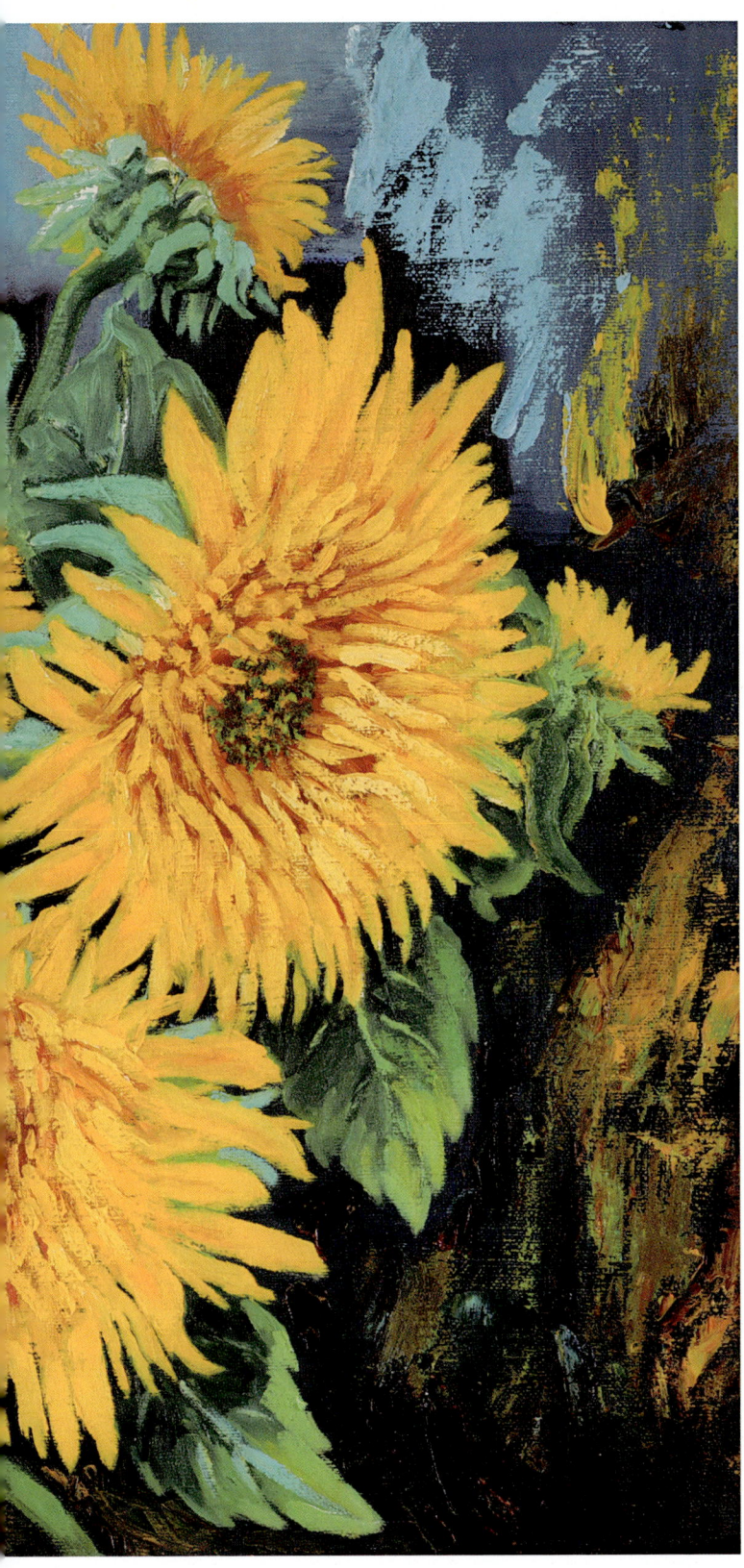

《나마스테》 *Namaste*
Oil on canvas, P10(40.9 × 53㎝), 2020

당신의 내면에 있는
신성함까지도
존경하고 사랑합니다.

늘
당신을 바라봅니다.

나마스테!

I honor and cherish
the divine within you.

Always,
I see you.

Namaste!

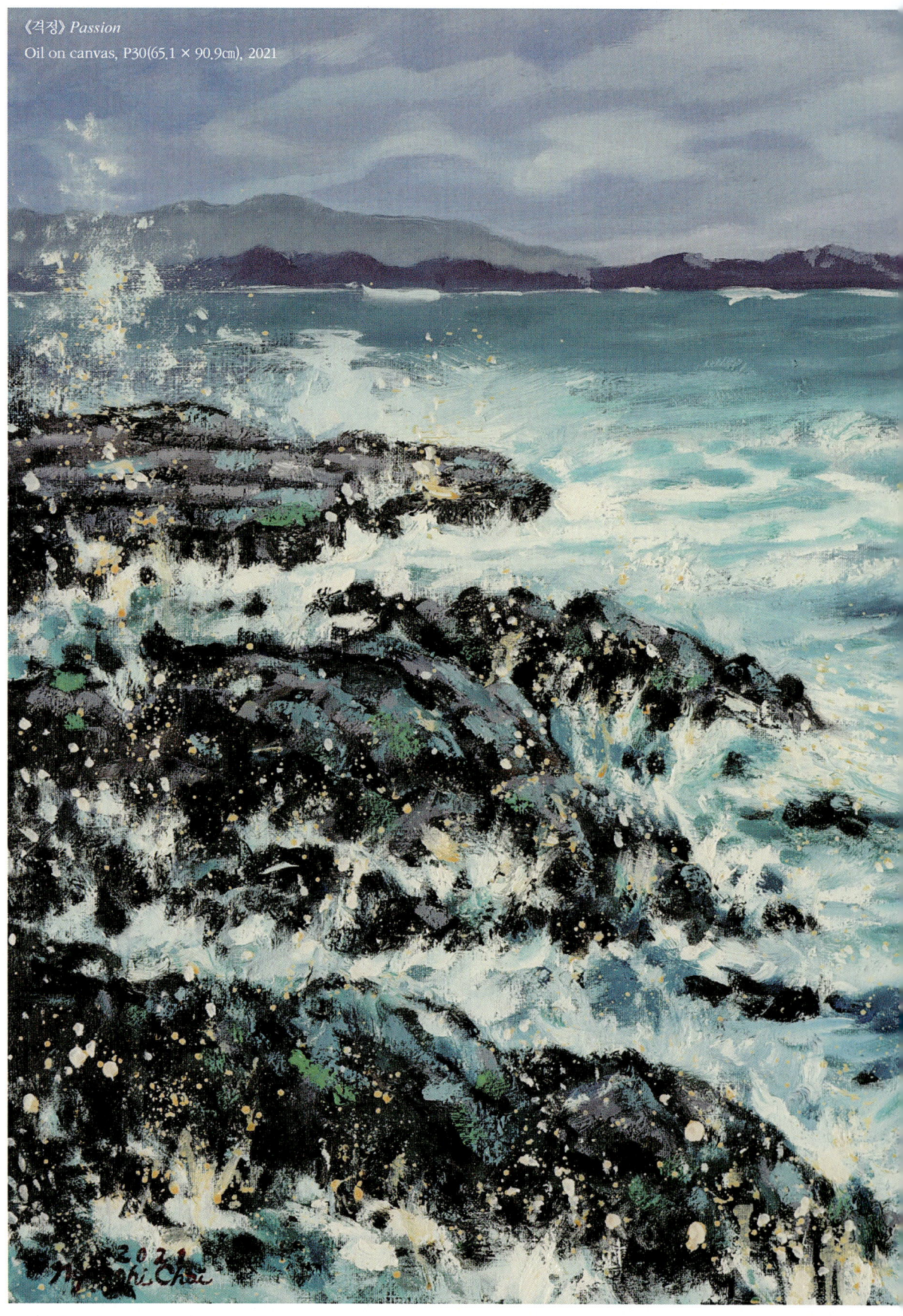

《격정》 *Passion*
Oil on canvas, P30(65.1 × 90.9㎝), 2021

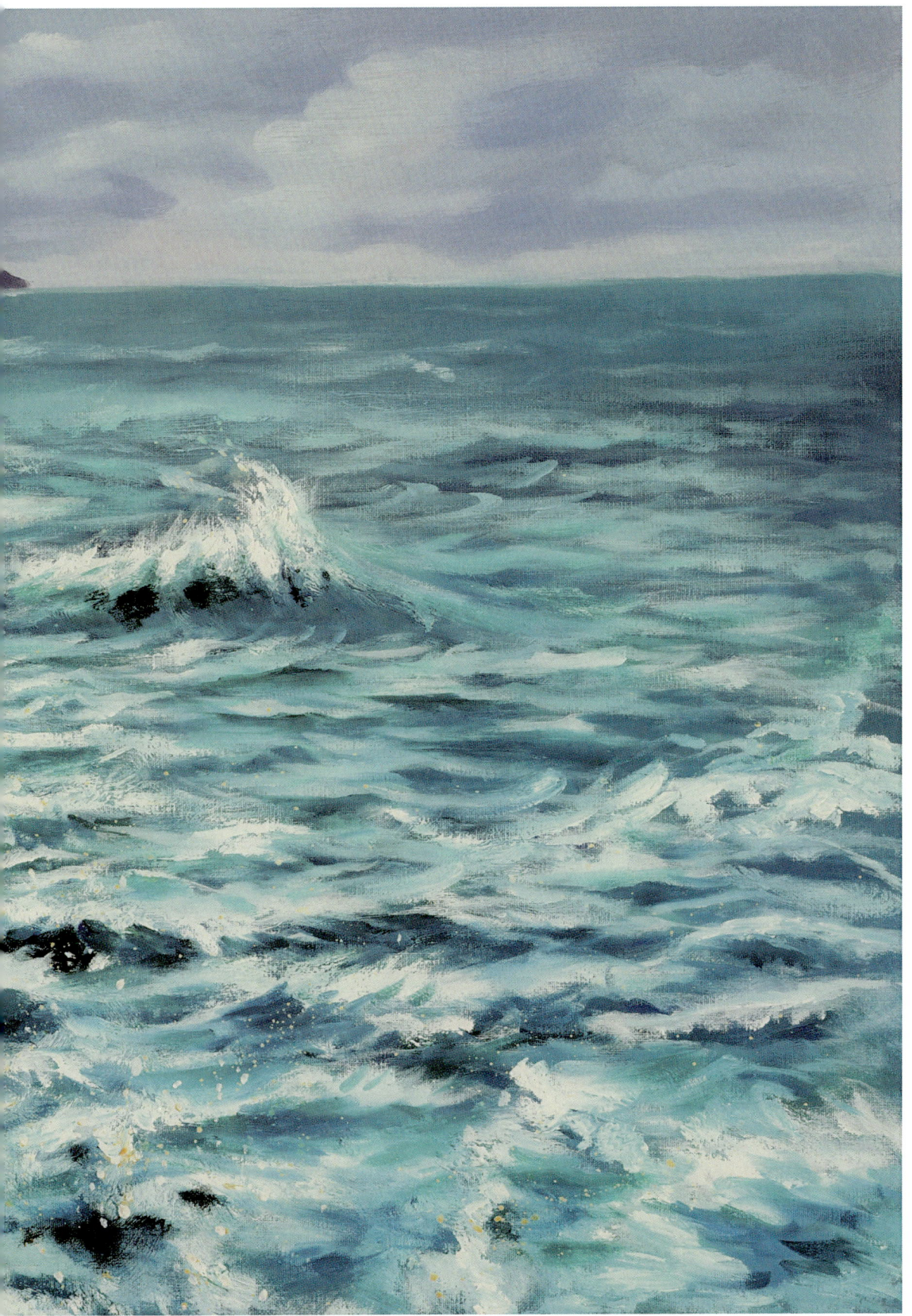

여름 바다는 격정의 바다.

까마득히 먼 시원始原에서
쉼 없이 달려온
파도는 단 한 번의 사랑에
제 몸이 산산이 부서져도
기꺼이 다시 달려온다.

나는—
누군가에게
그토록 뜨거웠던 적이 있었던가.

Summer sea—

a sea of passion.

From a distant origin,

the waves rush toward the shore.

Even knowing they may shatter

for a single moment of love,

they return,

again and again,

without hesitation.

And I—

have I ever been

that passionate

for someone?

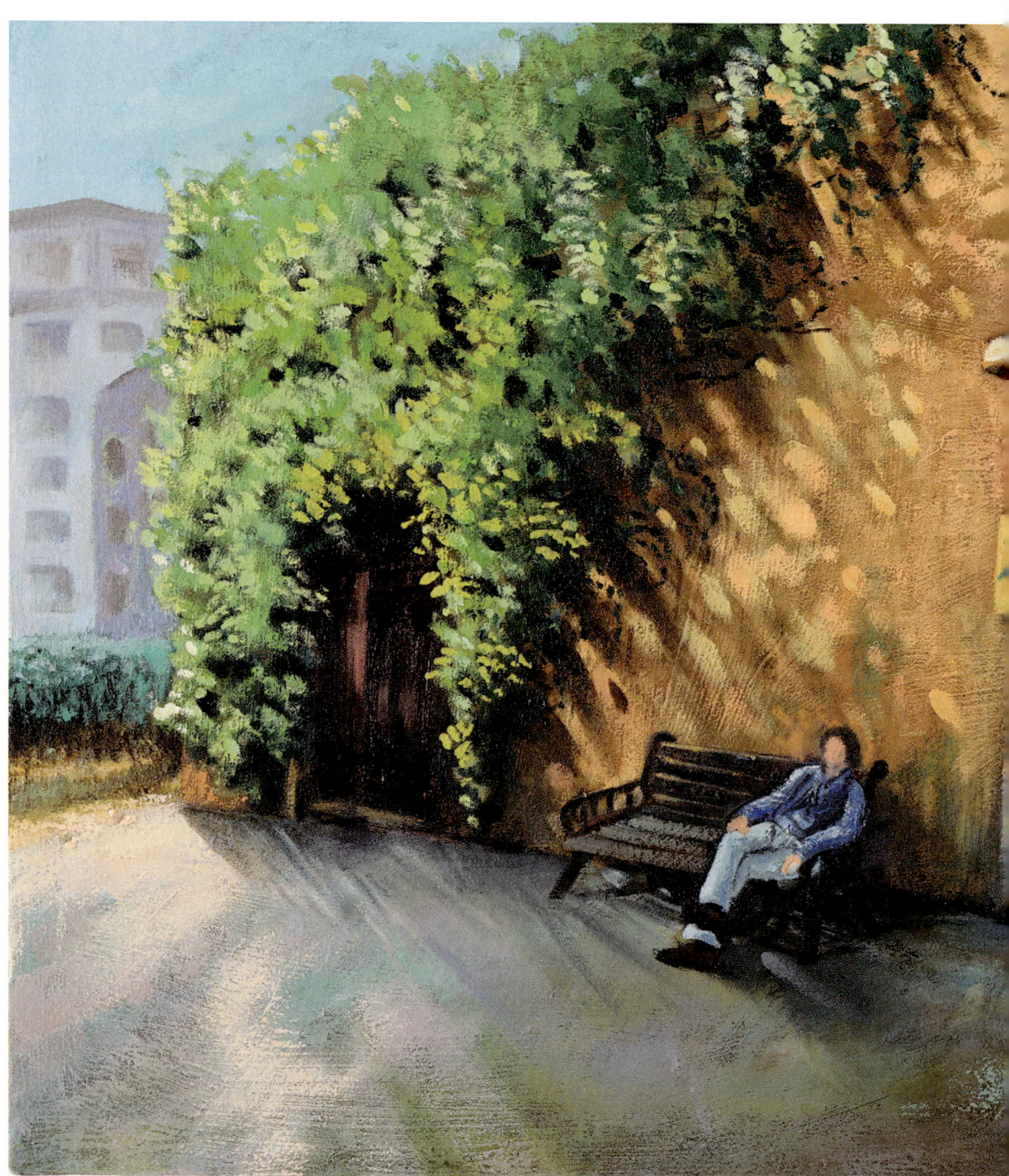

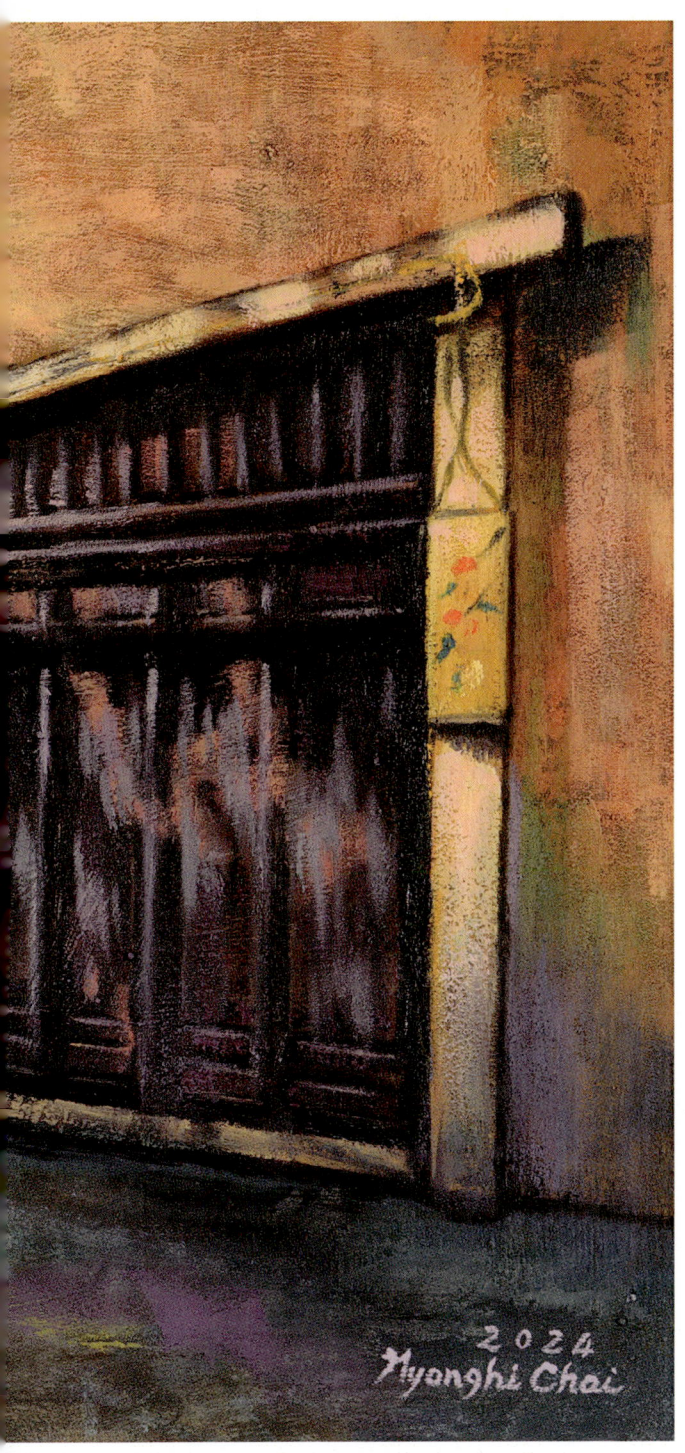

《잠시 멈춤》 *Pause*
Oil on canvas, P20(53 × 72.7㎝), 2024

뜨거운 여름,
그 격정의 시간이 지나간 뒤에는
쉼이 필요하다.

잠시 일을 내려놓고,
사람들로부터 물러나
한적한 곳에서
숨을 고른다.

다시 나아가기 위한,
잠시 멈춤.

After the blazing summer,
the season of fierce passion,
comes the need for rest.

Set your work aside,
step away from others,
and in a quiet, secluded place
catch your breath.

A gentle pause—
before moving on.

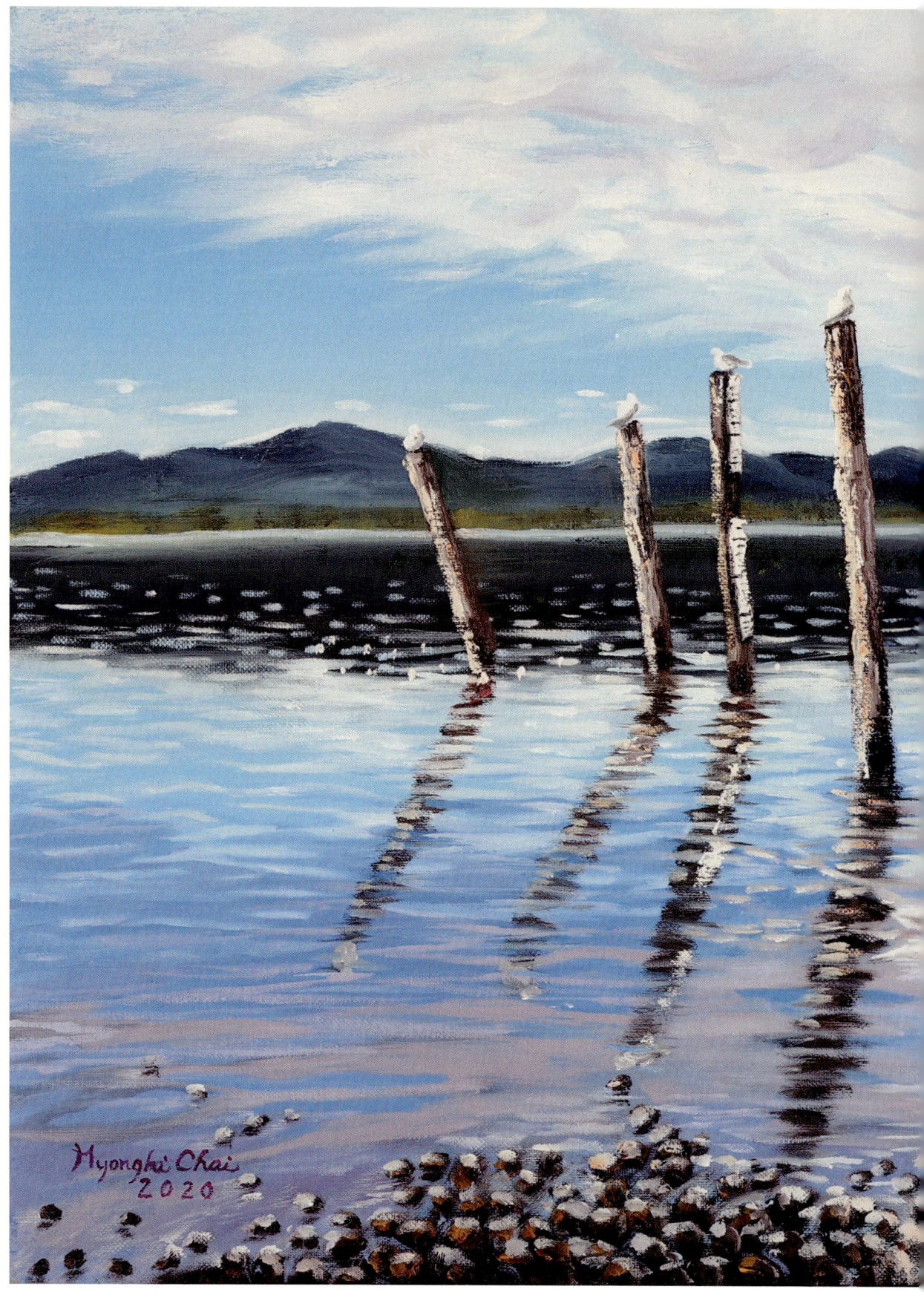

Myonghi Chai
2020

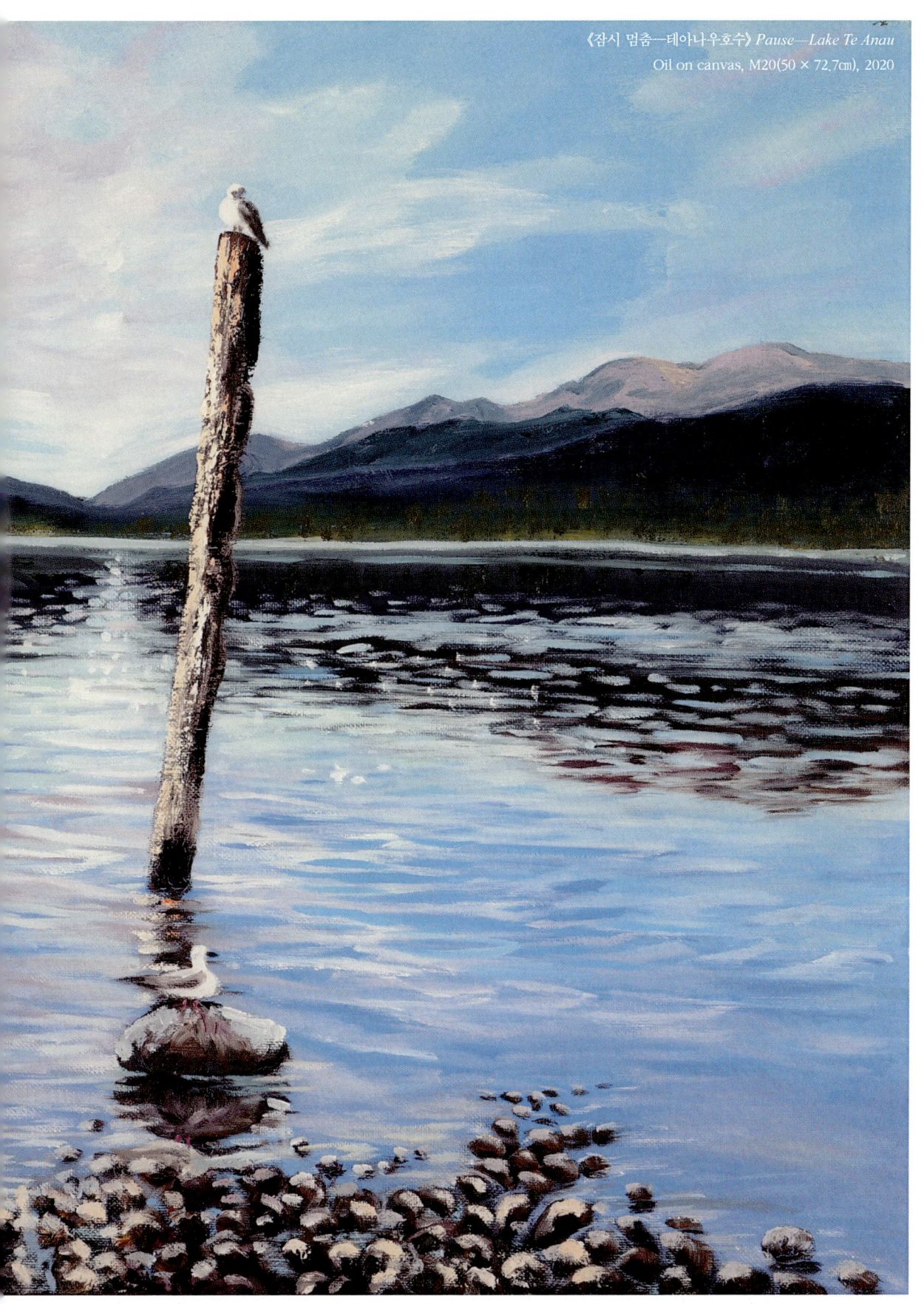

《잠시 멈춤—테아나우호수》 *Pause—Lake Te Anau*
Oil on canvas, M20(50 × 72.7㎝), 2020

잠시 멈춤이 필요한 존재는
우리만이 아니다.

먹이를 찾아,
천적을 피해
치열하게 날아다니던 새들도
마침내 안전한 곳에 내려앉아
날개를 접고
숨을 고른다.

모든 살아있는 존재에게
쉼은 필요하다.

We are not the only ones
who need to pause.

Birds, too—
after fierce flight in search of food,
or in escape from their hunters—
find a safe place to land,
fold their wings,
and catch their breath.

Every living being
needs rest.

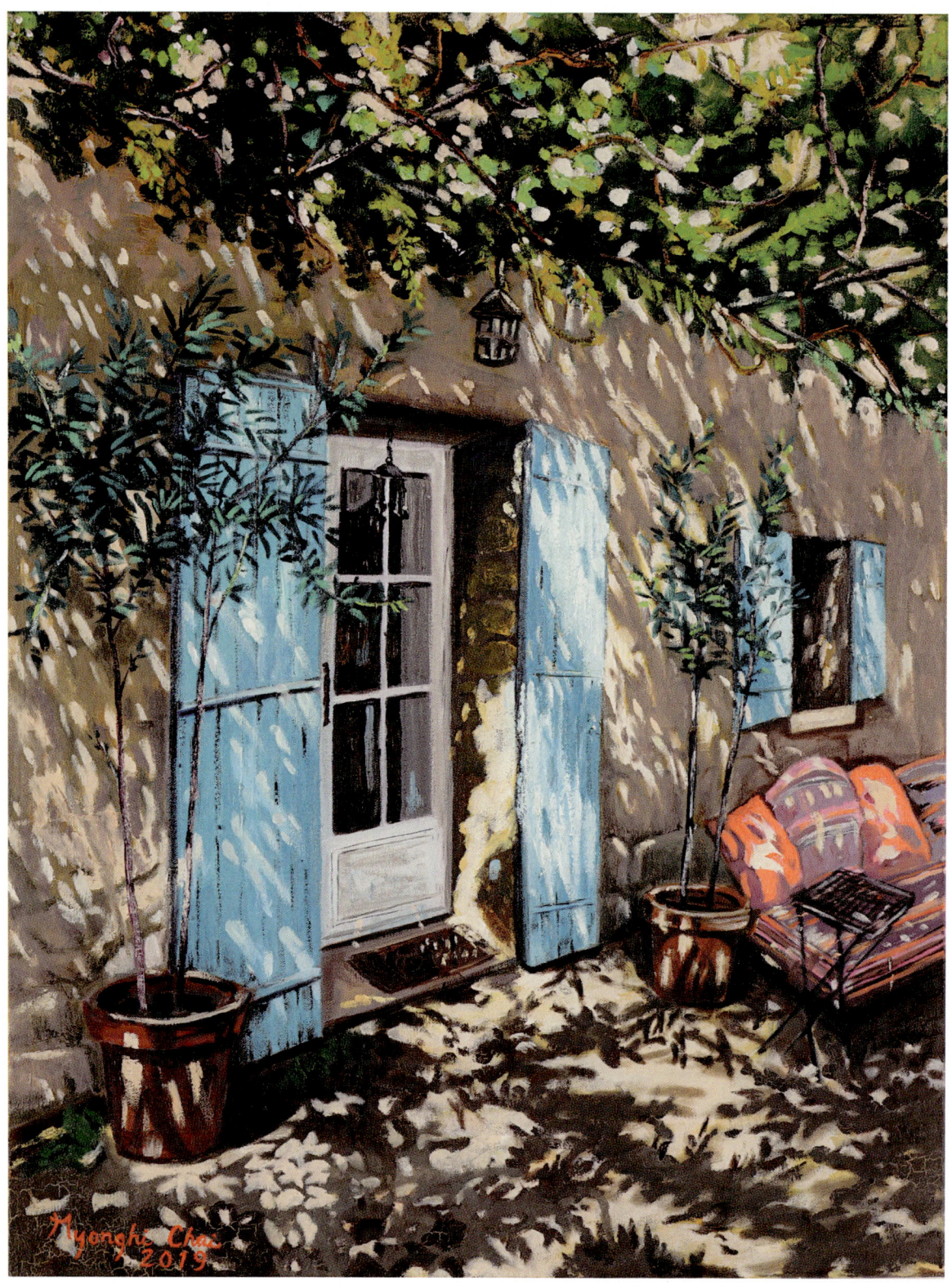

《그늘 아래》 *Under the Shade*
Oil on canvas, P20(72.7 × 53㎝), 2019

나무 그늘 아래
안락한 의자에 기대어
한숨 자도 좋고,

Under the shade,
lean back in a cozy chair—
and take a nap···

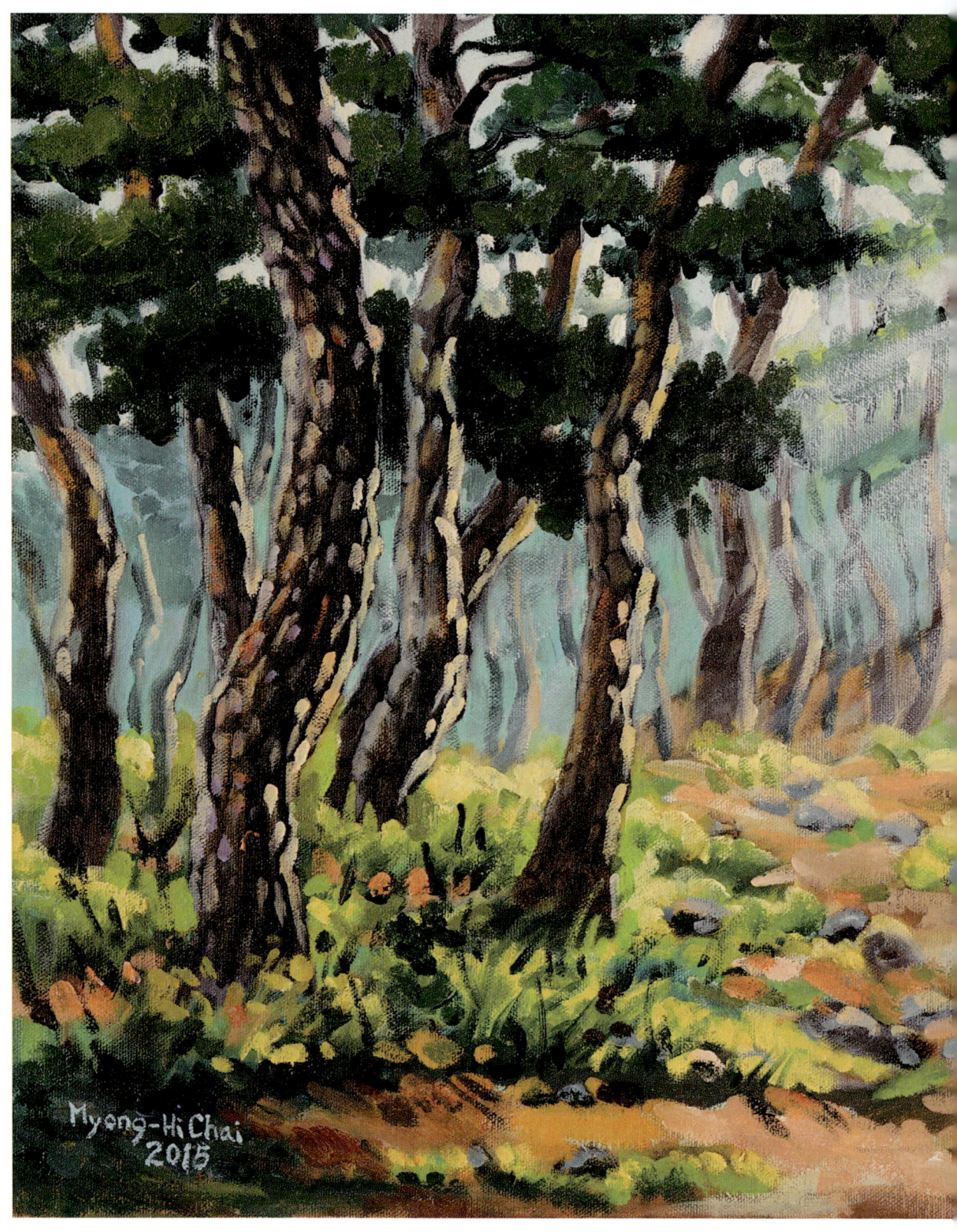

Myong-Hi Chai
2015

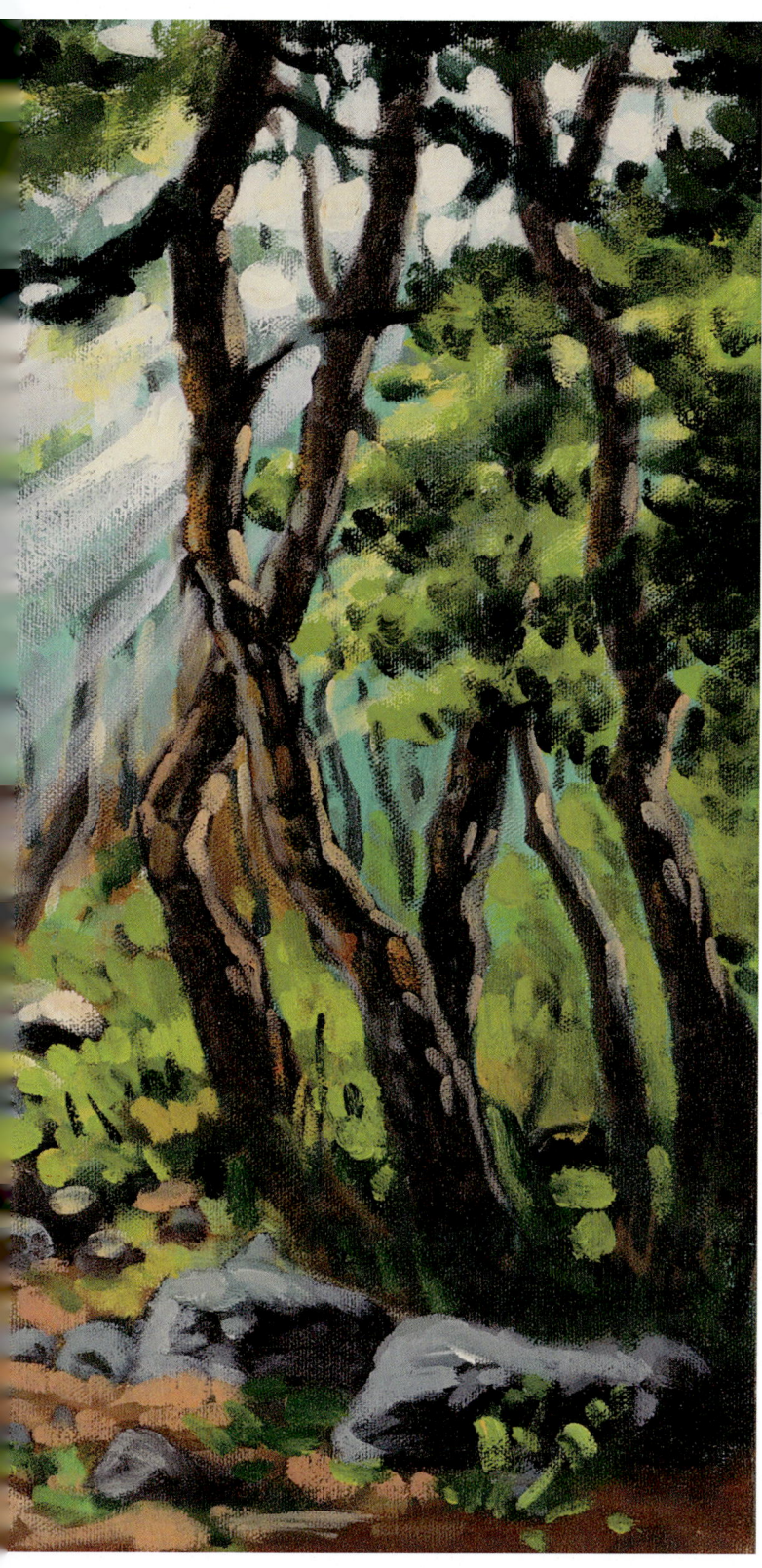

《숲길》 *Forest Trail*
Oil on canvas, P10(40.9 × 53㎝), 2015

고즈넉한 숲길을 따라
느린 걸음으로 거닐어도 좋고,

Or stroll slowly
along a quiet forest trail···

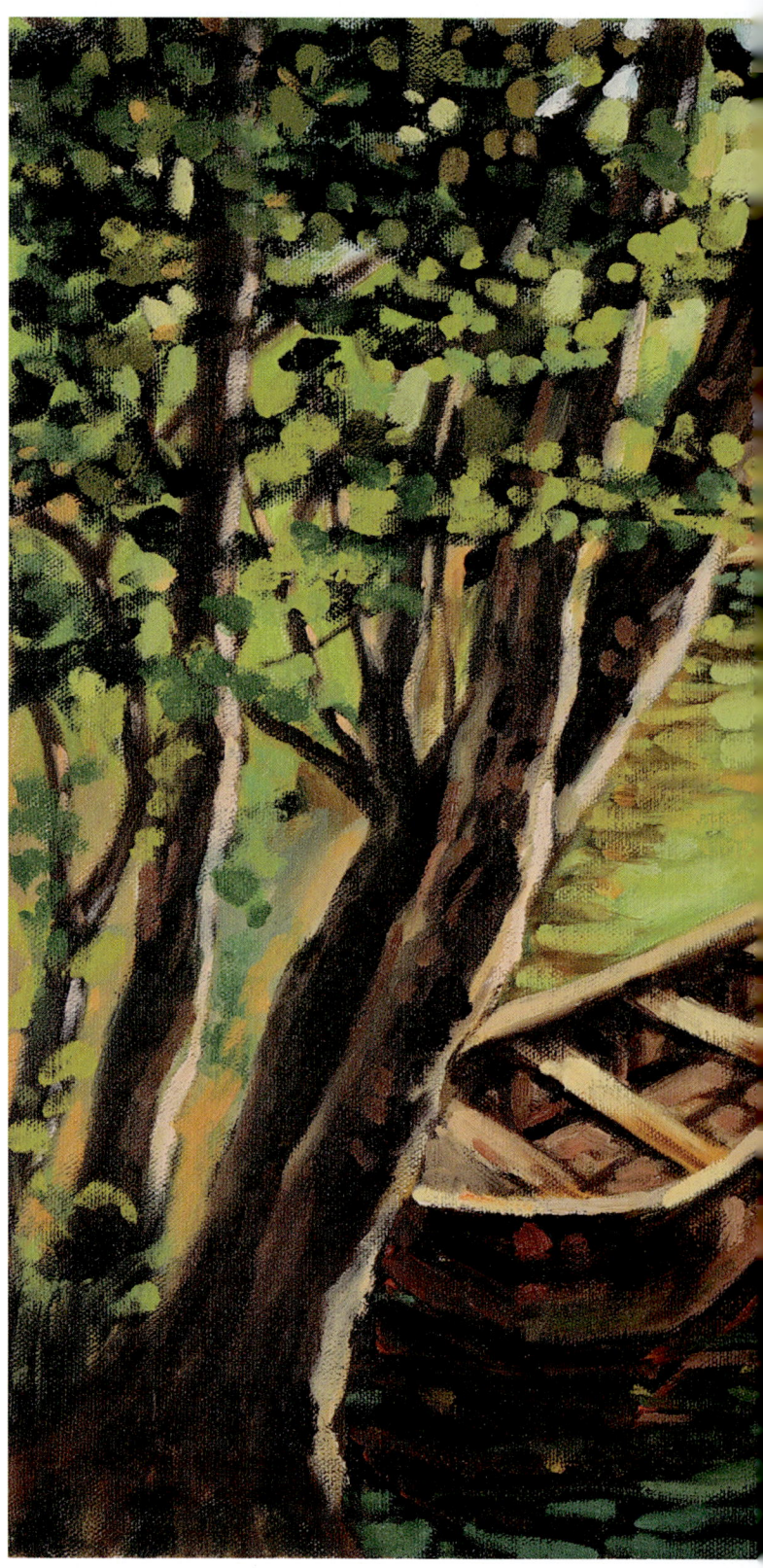

《쉼》 *The Rest*
Oil on canvas, P10(40.9 × 53㎝), 2014

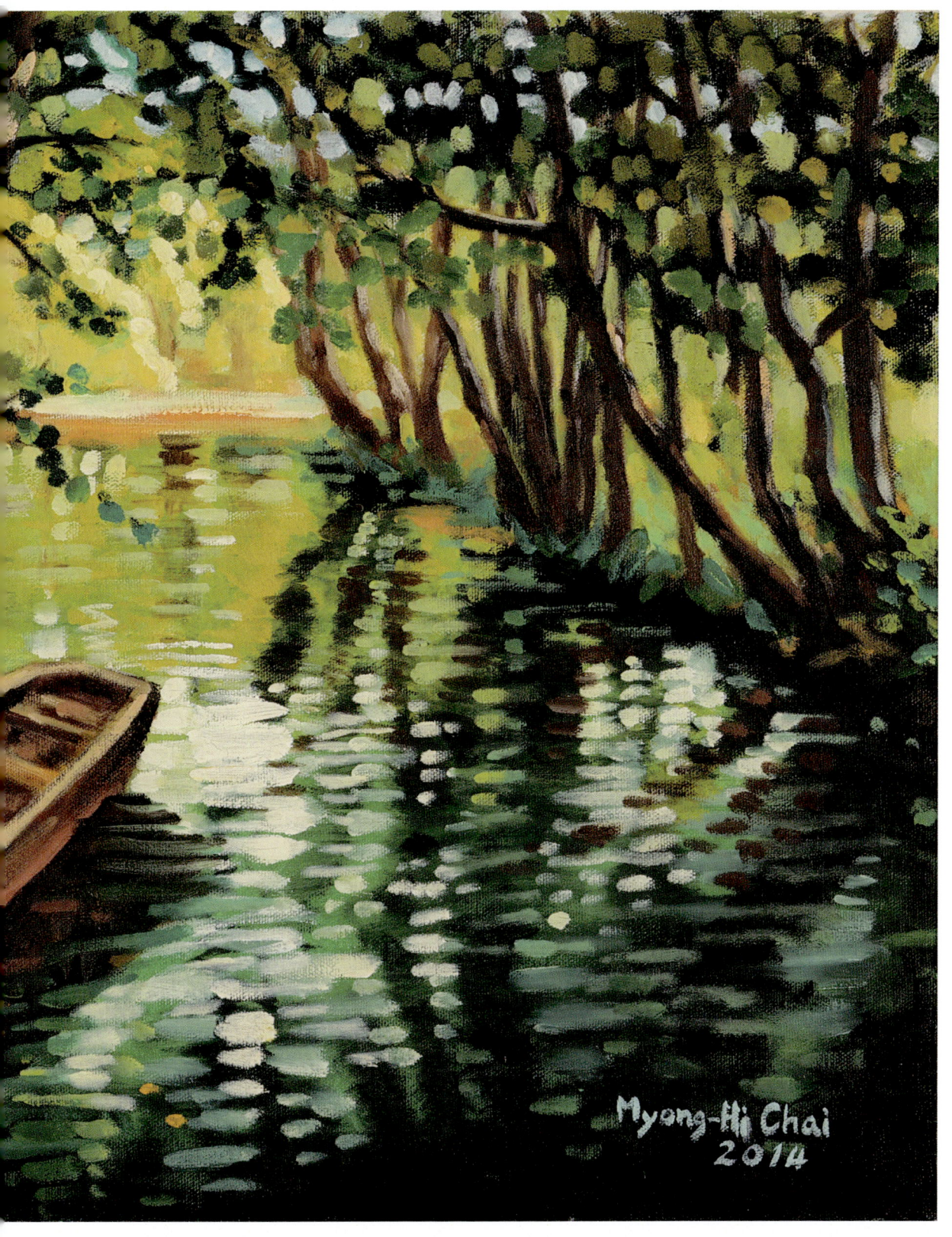

Myong-Hi Chai
2014

혹은
그저 멈추어
멍—하니 있어도 좋다.

당신만의
고요하고 한적한 쉼터는 어디인가?

Or just stop—
and simply··· be still.
That alone
is more than enough.

Where is your own
quiet, secluded place?

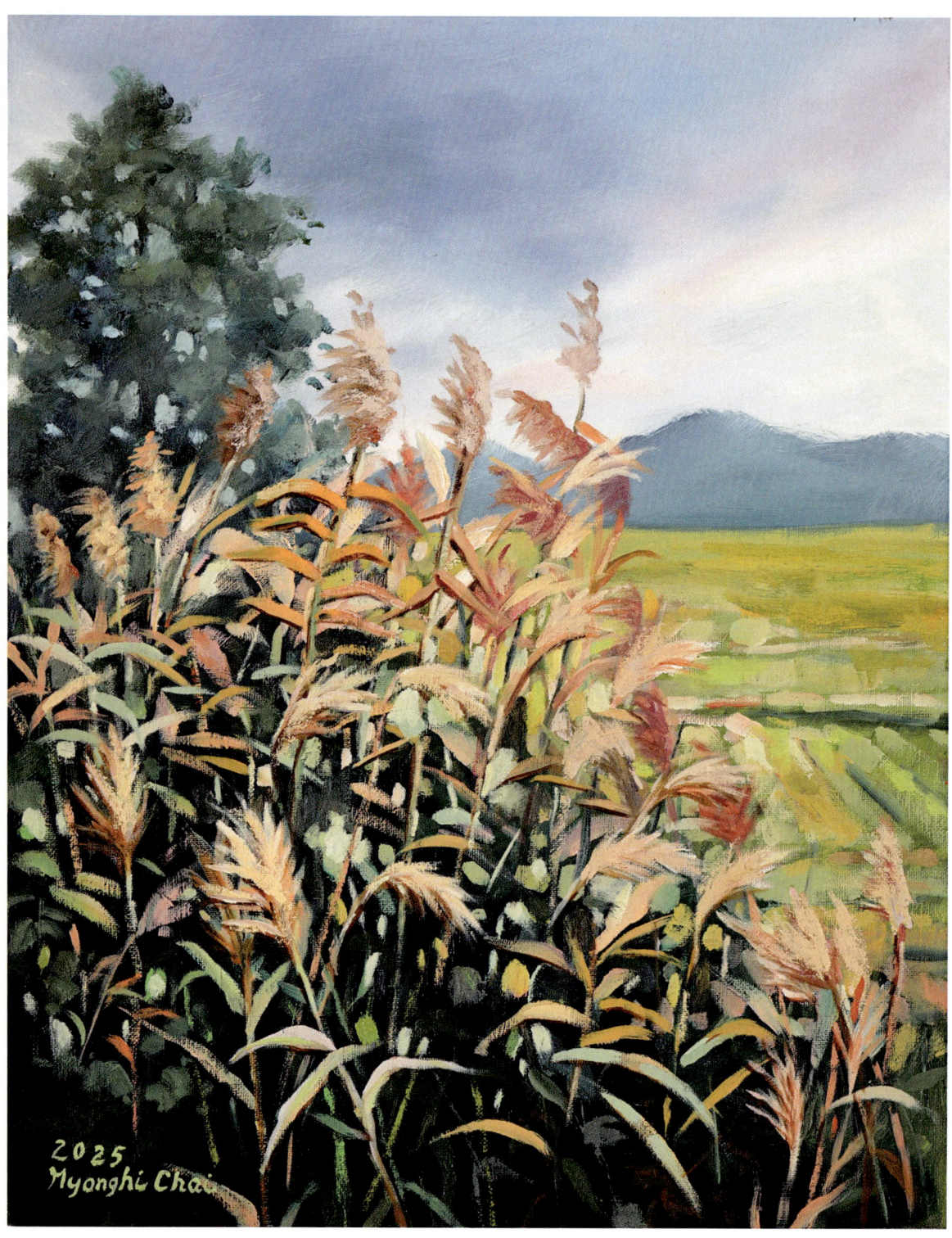

《바람의 노래—갈대》 *Song of the Wind—Reeds*
Oil on canvas, P10(53 × 40.9㎝), 2025

그렇게 잠시 멈추고 나면
어느덧 다시, 가을이다.

강가의 갈대는
바람의 노래에 맞춰
갈색 춤을 춘다.

여자의 마음이 갈대와 같다고 했던가.
쉽게 흔들리지만
쉽게 꺾이지 않는다.
한 번 뿌리 내린 마음은
좀처럼 거두지 않는다.

아, 그렇다.
여자의 마음은 갈대와 같다.

After such a gentle pause,
autumn returns.

By the riverside in fall,
the reeds dance a brown ballet
to the song of the wind.

They say a woman's heart is like the reeds—
easily moved, yet not easily broken;
once it takes root,
it is not easily uprooted.

Ah, indeed.
A woman's heart is like the reeds.

억새는 외로움을 타는 듯하다.
가을 산 어디에서나
무리를 지어,
바람의 노래에 맞춰
은빛 춤을 춘다.

격정의 짧은 군무가 끝나면,
간직한 모든 색을 토해내고
마른 갈색으로 스러져간다.

그러나 억새는 돌아온다.
그 자리로,
언제나.

The silver grasses seem to feel loneliness.
Across autumn's mountains,
they sway in silver
to the song of the wind—
always in a crowd, never alone.

When their brief, passionate dance is over,
they release the colors they held,
fading into dry brown.

Yet they return,
to that very spot,
always.

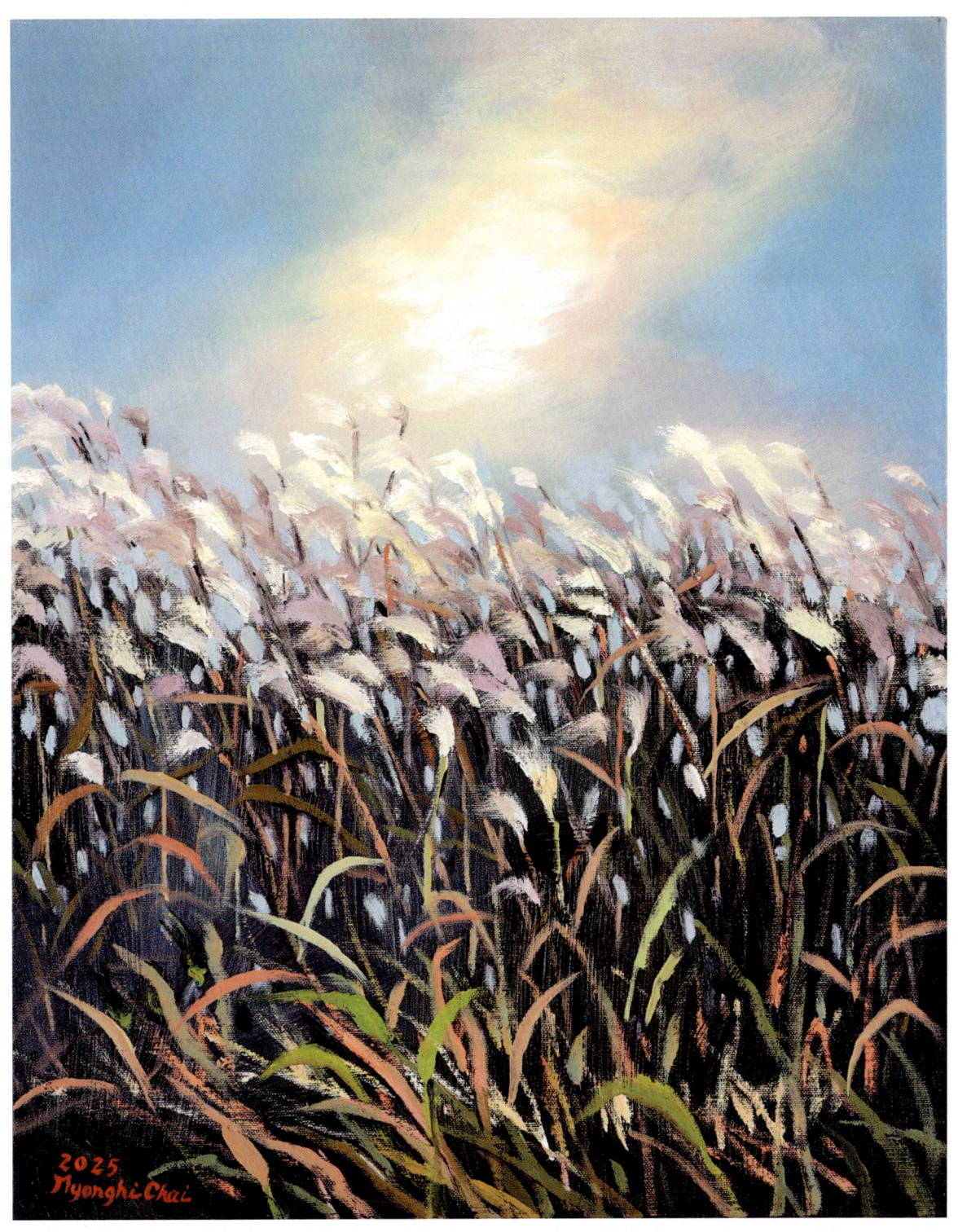

《바람의 노래—억새》 *Song of the Wind—Silver Grasses*
Oil on canvas, P10(53 × 40.9㎝), 2025

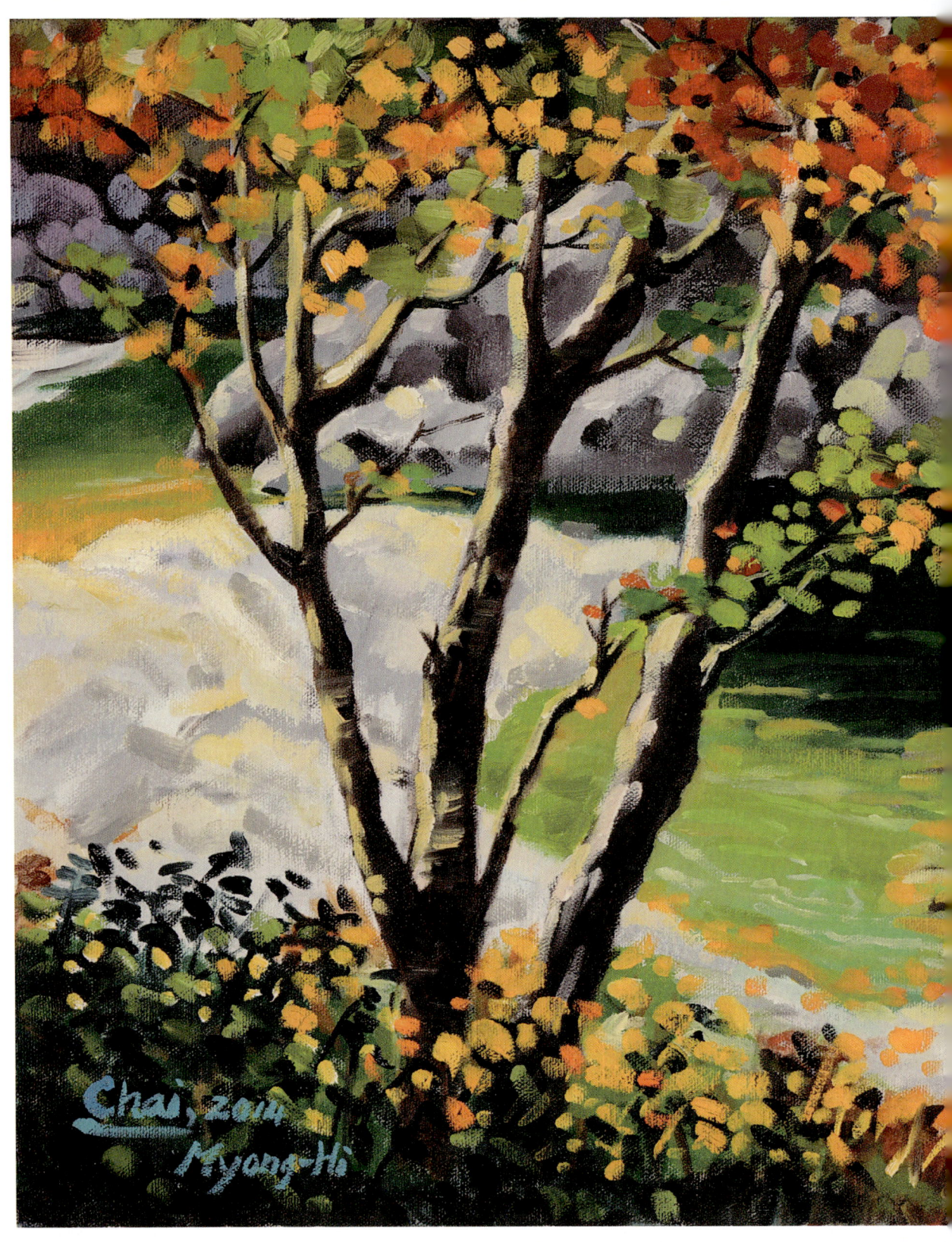

Chai, 2014
Myong-Hi

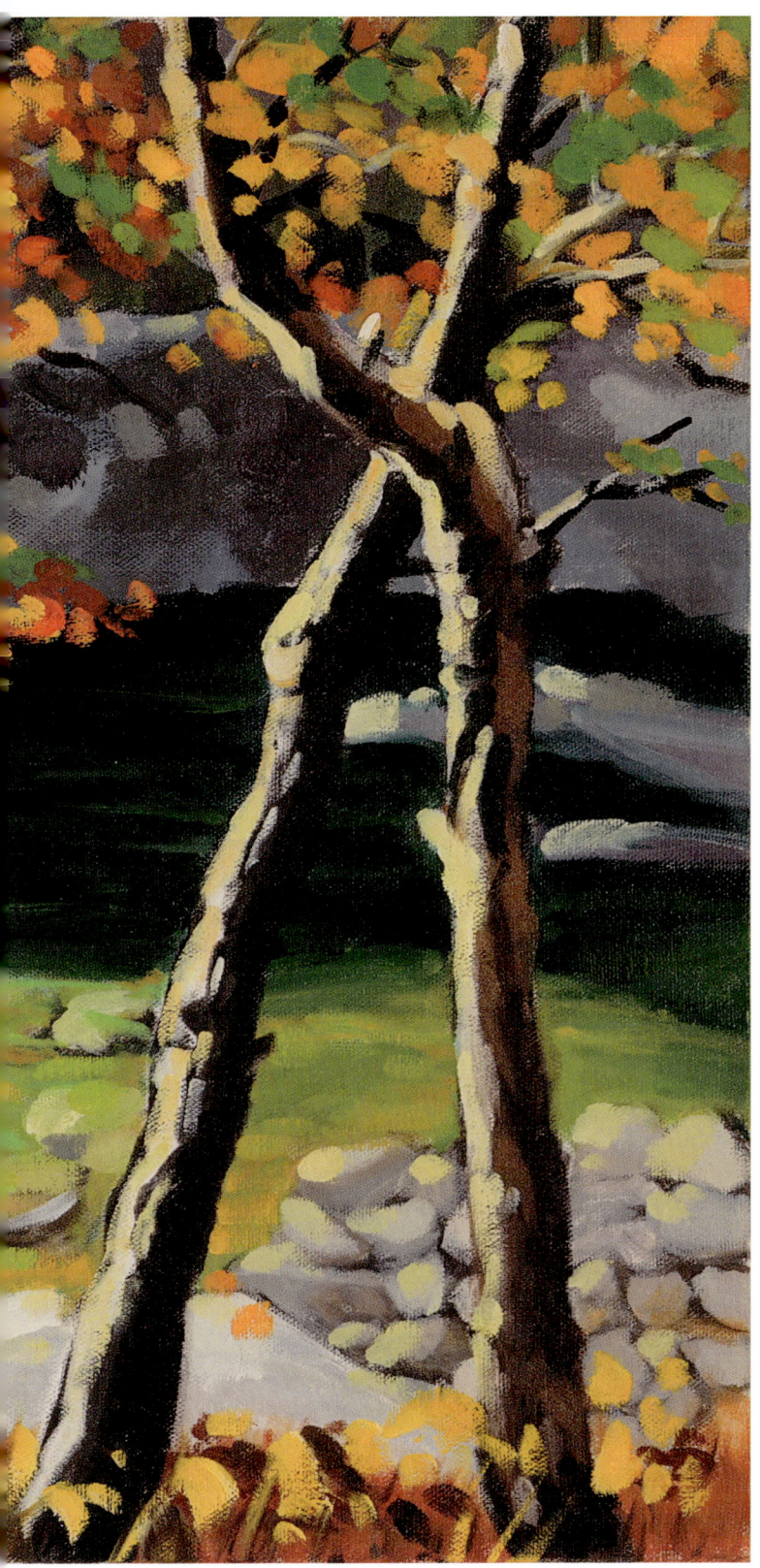

《계곡의 가을》 *Autumn in the Valley*
Oil on canvas, P10(40.9 × 53㎝), 2014

이렇게 가을은 깊어 간다.

알베르 카뮈는 말했다.
"가을은 모든 잎이 꽃이 되는 두 번째 봄이다."
아, 다시 봄인가?
아니다,
다시 가을이다.

계절의 순환,
생명의 연속성,
대자연에 대한 경외심,
그리고
그 속에 내가 있다는 안도감.

가을이,
참 좋다.

And thus, autumn deepens.

Albert Camus once said,

"Autumn is a second spring when every leaf is a flower."

Ah—

is it spring again?

No—

it is autumn, once more.

The cycle of seasons,

the continuity of life,

a reverence for the rhythms of nature,

and the quiet comfort of belonging within it.

Ah, autumn—

how I love it.

Part 2

삶—
함께 걷는 여정

여행은
일상을 잠시 멈추고
숨을 고르며
다시 나아갈 힘을 비축하는 시간

Part 2

Life—

A Shared Journey

Travel is a pause—

a quiet moment to step away from daily life,

to breathe,

and to gather strength before moving on

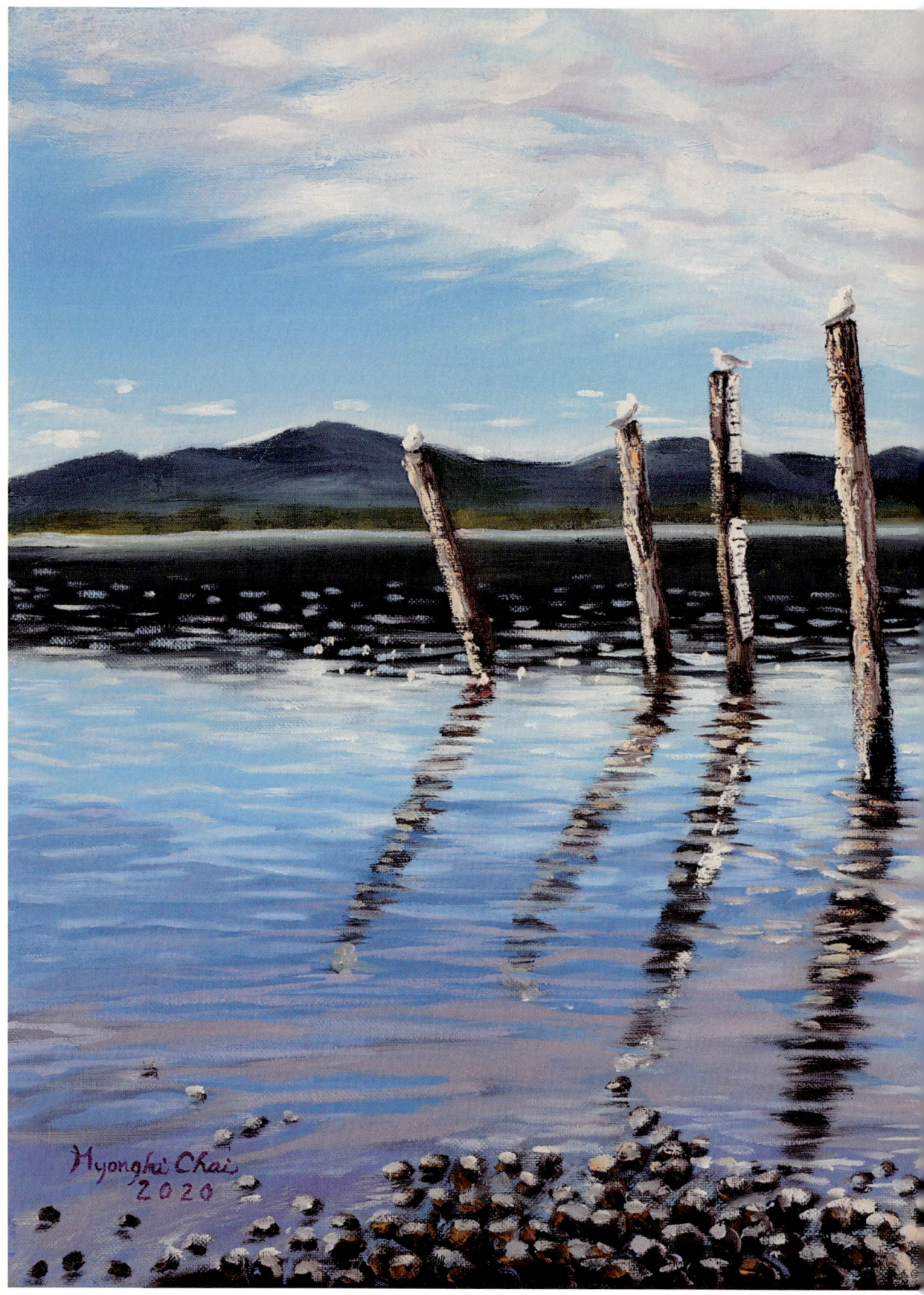

Myonghi Chai
2020

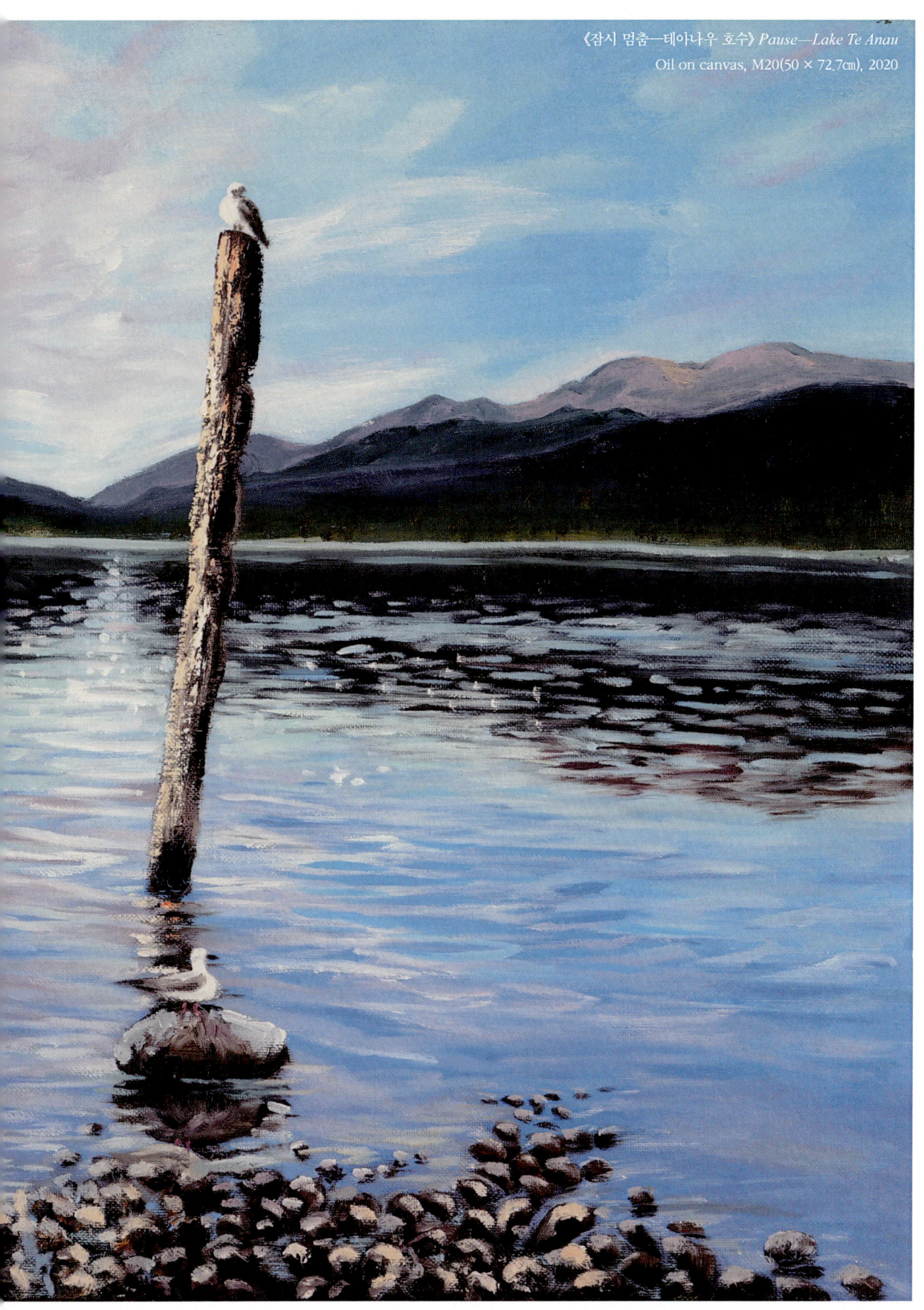

《잠시 멈춤—테아나우 호수》 *Pause—Lake Te Anau*
Oil on canvas, M20(50 × 72.7㎝), 2020

뉴질랜드 테아나우 호수 앞,
커피 한 잔을 위해 잠시 멈추었던 아침.

호수엔 하얀 새똥을 뒤집어쓴
나무 말뚝 몇 개가 물 위로 솟아 있었고,
말뚝 위엔 물새들이 하나씩 자리를 차지한 채
날개를 접고 고요히 쉬고 있었다.

근처 크고 작은 바위들도
또 다른 새들의 쉼터가 되어 있었고,
자리를 찾지 못한 새들은
주변을 서성이며 순서를 기다리는 듯했다.

저 새들도,
이곳에 잠시 멈춰 선 나처럼,
움직임을 멈추고
숨을 고르며
힘을 비축하고 있었다.

다음 비상을 위한
잠깐의 쉼.

One morning in New Zealand,
I paused for a cup of coffee by Lake Te Anau.

A few wooden poles rose from the water,
white with bird droppings.
Each one was claimed by a seabird,
perched still, wings folded.

Large and small rocks nearby
offered resting spots for others.
Some birds wandered around,
as if waiting for their turn.

They, too—like me—
had stopped for a while,
motionless,
breathing,
and recharging.

A brief pause
for the next flight.

《지베르니에서 모네를 추억하다》
Remembering Monet in Giverny
Oil on canvas, M20(50 × 72.7㎝), 2019

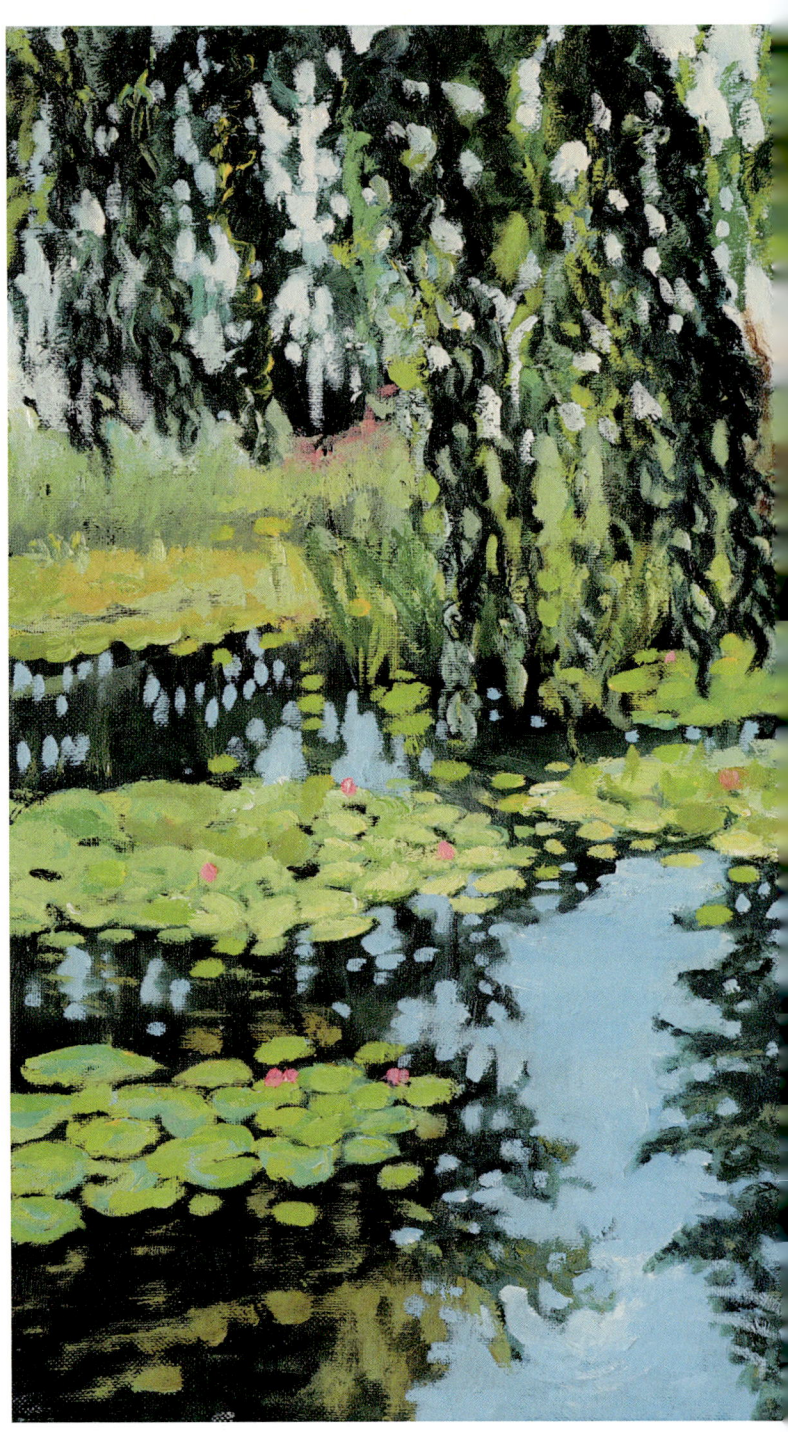

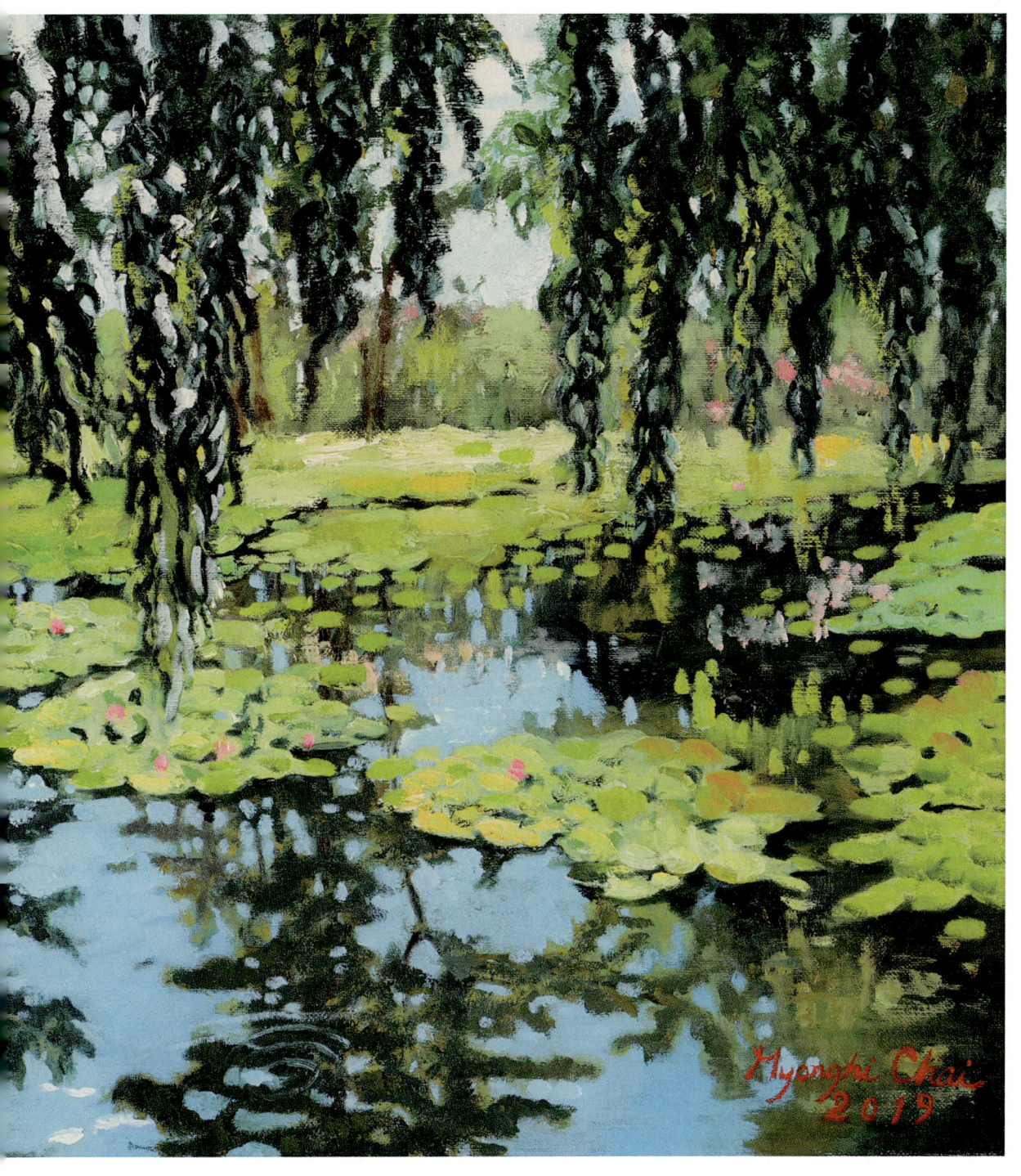

언젠가,
'인상주의 투어'라는 이름으로
유럽을 여행한 적이 있다.

프랑스 지베르니,
모네의 수련정원 앞에 섰을 때—
마치 그의 캔버스 속으로 들어간 듯했다.

바로 그 순간,
모네가 내 곁에 서 있는 것처럼 느껴졌다.
그 자리에 서서
시시각각 변하는 빛과 물결,
그리고 수련을 화폭에 담고 있는
모네가 말이다.

Once,

I traveled through Europe

on an "Impressionist Art Tour."

Standing before the water garden

at Monet's home in Giverny, France,

I felt I had stepped into his canvas.

In that moment,

I could almost see Monet right beside me—

capturing on his canvas

the shifting light,

the gentle ripples,

and the blooming water lilies.

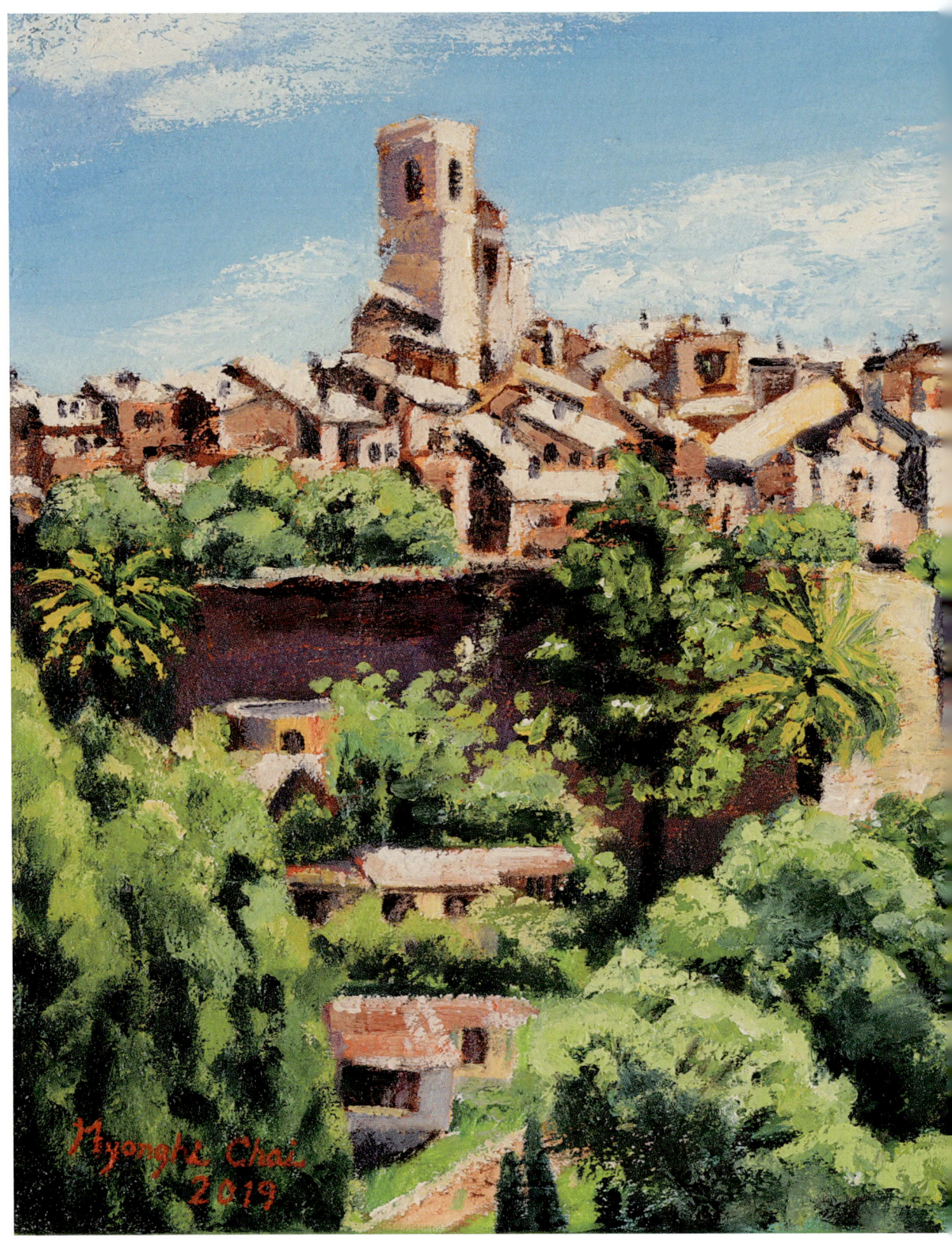

Myonghi Chai
2019

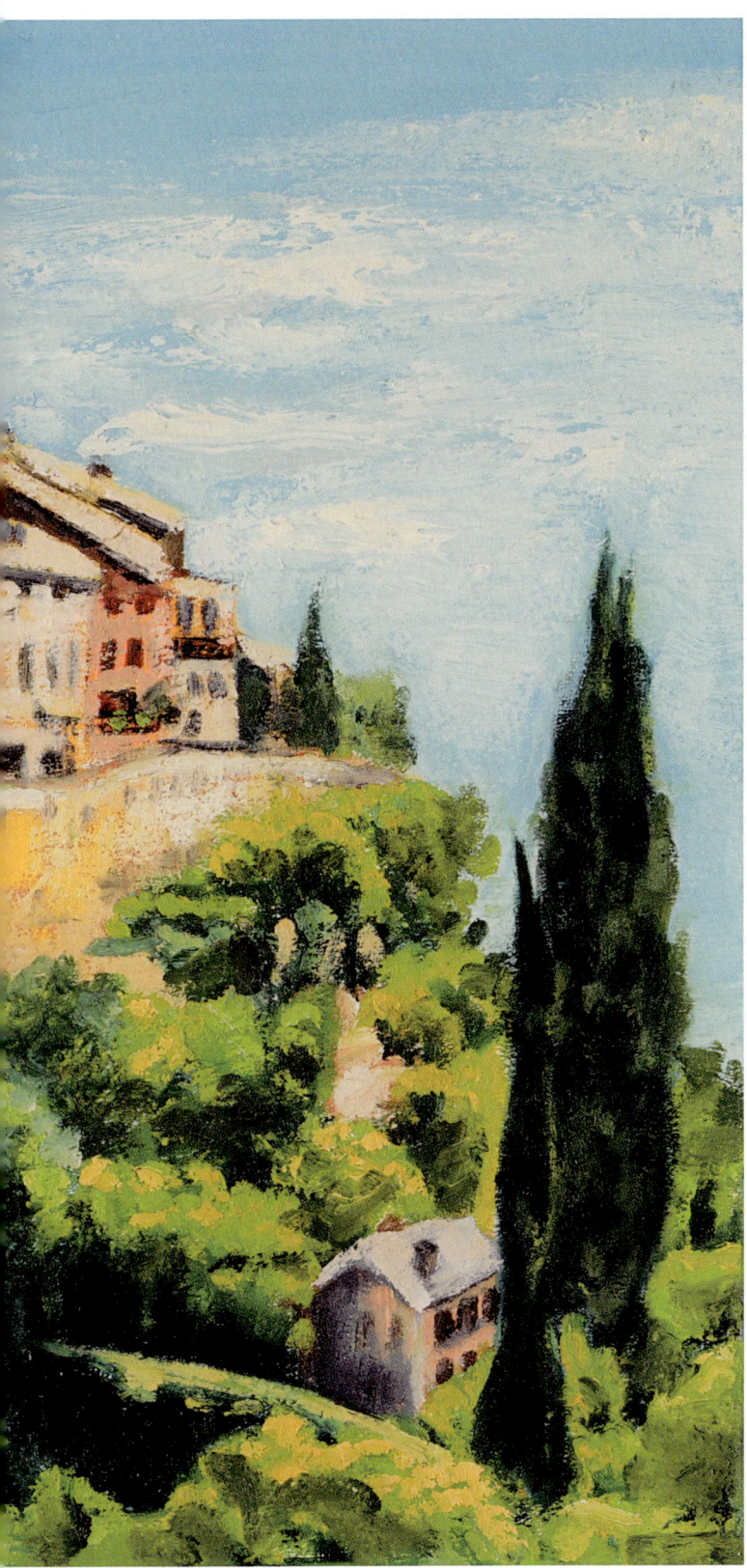

《샤갈의 마을—생폴드방스》
The Village of Chagall—Saint-Paul-de-Vence
Oil on canvas, P10(40.9 × 53㎝), 2019

생폴드방스—
'색채의 마술사' 마르크 샤갈이
살았고, 또 잠들어 있는 곳.
그래서 사람들은 이곳을
'샤갈의 마을'이라 부른다.

언덕 위에 자리한 이 중세 마을은
지중해를 굽어보며,
샤갈의 그림 속에도 자주 등장한다.

그 마을이 한눈에 들어오는 자리에 서니,
문득 생각이 스친다.
언젠가 샤갈도
이곳 어딘가에 앉아,
저 마을을 바라보았으리라.

Saint-Paul-de-Vence—
where Marc Chagall,
the *Magician of Color,*
once lived and now rests.
Hence, it is often called
The Village of Chagall.

This medieval hill town,
overlooking the Mediterranean,
often appears in his paintings.

Standing where the village unfolds below,
I wonder—
perhaps Chagall once sat here, too,
gazing at the same hillside town.

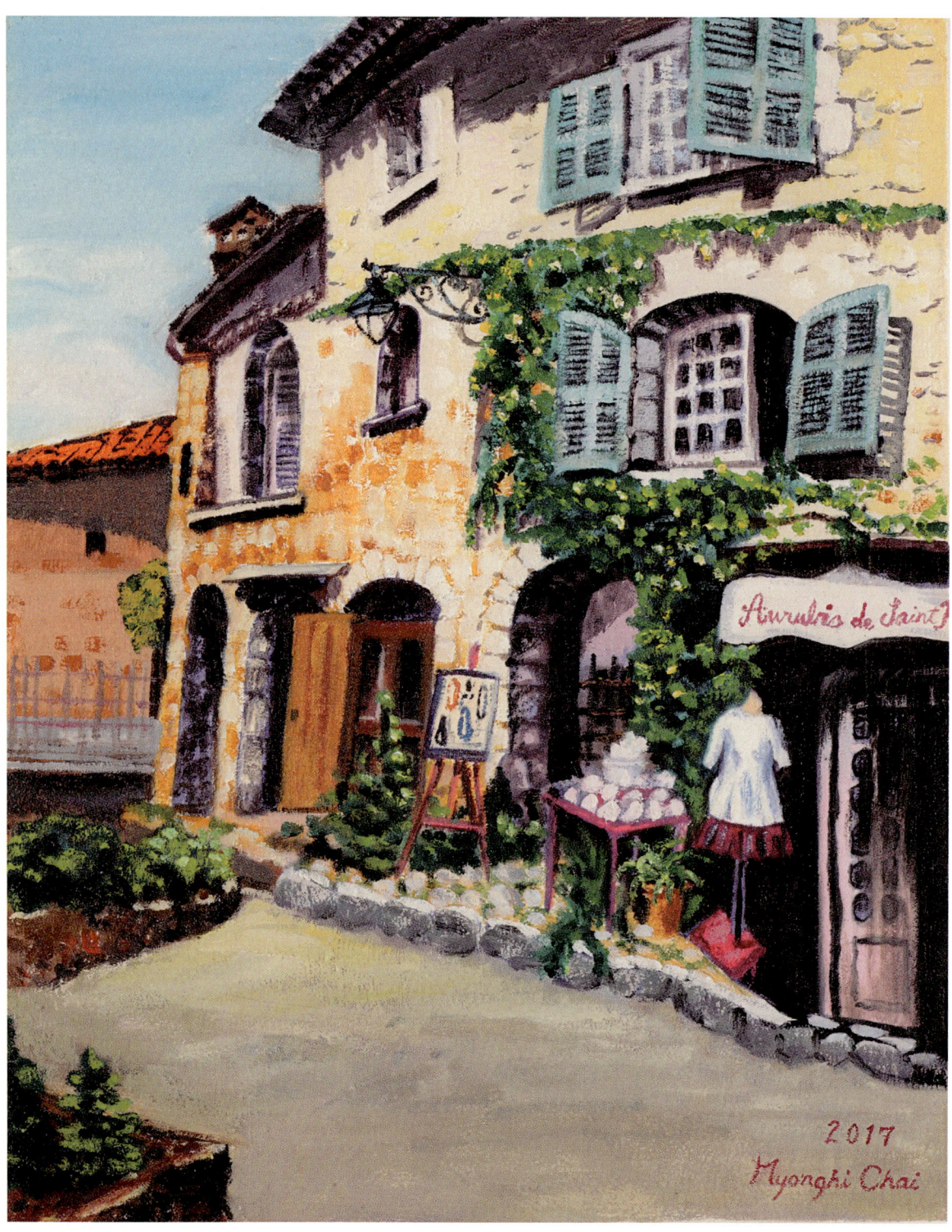

《생폴드방스》 *Saint-Paul-de-Vence*
Oil on canvas, P10(53 × 40.9㎝), 2017

생폴드방스의 좁고 구불구불한 돌계단을 오르다 보면
문득, 시간여행을 하는 듯하다.
오래된 돌담과 석조건물 사이로 비치는
지중해의 푸른빛이 눈부시다.

가난한 시절의 피카소와 동료들이
즐겨 찾았다는 작은 식당 안에는,
이제는 세계적으로 이름난 그들의 작품이
무심히 걸려있다.

중세의 건물 안에서 만나는
현대 예술의 숨결—
나는 역사와 예술 사이를 떠다니듯
황홀감에 잠긴다.

Walking the narrow, winding stone steps
of Saint-Paul-de-Vence,
I feel as though I've stepped back in time.
The cobalt blue of the Mediterranean,
glimpsed between old stone walls
and timeworn buildings,
dazzles the eyes.

Inside a small restaurant once frequented
by Picasso and his fellow artists—
struggling then, legendary now—
their paintings hang quietly on the walls.

Amid whispers of modern art
housed within medieval stone,
I drift in reverie—
suspended between history and art.

투레트쉬르루,
남프랑스 프로방스-알프-코트다쥐르에 자리한,
니스 근교 또 하나의 중세 마을.
생폴드방스보다 규모는 작지만
훨씬 조용하고 평화로워
오히려 걷기에는 더 아늑하다.

언덕 위에 자리한 이 마을 역시,
중세 석조 건물들 사이로 이어진
좁은 골목길을 따라 걷는 즐거움이 있다.
작고 아기자기한 수공예 상점들이
곳곳에서 발길을 붙든다.

이곳은, 현지 가이드가
살짝 귀띔해 준 숨겨진 보석 같은 마을이다.

Tourrettes-sur-Loup,
a medieval village near Nice,
nestled in the Provence-Alpes-Côte d'Azur region
of southern France.
Smaller than Saint-Paul-de-Vence,
yet quieter and more peaceful—
perhaps even more charming to wander through.

Perched on a hill,
this village, too, offers the quiet joy of wandering
through narrow alleys lined with old stone houses,
where tiny artisan shops await.

It was our local guide
who whispered to us about this hidden gem of a village.

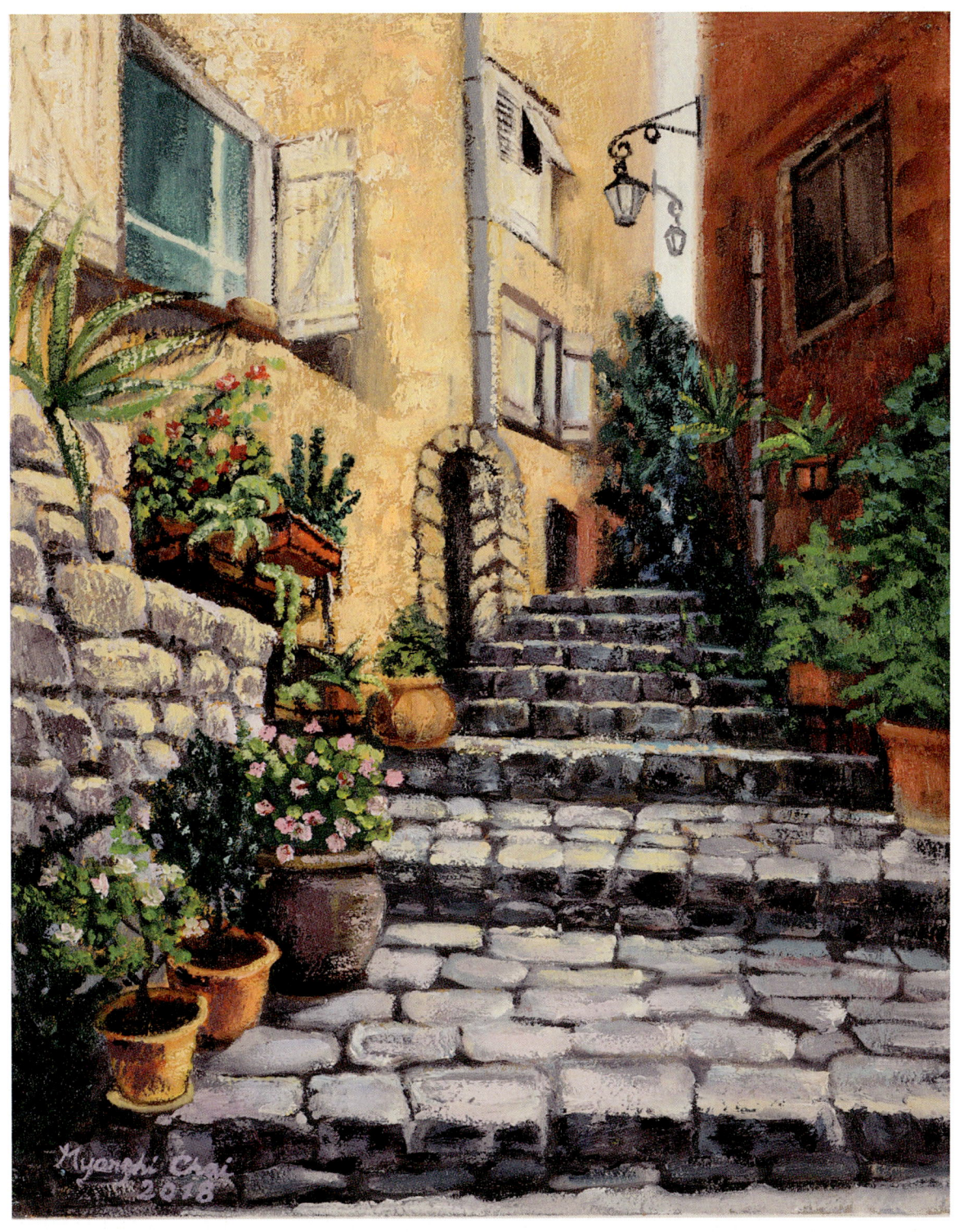

《투레트쉬르루》 *Tourrettes-sur-Loup*
Oil on canvas, P10(53 × 40.9㎝), 2018

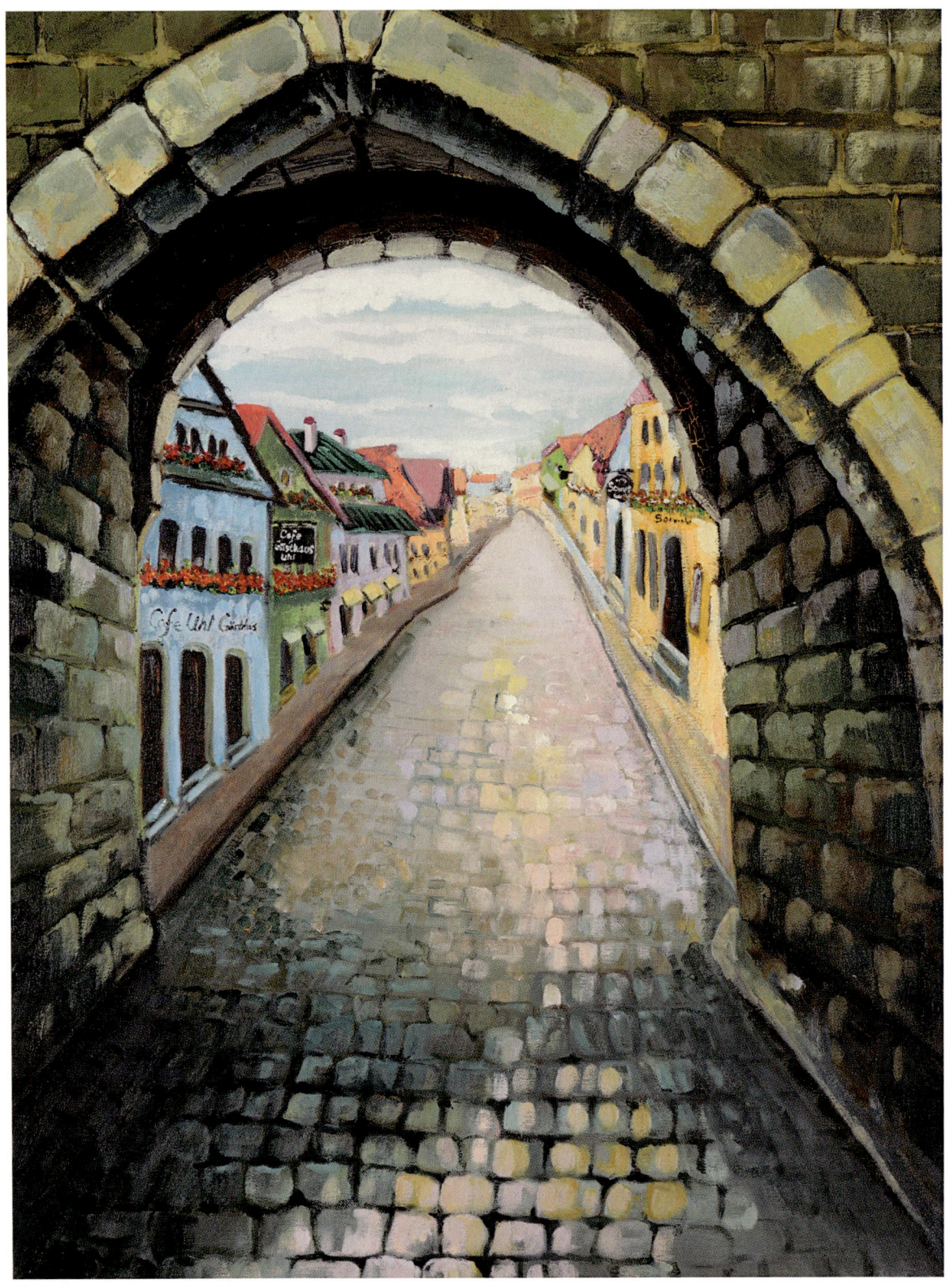

《로텐부르크》 *Rothenburg ob der Tauber*
Oil on canvas, P20(72.7 × 53cm), 2015

독일에도, 걷기 좋은 중세 마을이 많다.
그중 바이에른주의 로텐부르크는
중세의 성벽과 탑,
돌로 깔린 좁은 골목길이 고스란히 남아 있어
걸으며 둘러보는 재미가 있다.

게다가 이 마을은
독일의 '낭만가도' 위에 놓여 있어
여행길 자체가 이미 낭만적이다.

돌길을 오래 걷고 싶다면,
편한 신발은 필수다.

Germany, too, is home to many walkable medieval towns.
Among them, Rothenburg ob der Tauber in Bavaria
stands out—
with its well-preserved city walls and towers,
and narrow cobbled lanes
that invite you to explore on foot.

Set along Germany's famed "Romantic Road,"
this town truly lives up to its name.

If you plan to wander its cobbled paths for a while,
comfortable shoes are a must.

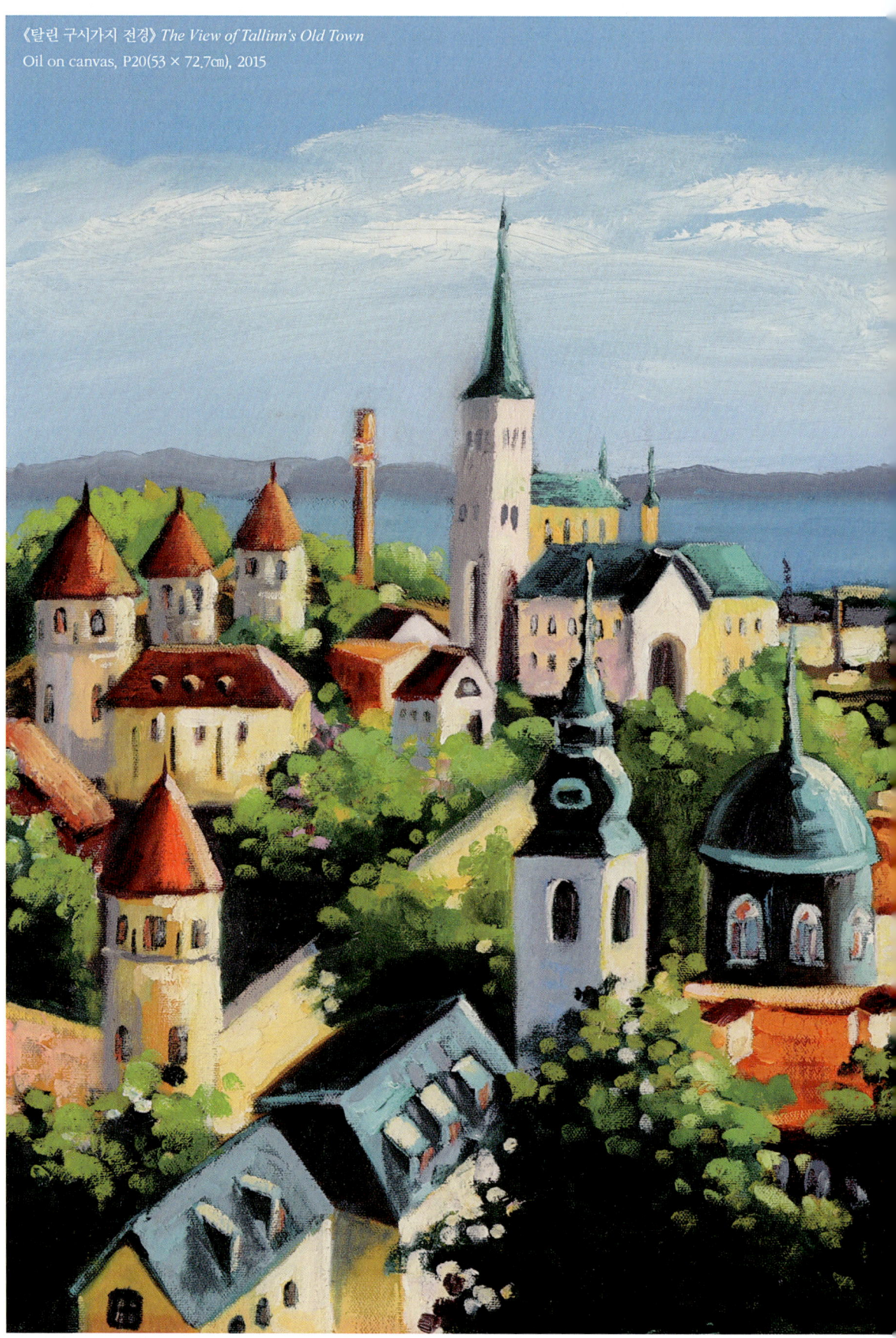

《탈린 구시가지 전경》 *The View of Tallinn's Old Town*
Oil on canvas, P20(53 × 72.7㎝), 2015

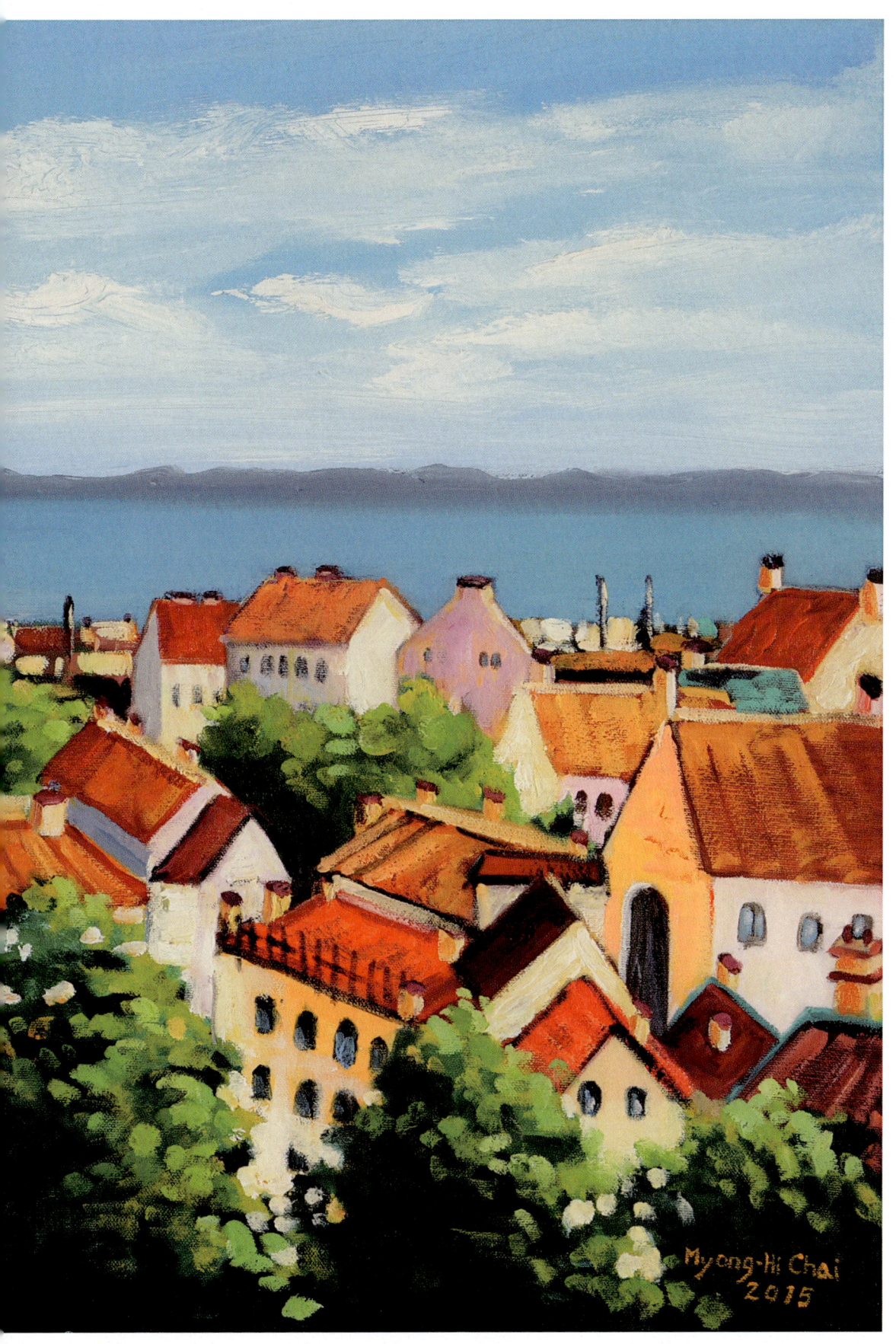

'발트 3국(에스토니아, 라트비아, 리투아니아)',
학창 시절 역사 시간에 들었던 이름.
그중 에스토니아의 수도 탈린은
도시 전체가 유네스코 문화유산으로 지정된 중세 도시다.

가장 높은 톰페아 언덕에 올라
붉은 지붕들과, 세월을 머금은 키 큰 나무들,
그리고 저 멀리, 드넓은 하늘 아래
펼쳐진 짙푸른 발트해를 바라본다.
마치 동화 속 한 장면 같다.

하지만,
항구로 들어오던 배들의 길잡이가 되어주었던
올레비스테 성당의 높은 첨탑과
식민 지배의 아픈 역사가 깃든 톰페아성의 망루들을 마주하니,
그 시절 탈린 사람들의 고단한 삶이 느껴져
문득 마음이 아려온다.

The name "the Baltic States"(Estonia, Latvia, Lithuania)—
I first heard it in a history class back at school.
Among them, Tallinn, the capital of Estonia,
is a medieval UNESCO World Heritage city.

From the highest point, Toompea Hill,
I look out over red rooftops and tall, timeworn trees.
Beyond them, beneath the wide open sky
spreads the deep blue Baltic Sea.
It seems like a scene from a fairy tale.

Yet, when I see the tall spire of St. Olaf's Church
once a guidepost for ships entering the harbor,
and the watchtowers of *Toompea Castle,*
still bearing the marks of foreign rule,
a quiet ache wells up within me—
imagining the hardships once endured
by the people of Tallinn.[3]

---

3   *St. Olaf's Church* is the English name for *Oleviste* Church. The alternative spelling *St. Olav's Church* follows the
Norwegian form.

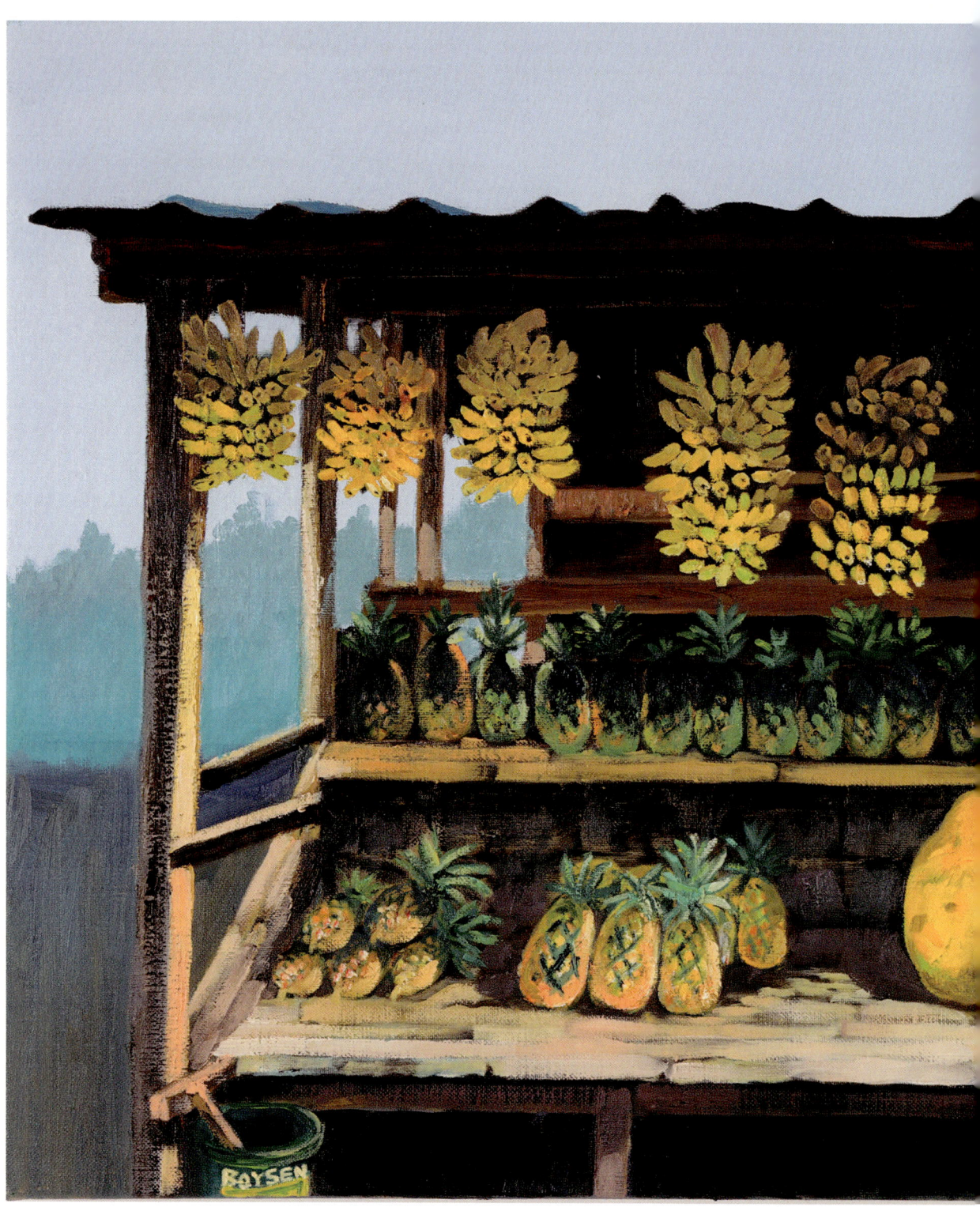

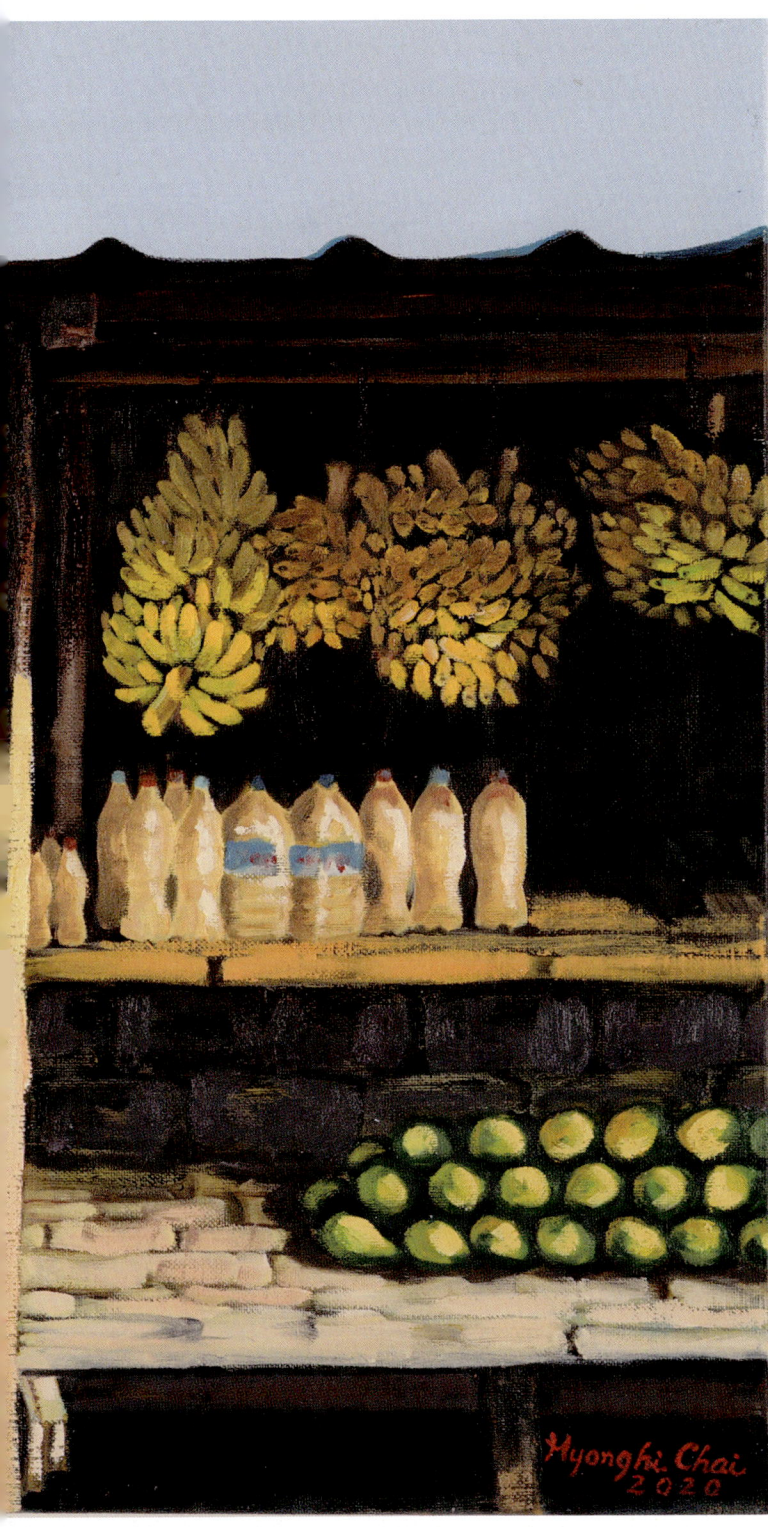

《따가이따이의 과일가게》
The Fruit Stand in Tagaytay
Oil on canvas, P20(53 × 72.7㎝), 2020

둘째 동생이 필리핀에 머물 때,
다른 자매들과 함께 그곳을 여행했다.
이름하여 "자매 여행"

유명 관광지인 따알 화산으로 향하는 길,
차 안은 자매들의 이야기꽃이 활짝 피었다.
창밖으로는 열대의 전원 풍경이
그림처럼 흘러갔다.

따가이따이의 시골 산길을 지날 무렵,
소박한 과일 가게 하나가 문득 시야에 들어왔다.
차를 멈추자,
윗옷도 걸치지 않은 채 순진한 미소로 반기던 사내들.

고단한 삶의 무게와 대비되듯
화사하게 빛나던 열대 과일들의 색감이
유독 오래 기억에 남는다.

I once traveled with my younger sisters
while one of them was living in the Philippines.
We called it our "Sisters' Journey."

On the way to the famous Taal Volcano,
the car was filled with chatter and laughter.
Outside the window,
the tropical countryside drifted by like a painting.

Along a quiet mountain road in Tagaytay,
a humble roadside fruit stand
suddenly came into view.
A few shirtless men
welcomed us with unguarded smiles.

The vivid colors of tropical fruit—
shining against the weight of daily life—
have lingered in my memory ever since.

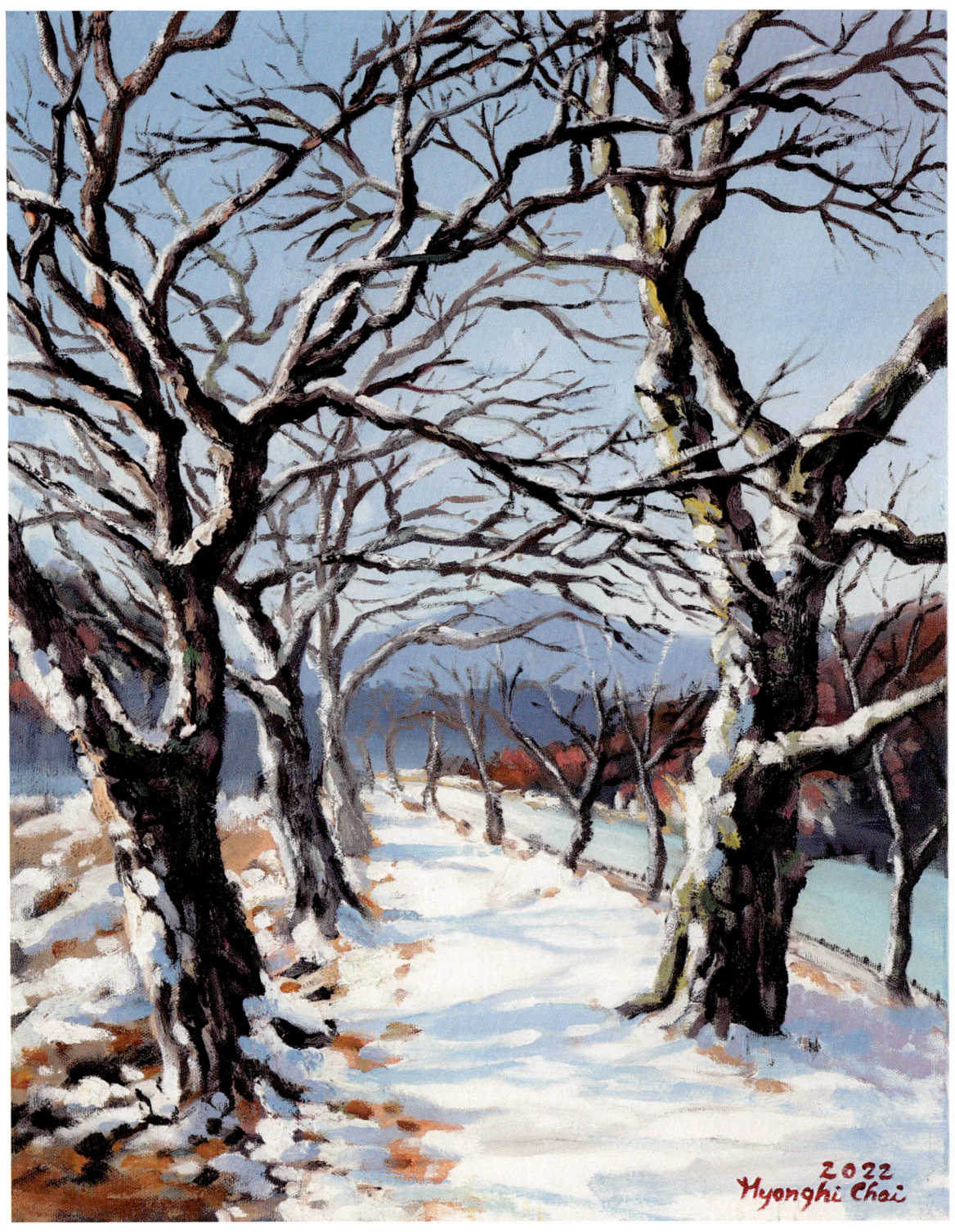

《담양 관방제림 106번 나무》 *Tree No. 106 in Gwanbangjerim, Damyang*
Oil on canvas, P10(53 × 40.9㎝), 2022

담양에 작업실을 마련한 후,
관방제림은 자주 찾는 산책길이 되었다.[4]

눈이 제법 내린 다음 날 아침,
등산화 끈을 단단히 묶고 관방제림을 찾
았다.
경사면에는 썰매 타는 아이들의
즐거운 함성이 울려 퍼졌다.

아침 햇살이 손을 내밀자,
겨울 나목은 하얀 솜이불 밖으로
살며시 얼굴을 내민다.

어느덧
내 마음도 따뜻하고 평안해진다.

After setting up my studio in Damyang,
Gwanbangjerim soon became my favorite
walking path.[5]

The morning after a heavy snowfall,
I tightened the laces of my hiking boots
and headed toward Gwanbangjerim.
From the hillside came the joyful shouts
of children racing down on sleds.

When the morning sun stretched out its
hand,
the bare winter trees shyly peeked out
from beneath their white cotton quilt.

Before I knew it,
my heart too felt warm—and at peace.

---

4   관방제림은 전라남도 담양군에 있는 인공림으로, 조선
시대에 홍수 방지를 위해 조성되었으며 현재 천연기념물
제366호로 지정되어 있다.

5   Gwanbangjerim is an artificial forest in Damyang,
created during the Joseon Dynasty to prevent
floods, and is now designated as Natural Monument
No. 366. Damyang, a county in Jeollanam-do,
Korea, is renowned for bamboo forests and nature
trails.

봄보다 가을.

가을은 찬란했던 초록을 열매로 바꾸고,
자신만의 색으로 물들며
조용히 다음 겨울을,
아니, 다시 봄을 준비한다.

나는 그 의연함이 좋다.

내 인생의 가을날도
그렇게 의연하길.

Autumn,
rather than spring.

Autumn trades its brilliant green for fruit,
takes on its own colors,
and quietly prepares for winter—
or for the spring to come.

I admire that quiet dignity.

May the autumn of my own life
be just as steadfast.

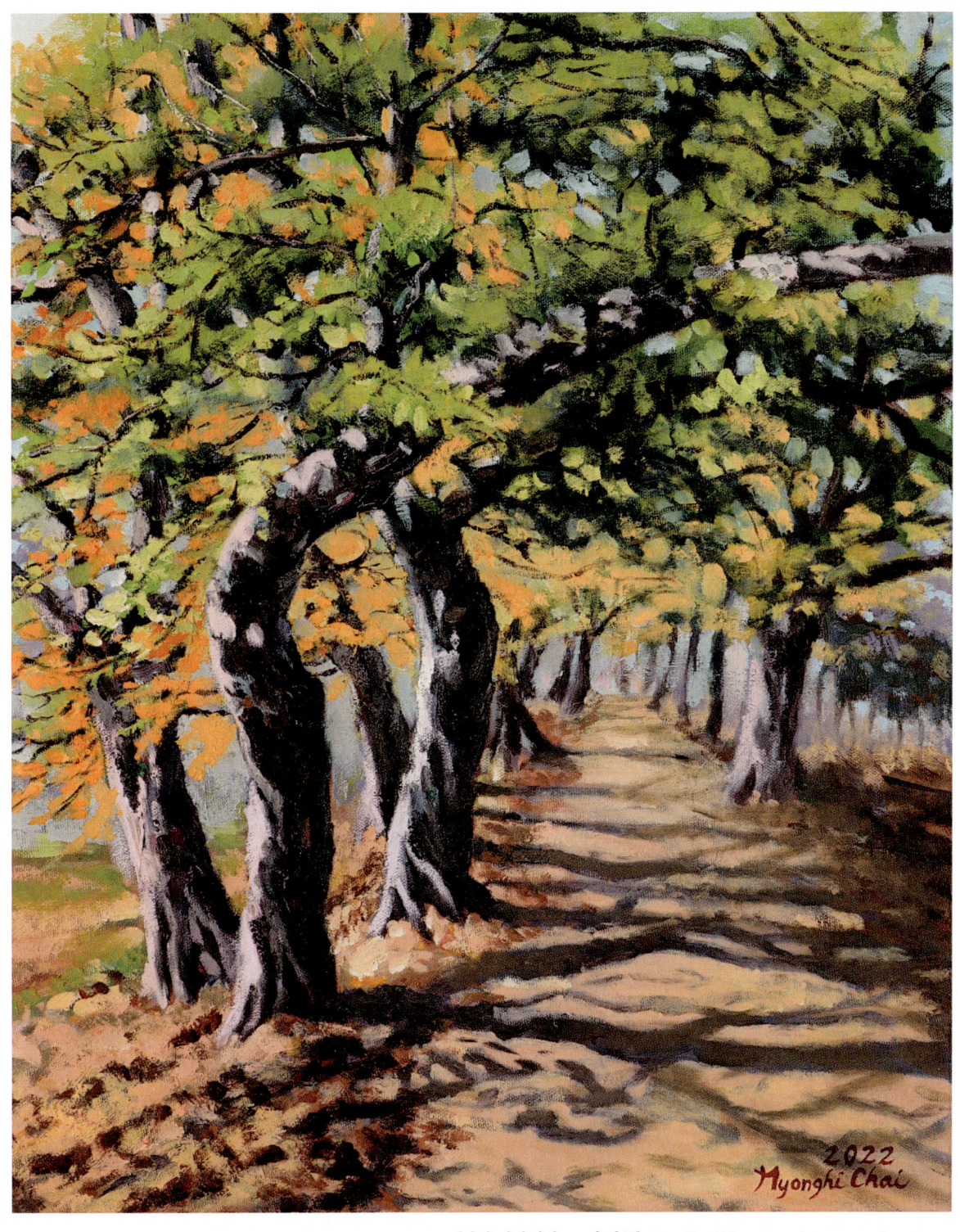

《담양 관방제림 135번 나무》 *Tree No. 135 in Gwanbangjerim, Damyang*
Oil on canvas, P10(53 × 40.9㎝), 2022

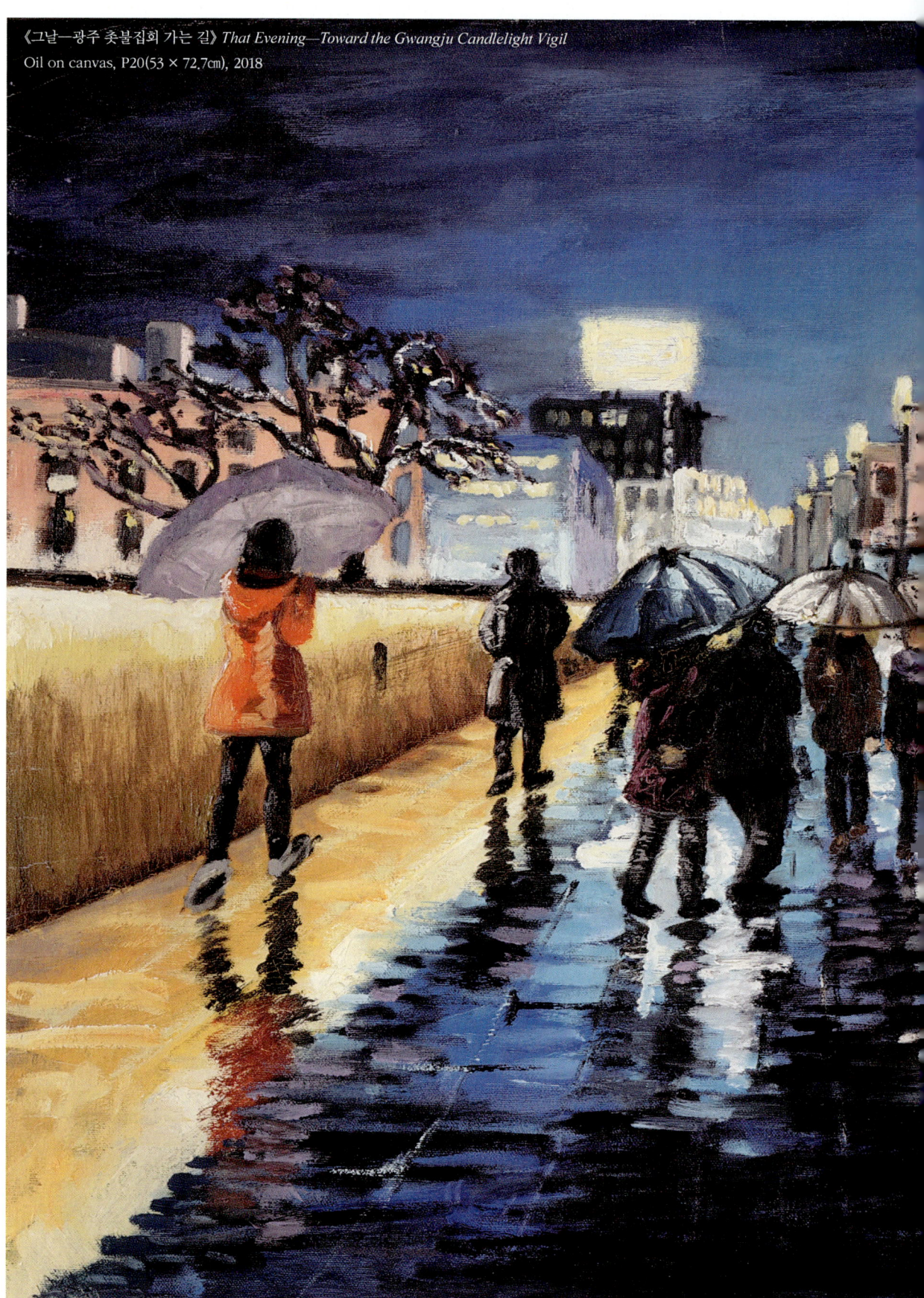

《그날—광주 촛불집회 가는 길》 *That Evening—Toward the Gwangju Candlelight Vigil*
Oil on canvas, P20(53 × 72.7㎝), 2018

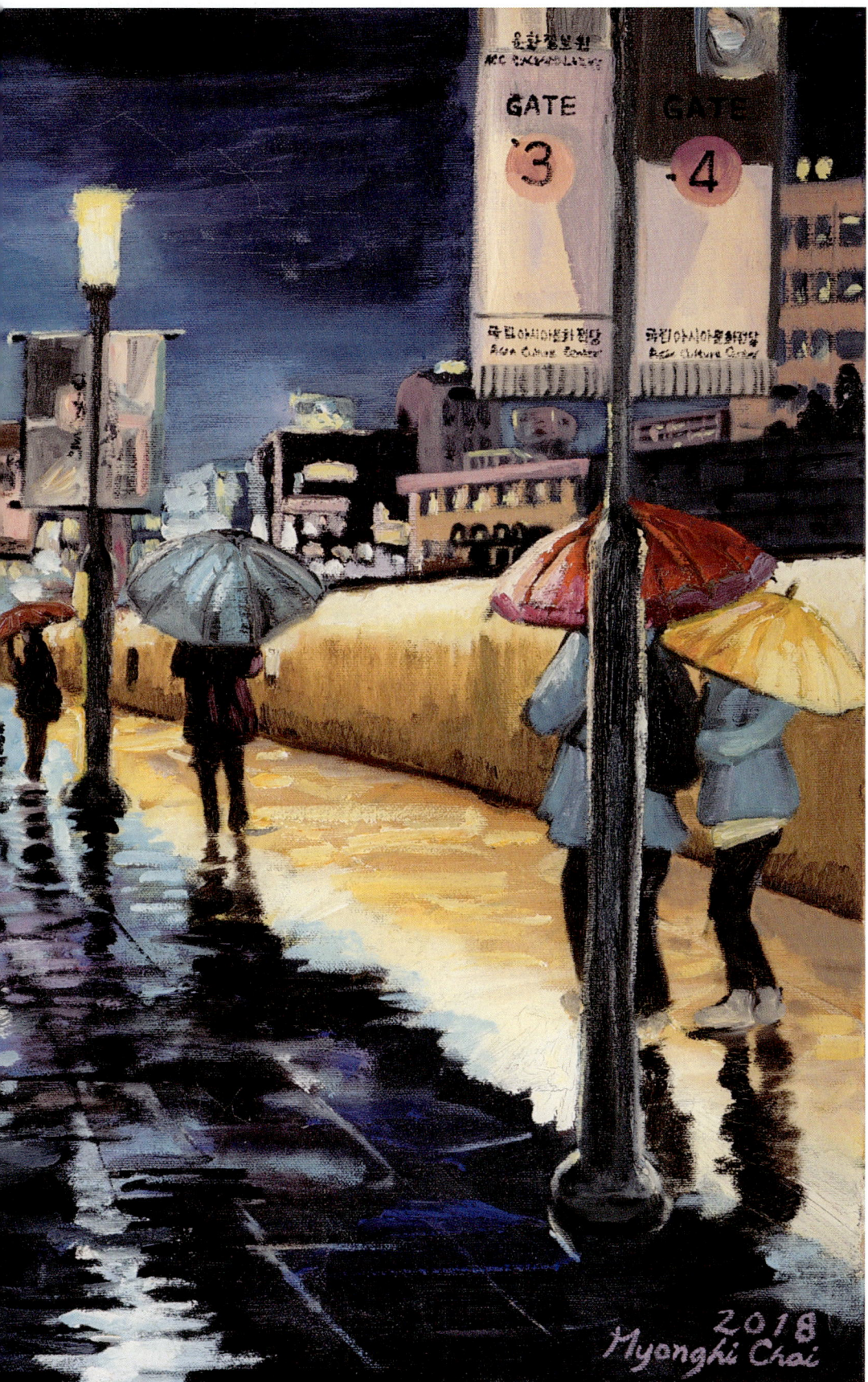

GATE 3

GATE 4

국립아시아문화전당
Asia Culture Center

국립아시아문화전당
Asia Culture Center

2018
Myonghi Chai

2016년 겨울,
대한민국은 정치적 소용돌이에 휩싸여 있었다.
광주 역시 예외는 아니었다.
매일 저녁, 시민들이 금남로에 모여
민주주의를 외쳤다.

그날도 퇴근 후,
나는 촛불집회 현장으로 향했다.
가랑비가 내리고 있었다.

ACC 앞 도로에 들어선 순간,
발걸음이 멈췄다.
짙푸른 어스름 속 저녁 하늘 아래,
가로등 불빛은 가랑비에 춤을 추고,
사람들은 말없이, 한 방향으로 걸어가고 있었다.[6]

그 마음을 아는지 모르는지,
풍경은 아이러니하게도
아프도록 아름다웠다.

---

6   ACC: 국립아시아문화전당(Asia Culture Center). 광주광역시 동구에 위치한 복합 문화기관으로, 아시아 문화예술의 교류와 연구를 위한 공간이다.

In the winter of 2016,

South Korea was swept into political turmoil,

and Gwangju was no exception.

Each evening, citizens gathered on Gumnam-ro,

raising their voices for democracy.[7]

That evening too, after work,

I headed toward the candlelight vigil.

A light rain was falling.

As I stepped onto the road in front of the ACC,

my feet came to a halt.

Beneath the deep blue dusk,

streetlights shimmered in the drizzle,

and people walked silently in the same direction.[8]

Whether the scene knew their hearts or not,

it was—ironically—achingly beautiful.

---

[7]   Gwangju is a metropolitan city in Korea, historically known for the May 18 Democratization Movement of 1980.

[8]   ACC stands for Asia Culture Center, a major cultural complex located in Gwangju, South Korea, dedicated to Asian arts, culture, and exchange.

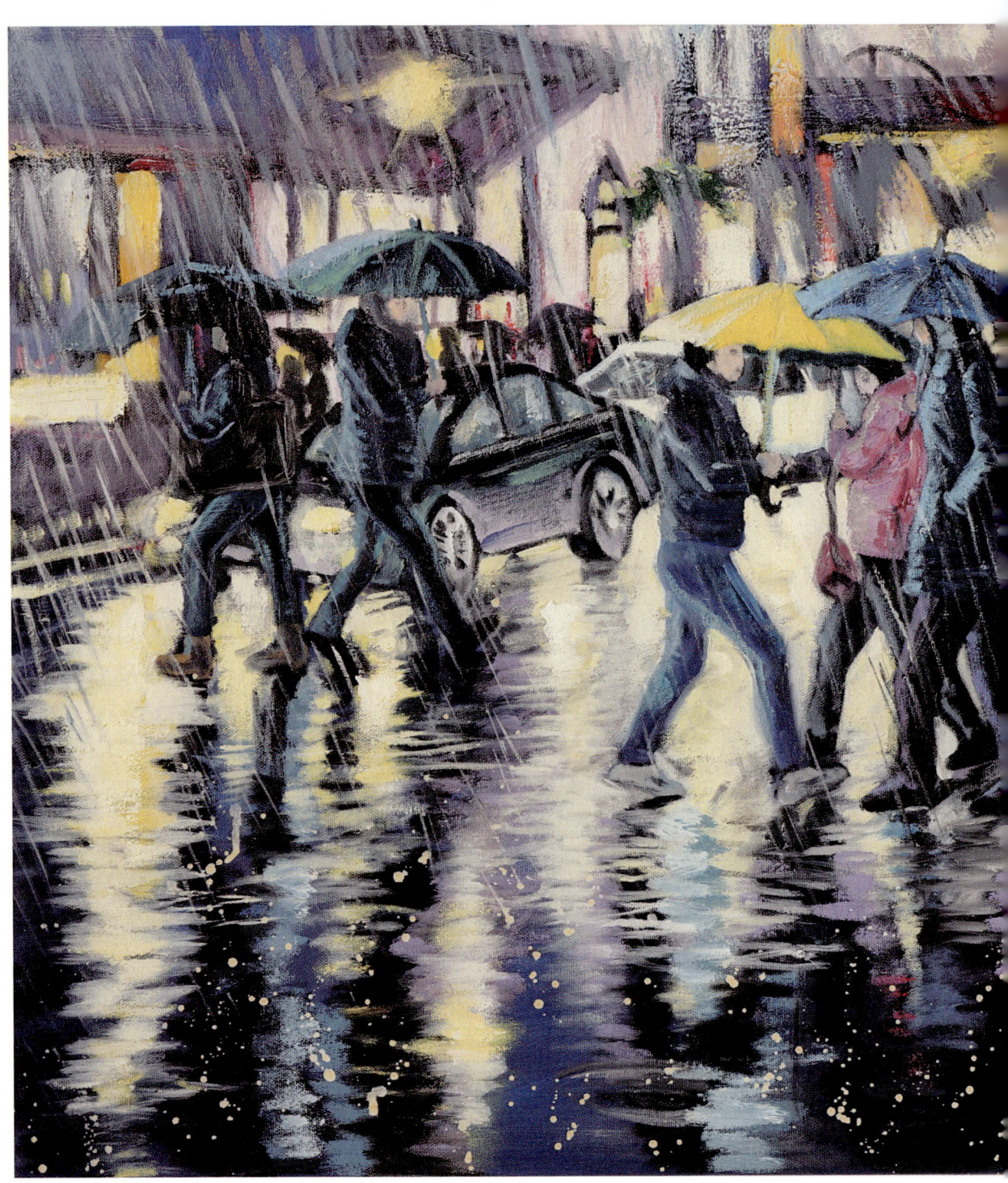

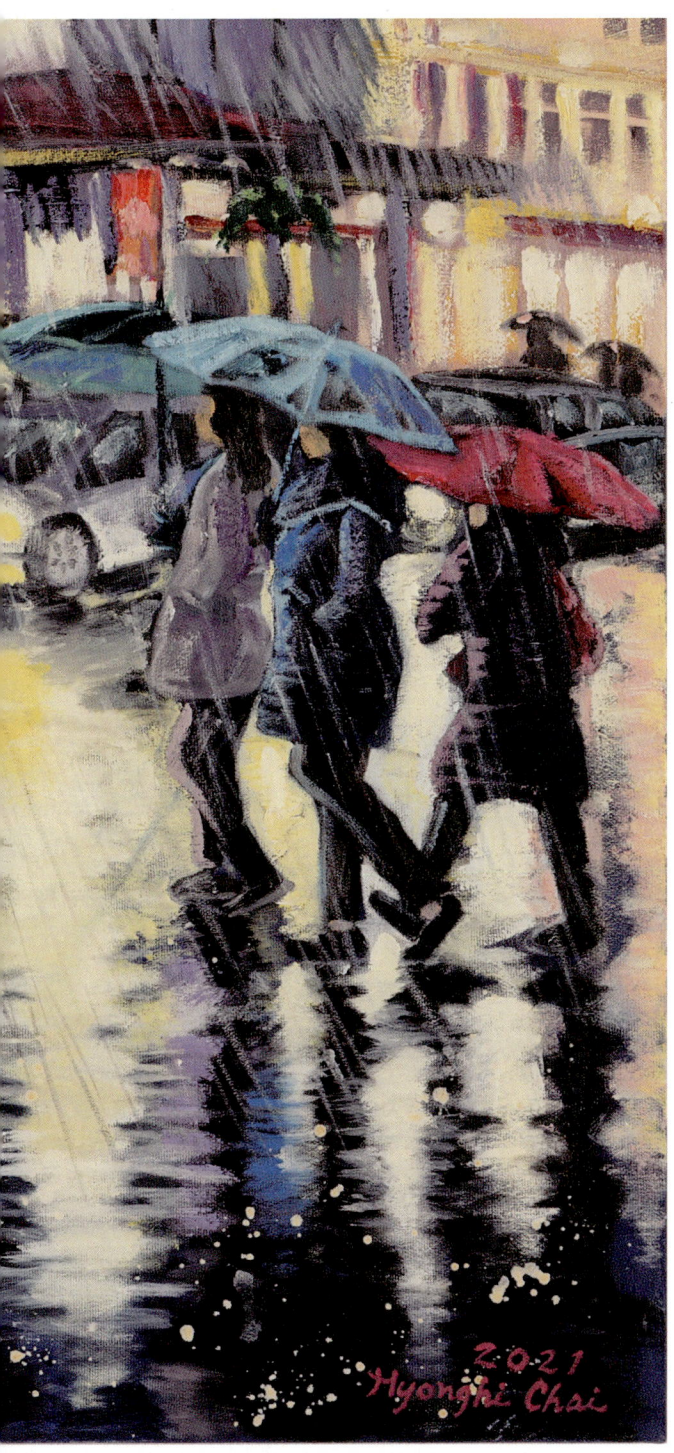

《비 내리는 도시의 밤》 *Rainy Night in the City*
Oil on canvas, P20(53 × 72.7㎝), 2021

153

어둠이 내려앉은 도시의 밤에
비가 내리면,
귀가를 서두르는 자동차의 불빛과
손님을 유혹하는 화려한 네온사인과 가게 조명,
저마다의 목적지를 향해
우산 아래서 발걸음을 재촉하는 사람들로
거리는 부산해진다.

비 내리는 도시의 밤거리는
그렇게 분주하기에
오히려 더 매혹적이다.

When rain falls on the city at night,

the streets come alive with

headlights rushing through the rain,

neon signs and shop lights luring passersby,

and people with umbrellas,

each hurrying to their own destination.

A rainy night in the city—

so restless,

and all the more alluring.

《별 내리는 밤》 *Starry Night*
Oil on canvas, P10(40.9 × 53㎝), 2015

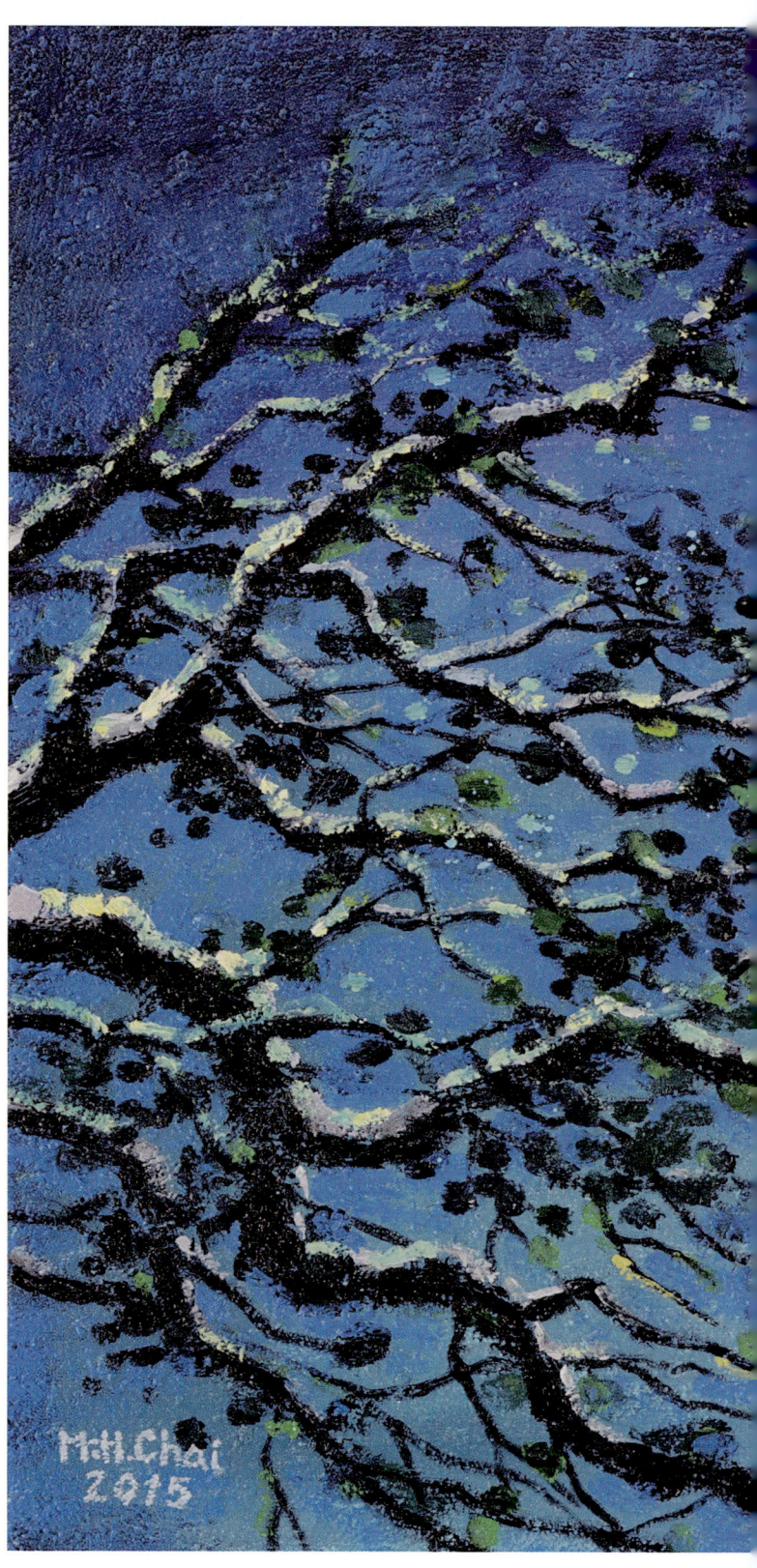

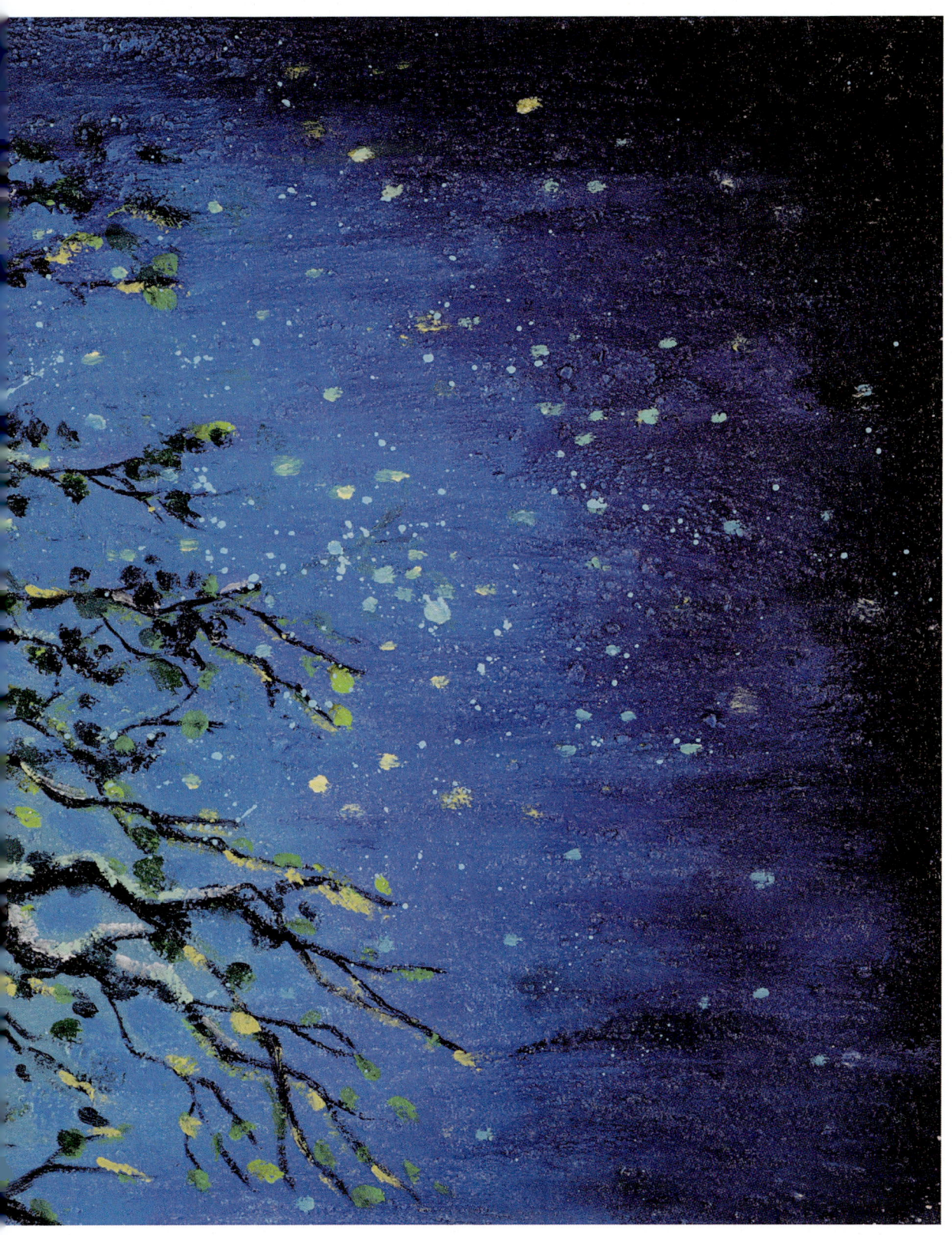

물기를 머금은 어둠이 걷히고
비 대신 별빛이 쏟아져 내리는 밤,
짙푸른, 고요한 하늘 아래
이보다 좋을 순 없다.

The damp darkness recedes,
and starlight, instead of rain, begins to fall—
under the deep, serene night sky,
nothing could be more perfect.

《증도에서 본 석양의 바다》 *Sea of Dusk from Jeungdo*
Oil on canvas, P10(40.9 × 53㎝), 2018

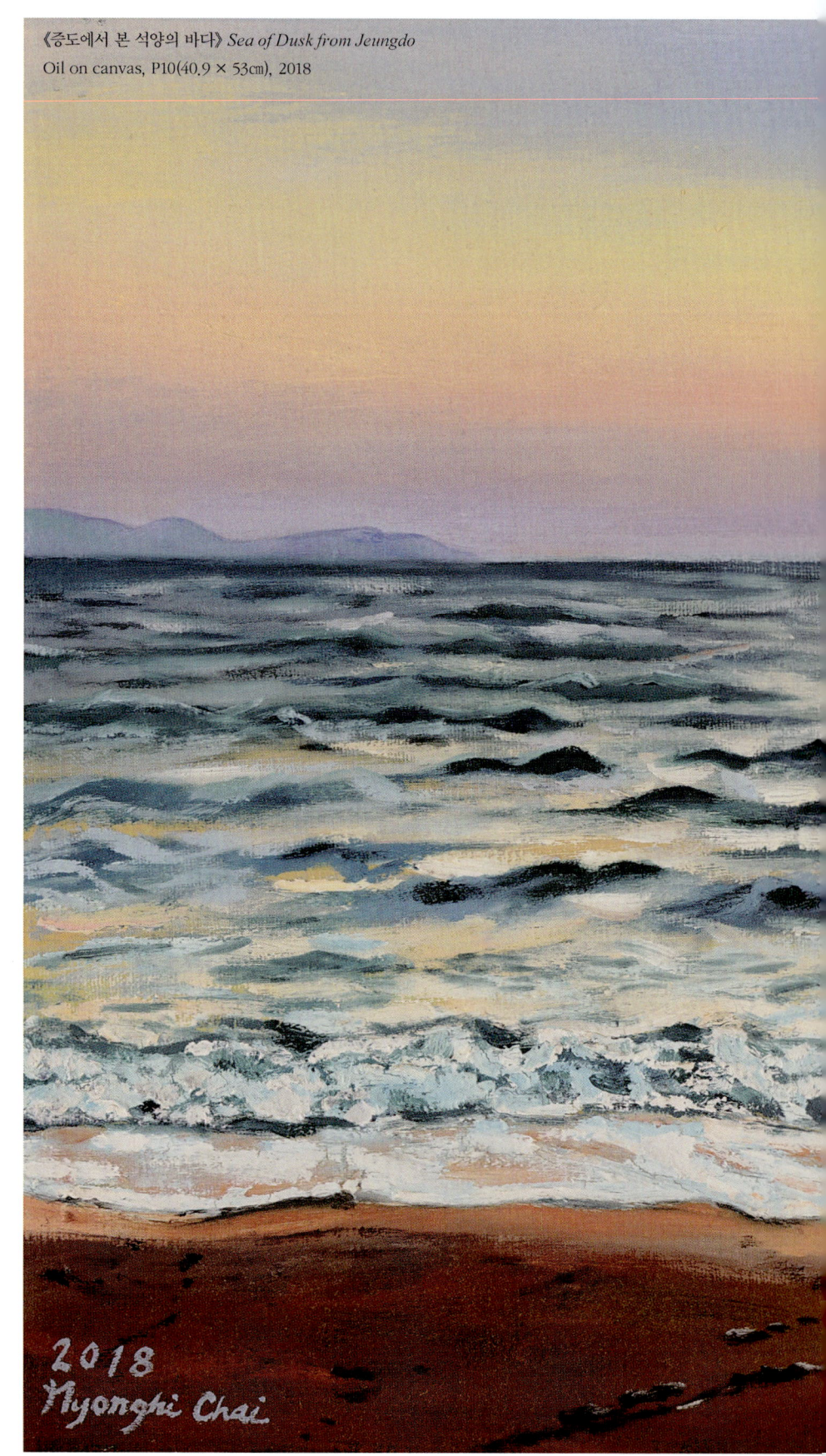

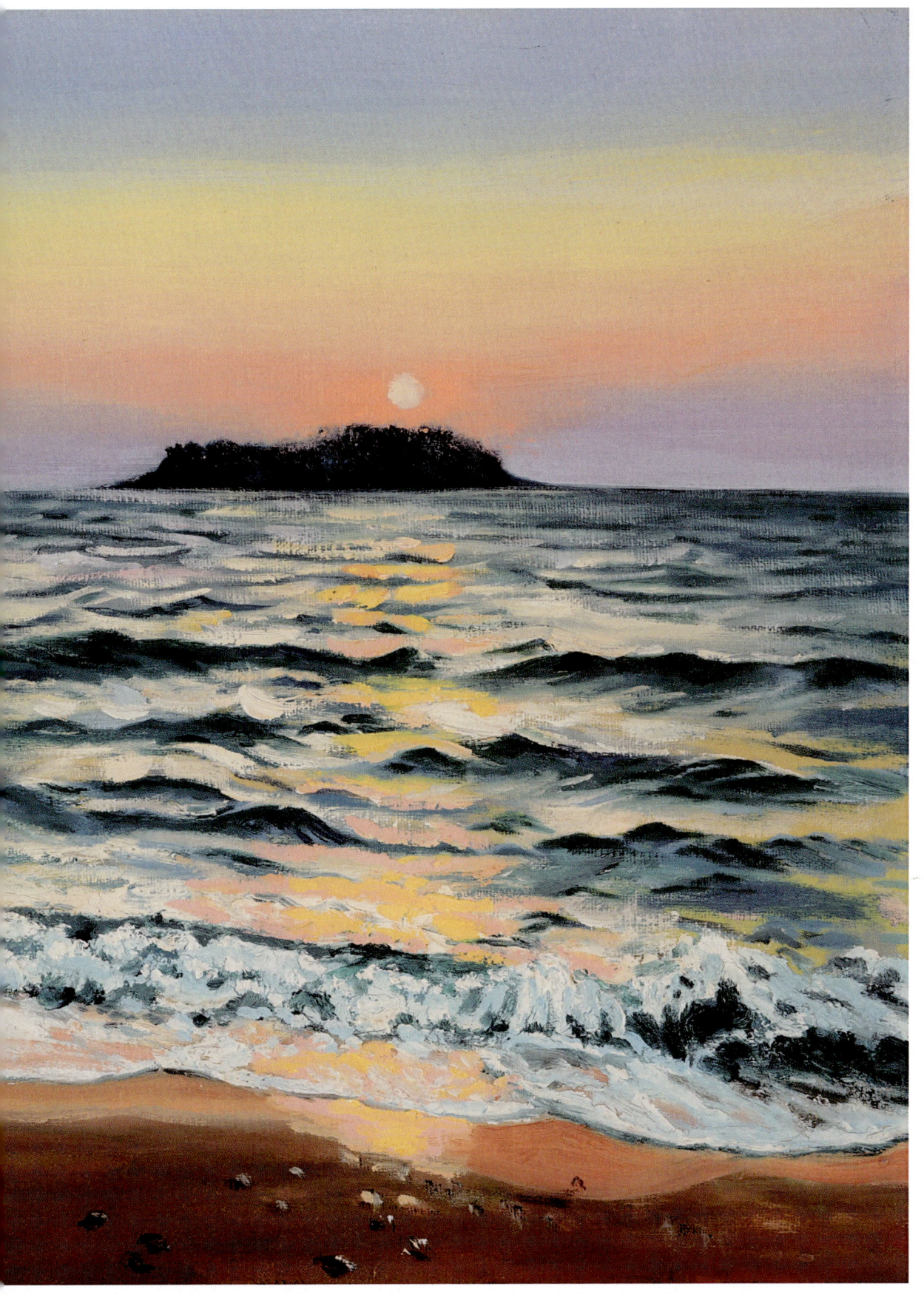

남쪽 끝, 신안 중도로 가족여행을 간 적이 있다.
해변에서 저녁 바비큐를 즐기던 중,
우리는 잊을 수 없는 석양의 바다를 만났다.

하늘에선 노랑, 주황, 보라,
그리고 점점 밀려나는 하늘빛까지
색의 향연이 펼쳐지고,
바다 위에선, 분주한 파도와 함께 춤추는
찬란한 빛들의 잔치가 열렸다.

나도, 삶의 끝자락을
이렇게,
눈부신 잔치처럼 마무리할 수 있다면.

In the far south, we once took a family trip
to Jeungdo, a small island in Sinan.
While barbecuing on the beach,
we encountered a sea at dusk I'll never forget.

In the sky—a banquet of colors:
yellow, orange, violet,
and fading hues of blue retreating into night.
On the sea—a festival of light,
dancing with the restless waves.

At the end of my life,
may it be just like this—
a radiant celebration.

《여명의 바다》 *Sea of Dawn*
Oil on canvas, P10(40.9 × 53㎝), 2018

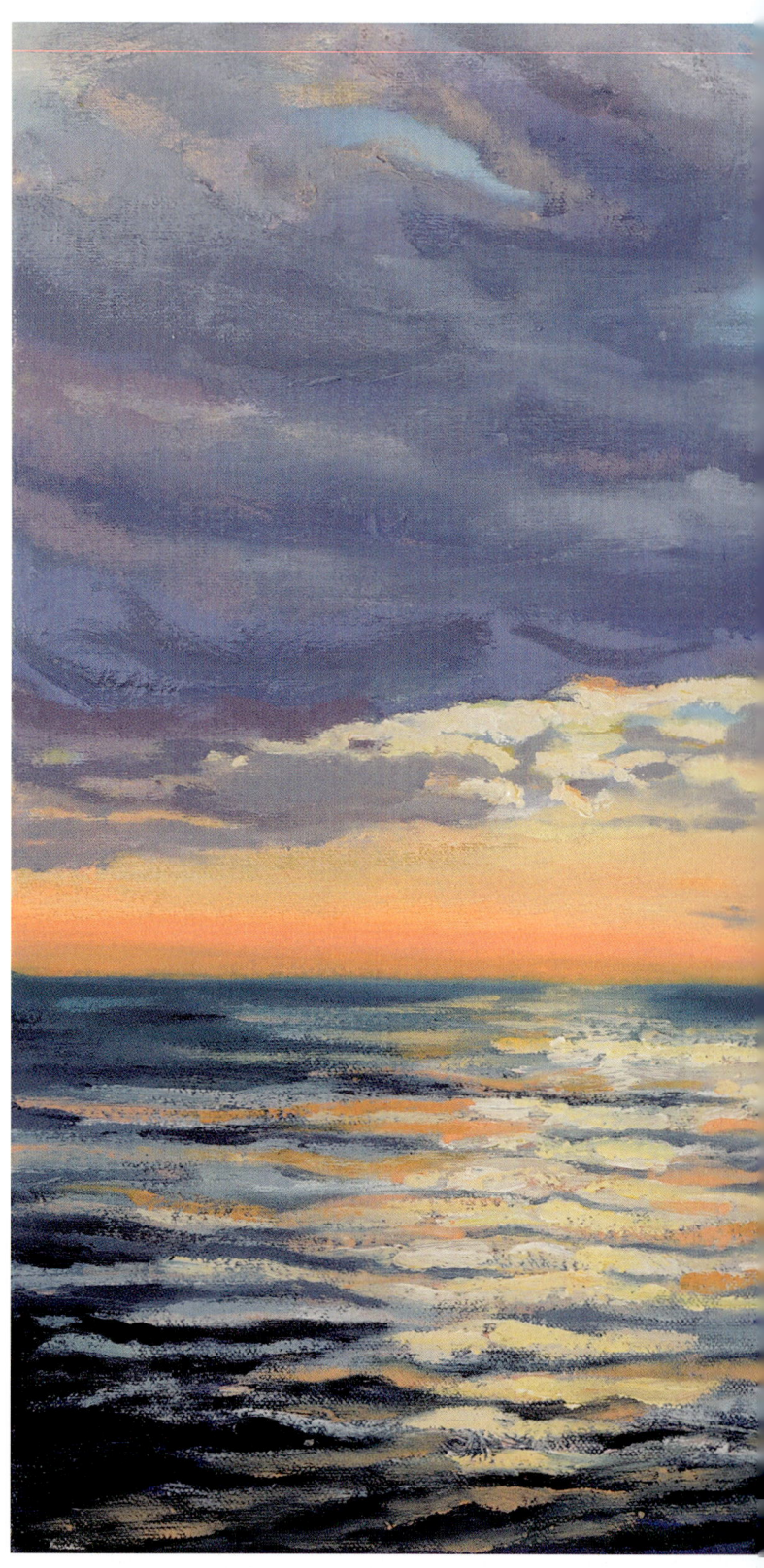

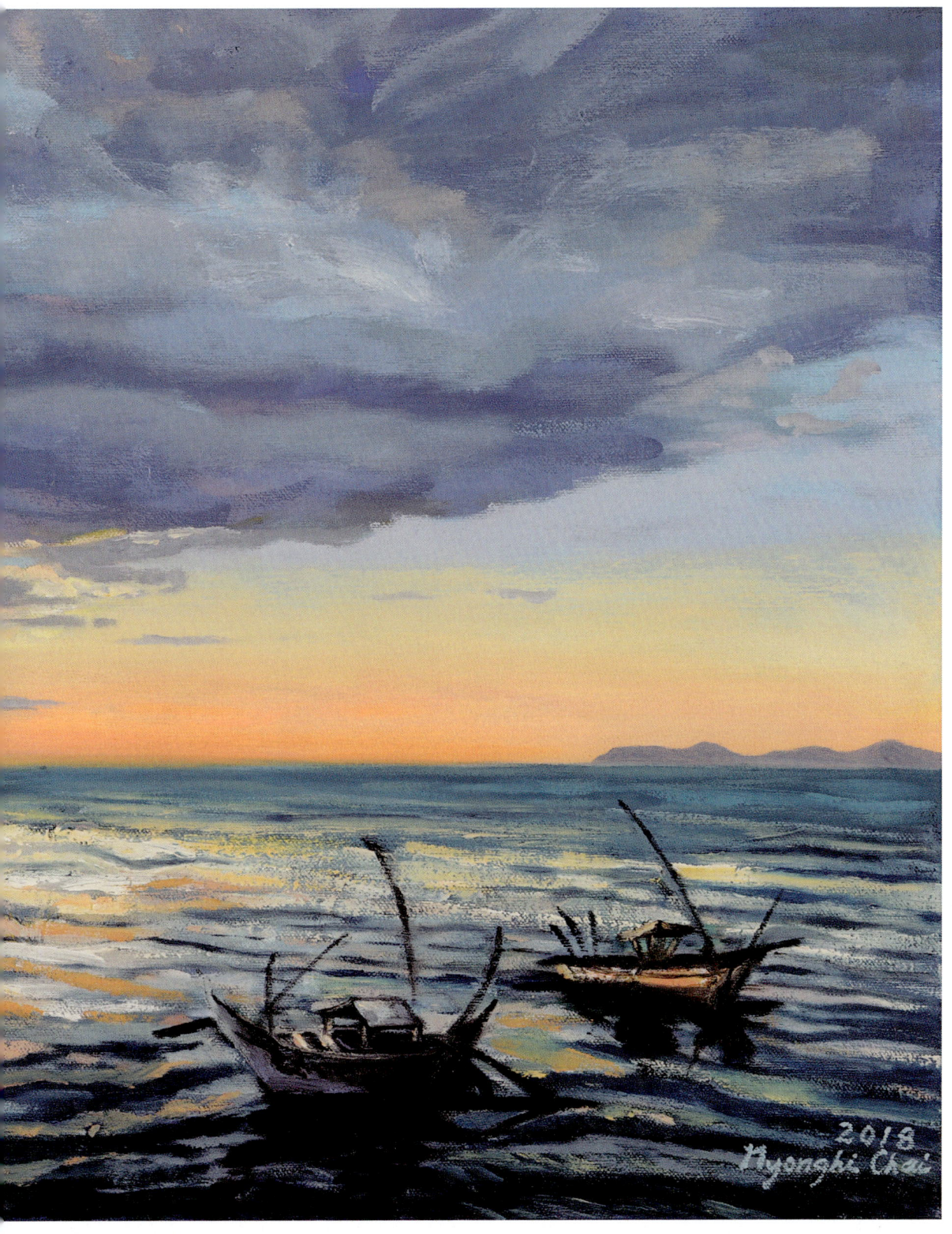

2018
Myonghi Chai

하나의 저묾은
또 다른 것의 시작을 잉태한다.

순환하는 대자연,
그 안에 속해 있음이 다행이다.

어제의 나는 저물고,
오늘 다시 새로워진 내가 태어나길.

One setting

gives birth to another.

Within the great cycle of nature,

I am grateful to belong.

May the me of yesterday fade,

and a new me rise today.

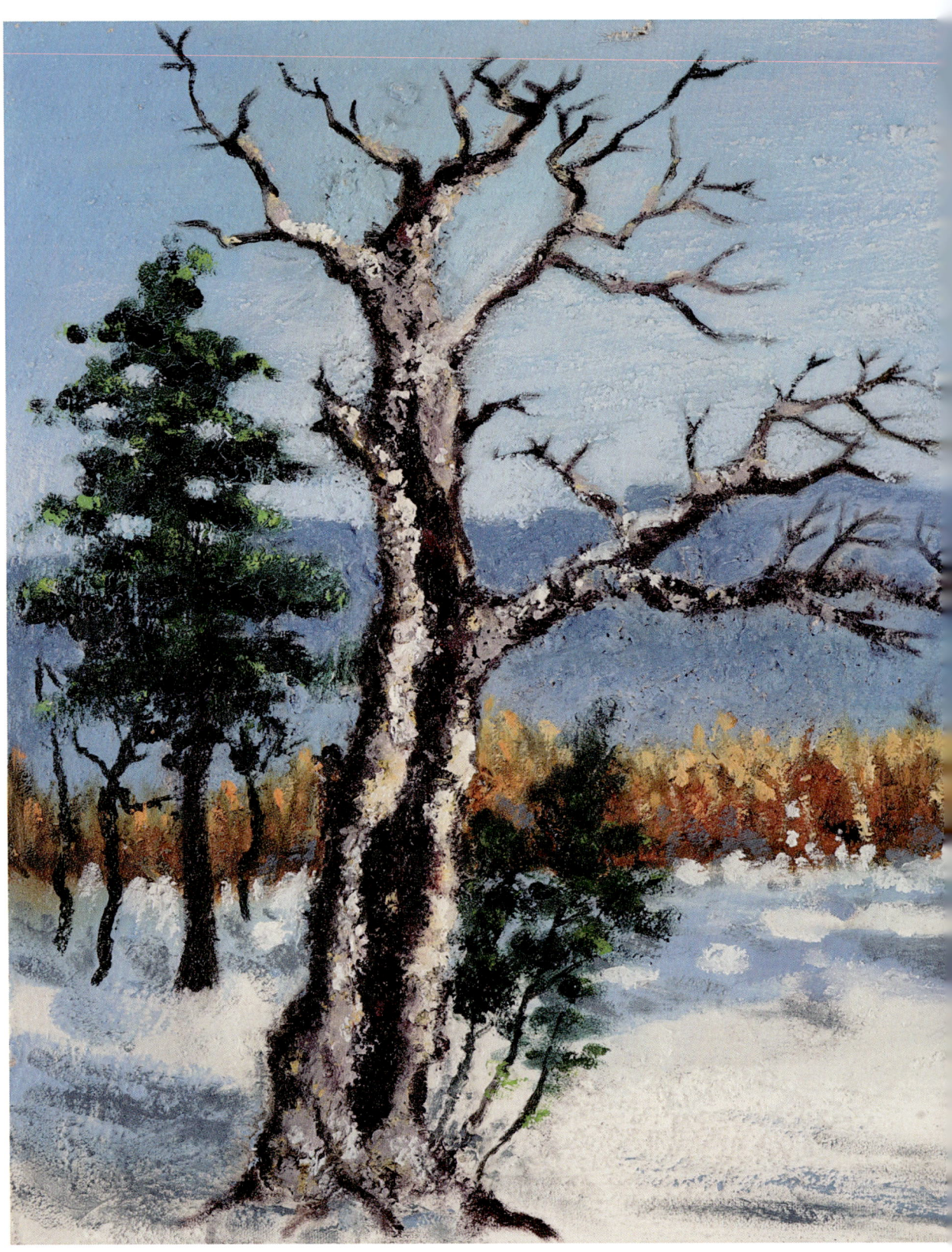

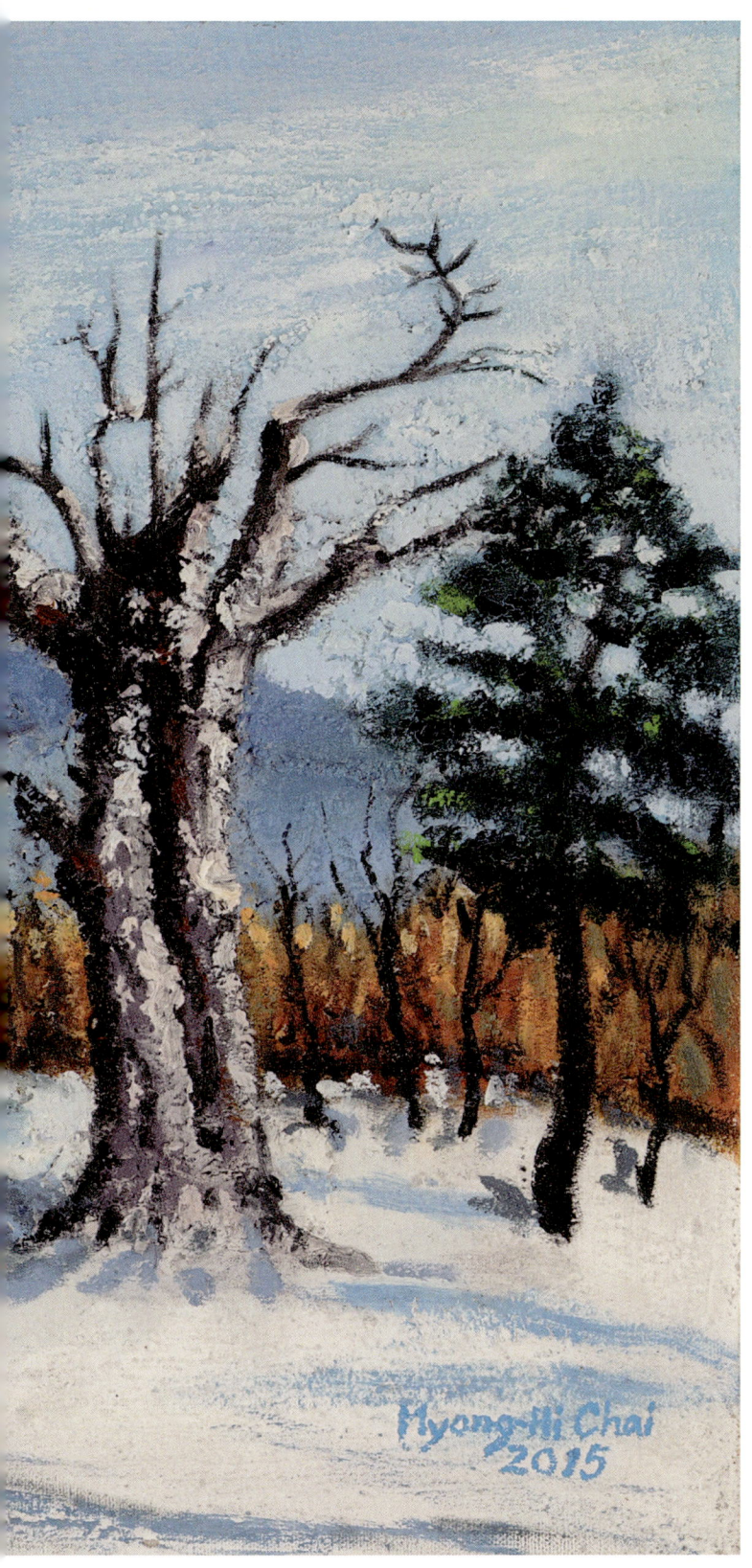

《늘 그 자리에 II》 *As Always II*
Oil on canvas, P10(40.9 × 53㎝), 2015

태백산에 오르면
주목 군락을 만난다.
살아서 천 년,
죽어서 천 년을 산다는 나무.

한겨울 푸른 기운을 잃지 않고
우뚝 선 자태도 인상적이지만,
죽어서도 이파리 하나 없이
맨몸으로 버티는 모습은 더욱 근사하다.

고사목이 되어서도
몸이 다 스러질 때까지
늘 그 자리에,
서로를 향해 마주 선
두 그루의 주목을 바라본다.

나, 감히,
저러한 사랑을 꿈꿀 수 있을까.

Upon Mt. Taebaeksan's summit
stands a grove of yew trees.
They are said to live a thousand years in life—
and another thousand beyond death.[9]

Even in the heart of winter,
their evergreen dignity inspires awe—
but more moving still
are those stripped bare,
enduring quietly beyond death.

Look at the two ancient trunks,
still standing there, as always,
facing each other,
never parting.

Could I dare
to dream of such love?

---

9   Taebaeksan, in Gangwon-do, is one of the major peaks along the Baekdudaegan mountain range.

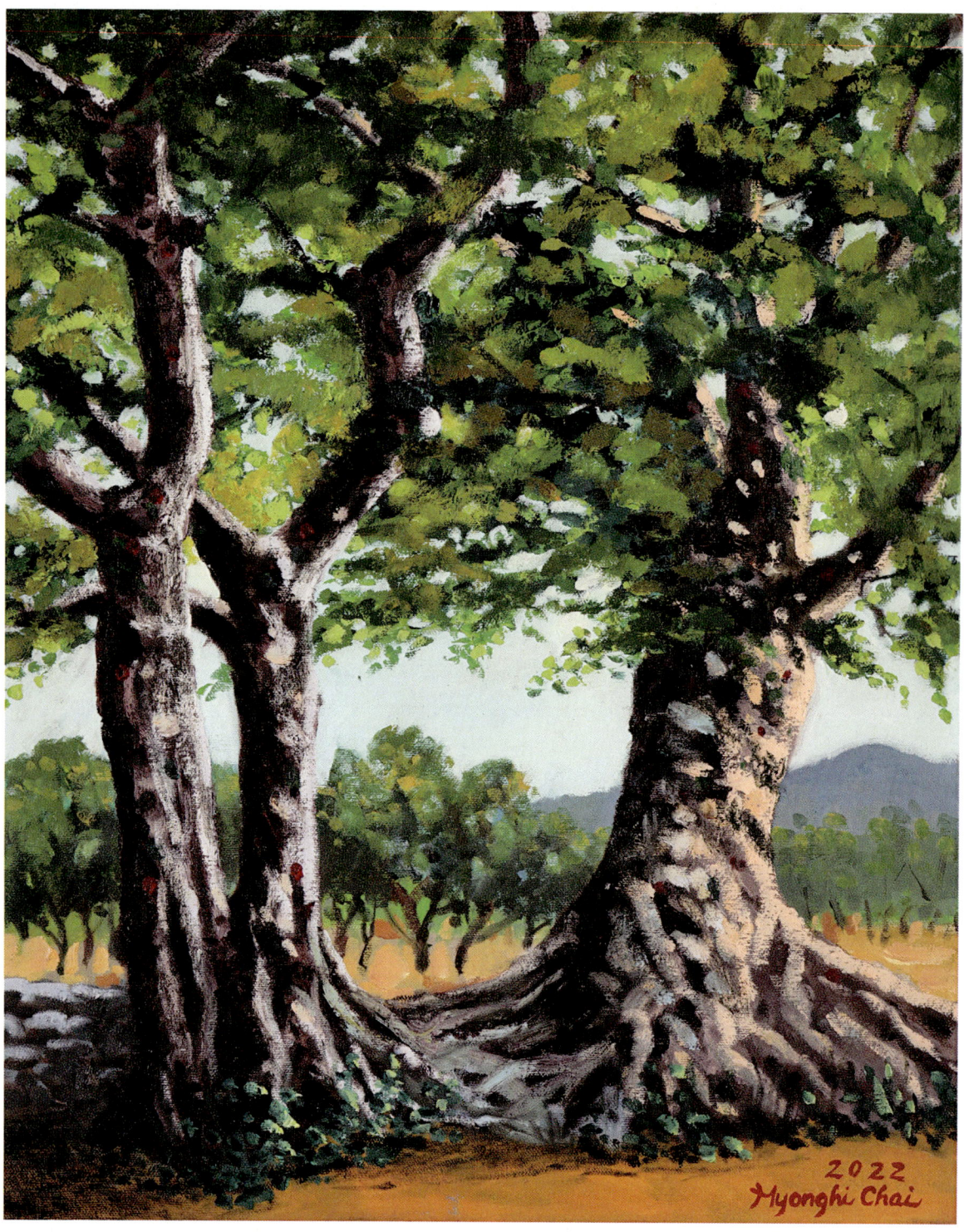

《늘 그 자리에》 *As Always*
Oil on canvas, P10(53 × 40.9㎝), 2022

해남 대흥사에 가면
느티나무 연리근 한 쌍을 만난다.

생김새는 전혀 다르지만
오백 년을 함께 지내다 보니,
뿌리가 맞닿아, 기어이 하나가 되었다.
드렁칡도 아니면서.

이쯤은 되어야,
비로소 '사랑 나무'라 불릴 수 있지 않을까.

At Daeheungsa Temple in Haenam,
you'll find a pair of zelkova trees
whose roots have intertwined.

So different in form,
yet after 500 years together,
their roots finally have grown into one—
and they are not even vines.

Perhaps only this
deserves to be called
the "Tree of Love."

엄마의 프로필 사진은
왜 늘 꽃밭이냐는
어느 노랫말처럼.[10]

조선대 장미원에서,
섬진강 장미원에서,
돌아가신 엄마는
늘 꽃 앞에서 웃고 계신다.
장미보다 더 활짝.[11]

이렇게 꽃밭에 심긴
가슴 시린 그리움 하나쯤은 있어야
이 힘든 세상을
견뎌낼 수 있지 않을까.

Like the song that asks,
why does Mom's profile photo
always show a garden of flowers?[12]

At The Rose Garden of Chosun University,
or again by the Seomjin River,
my late mother
is always smiling before the flowers—
brighter than the roses.[13]

Perhaps we all need
at least one bittersweet memory
rooted in a garden of blossoms,
to help us carry on
in this harsh world.

---

10 김진호(SG워너비)의 노래, 「엄마의 프로필 사진은 왜
꽃밭일까」의 가사에서 인용.

11 섬진강은 대한민국의 남부를 흐르는 강으로, 아름다운
강변 장미원으로도 유명하다.

---

12 From the song "엄마의 프로필 사진은 왜 꽃밭일
까?"(*Why Is Mom's Profile Photo Always a Flower
Garden?*) by Jinho Kim of SG Wannabe.

13 The Seomjin River, flowing through southern
Korea, is known for its scenic beauty and rose
gardens along its banks.

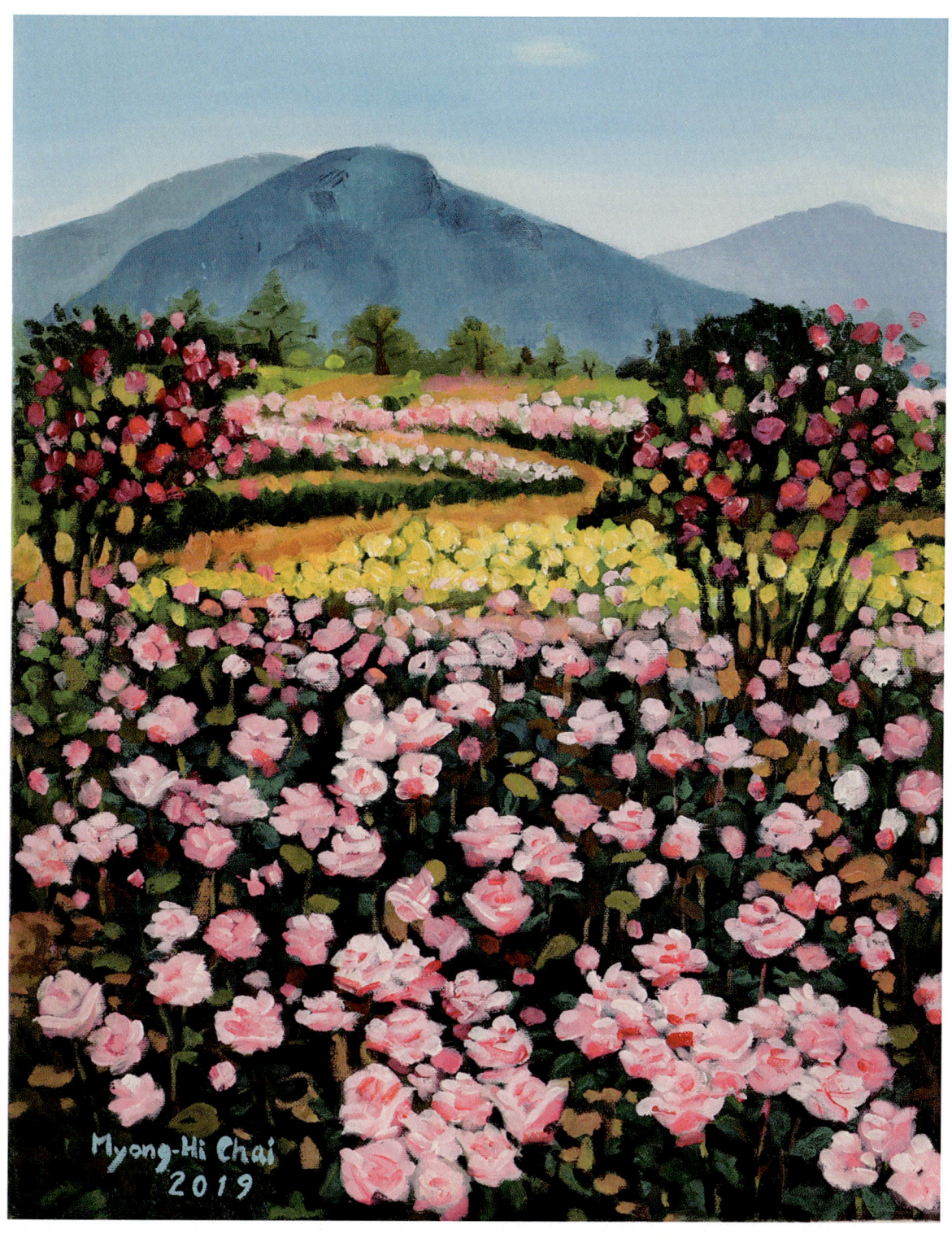

《장미원의 추억》 *Rose Garden*
Oil on canvas, P10(53 × 40.9㎝), 2019

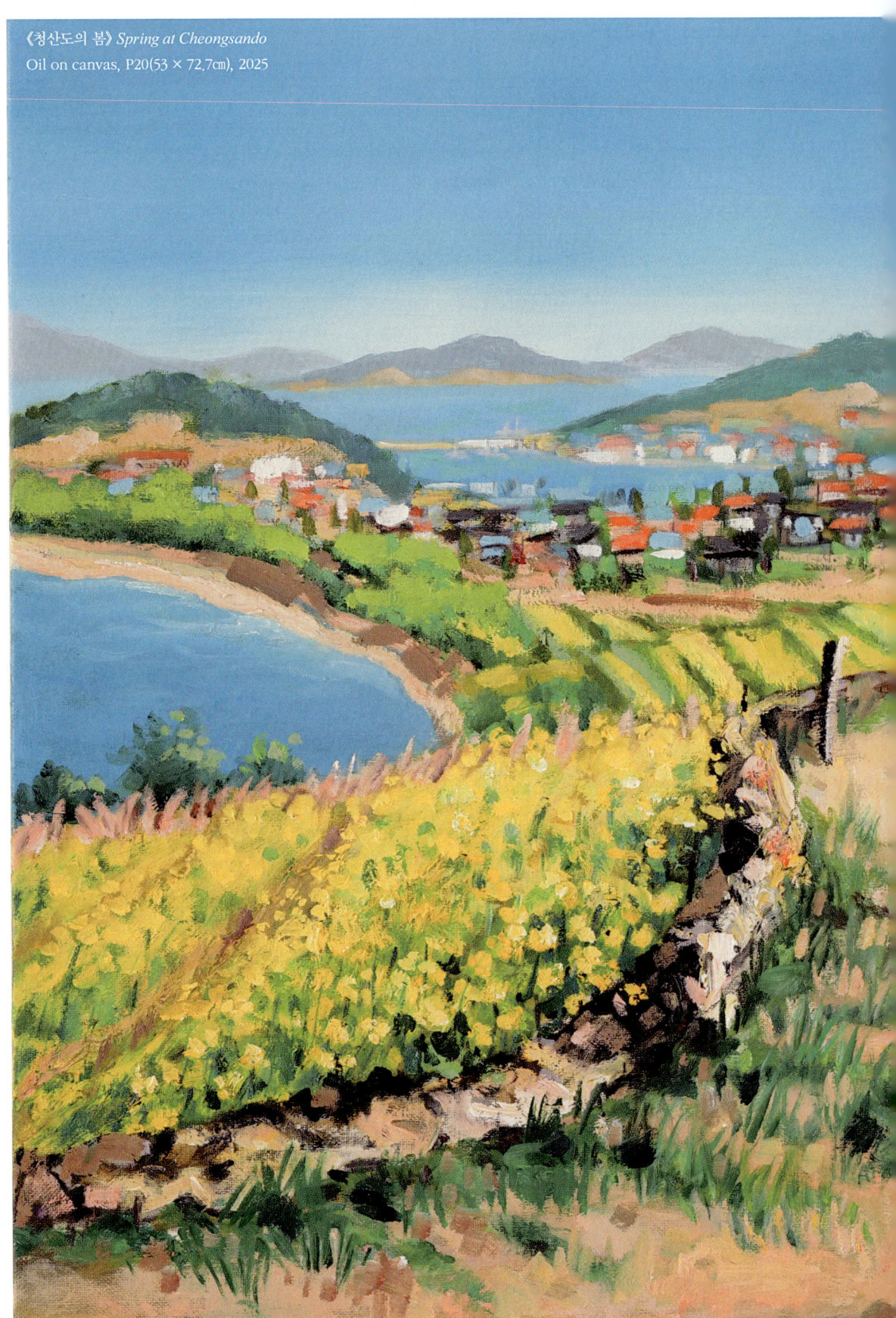

《청산도의 봄》 *Spring at Cheongsando*
Oil on canvas, P20(53 × 72.7㎝), 2025

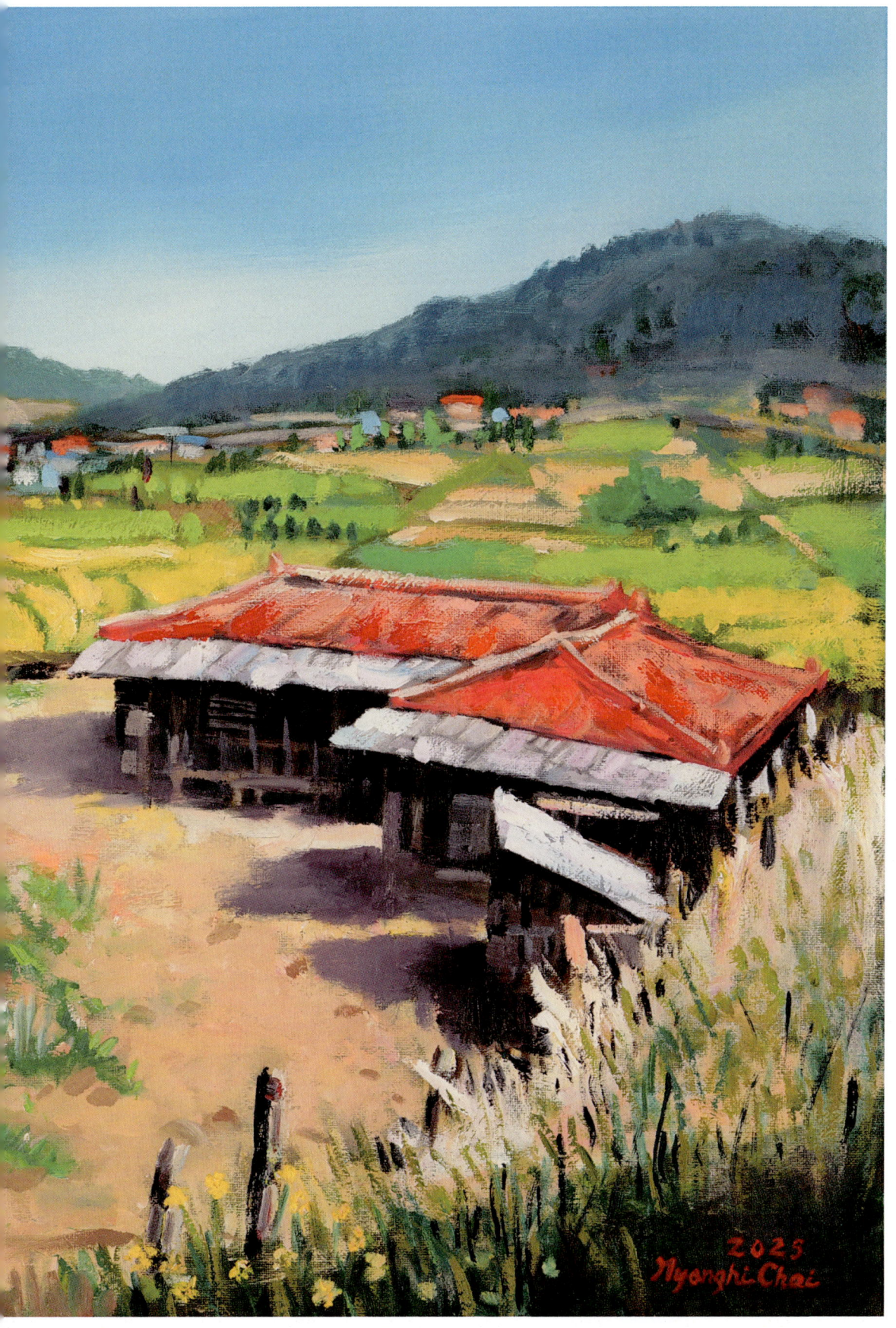

2025
Nyonghi.Chai

남녘의 작은 섬, 청산도의 봄을 맞으려면
새벽부터 서둘러야 한다.
완도항에서 하루 몇 편뿐인 배를 타야 하니까.

전기 자전거를 빌려 섬을 돌다 보면
순간순간 고개를 돌리게 된다.
굽이진 길모퉁이에선 송화의 진도아리랑이,
언덕 위 하얀 집에선 재하의 피아노 선율이,
돌담 아래 유채밭 사이에선 인하와 달포의 웃음소리가
들리는 듯해서.[14]

이 설레는 풍경에 문득 그리워진다.
보고파 하면,
그리워하면,
반드시 만나게 된다고 했던가.[15]

아, 섬에서 태어난 울 엄마는
이곳 청산도에 와보셨을까?
이토록 찬란한 노란 봄을
단 한 번이라도 누리셨을까?

왜일까.
이곳 청산도에서
불현듯 엄마가 보고파지는 것은.
그땐, 내가 너무 어렸다.

---

14 송화: 영화 《서편제》에 등장하는 소리꾼. (청산도 촬영)
　　재하: 드라마 《봄의 왈츠》의 주인공 피아니스트. (청산도 배경 및 촬영)
　　인하, 달포: 드라마 《피노키오》의 두 주인공. (청산도 촬영)
15 "보고파 하면, 그리워하면, 반드시 만나게 된다." — 드라마 《봄의 왈츠》의 주인공 재하와 은영의 대사에서 인용.

To greet the spring on Cheongsando,

a small island off Korea's southern coast,

one must set out early.

The ferry from Wando Port

runs only a few times a day.[16]

Riding a rented electric bicycle around the island,

I keep turning my head.

At a winding corner, I seem to hear Songwha's *Jindo Arirang;*

from the white house on the hill, Jaeha's piano;

and beyond the stone walls, in the canola fields,

the laughter of Inha and Dalpo.[17]

The stirring scenery brings a sudden longing.

They say, if you yearn,

if you truly long,

you are sure to meet again.[18]

Ah... had my mom,

born on an island herself,

ever come to Cheongsando?

Had she ever seen

such radiant, golden spring?

Why is it, I wonder,

that here on Cheongsando

my mother returns so vividly to my heart?

Back then, I was too young.

---

16 Cheongsando(청산도), in Wando County, Jeollanam-do, is Korea's first designated "Slow City."

17 Songhwa: singer in the film *Seopyeonje (1993)*, filmed on Cheongsando.
Jaeha: pianist in the drama *Spring Waltz (2006)*, set and filmed here.
Inha and Dalpo: protagonists in the drama *Pinocchio (2014)*, also filmed on the island.

18 "If you yearn, if you truly long, you are sure to meet again" — from a dialogue between Jaeha and Eunhyeong in *Spring Waltz*.

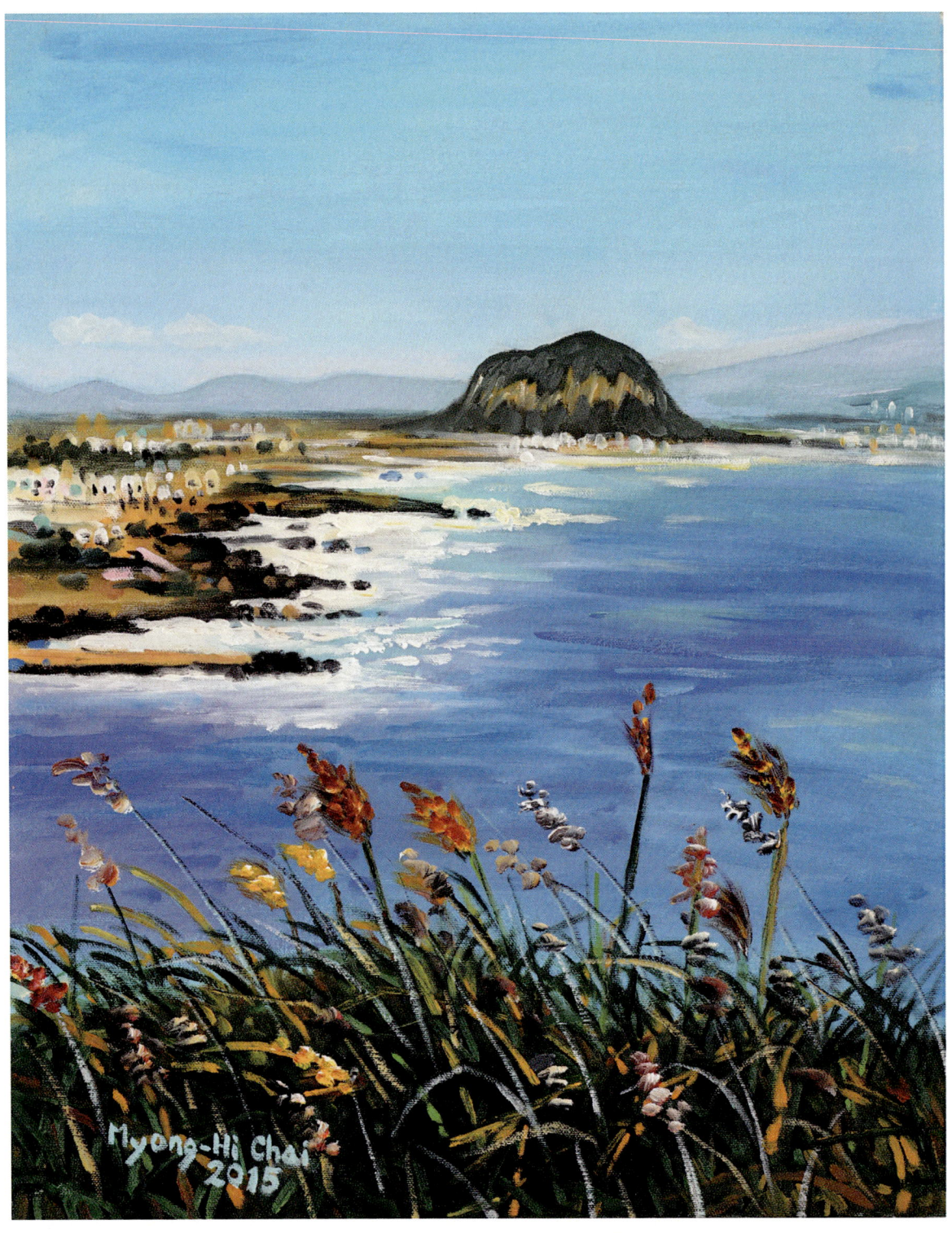

《제주 송악산에서 본 산방산》 *Sanbangsan Seen from Songaksan, Jeju*
Oil on canvas, P10(53 × 40.9㎝), 2015

가을에는
바람의 섬, 제주를 찾아야 한다.

그해 가을,
어느 바람 부는 날
우리는 제주 절울이오름에 올랐다.[19]

상쾌한 바닷바람에 춤추던 갈대,
푸른 물결 위를 쉼 없이 달려오던 하얀
옷의 파도,
옹기종기 모여 앉은 집들,
한라산 품에 안긴 산방산.[20]

가을이 오면,
제주의 오름에 올라야 한다.

In autumn,
one must go to Jeju, the island of wind.[21]

One breezy day that autumn,
we stood atop Jeolwoolioreum in Jeju.[22]

The reeds danced in the fresh sea breeze,
the white-capped waves raced endlessly
across the blue water,
the little houses huddled close together,
and Sanbangsan rested in the embrace
of Hallasan—
the scene was unforgettable.[23]

When autumn comes,
we must walk Jeju's *oreum*s.

---

[19] 절울이오름: 제주 서귀포시에 있는 완만한 능선의 화산체로, '송악산'의 다른 이름.
오름: 작은 화산체를 가리키는 제주 방언.

[20] 산방산: 한라산 자락에 있는 돔 모양의 용암돔 (volcanic dome)으로, 송악산에서 멀리 바라보인다.

---

[21] Jeju: Korea's largest island and a UNESCO World Natural Heritage Site.

[22] Jeolwoolioreum: another name for Songaksan, a low volcanic hill in Seogwipo, Jeju.
Oreum is a Jeju dialect for a small volcanic cone.

[23] Sanbangsan: a dome-shaped lava mountain at the foot of Mt. Hallasan, visible from Songaksan. Hallasan, at 1,950 m, is the highest mountain in South Korea.

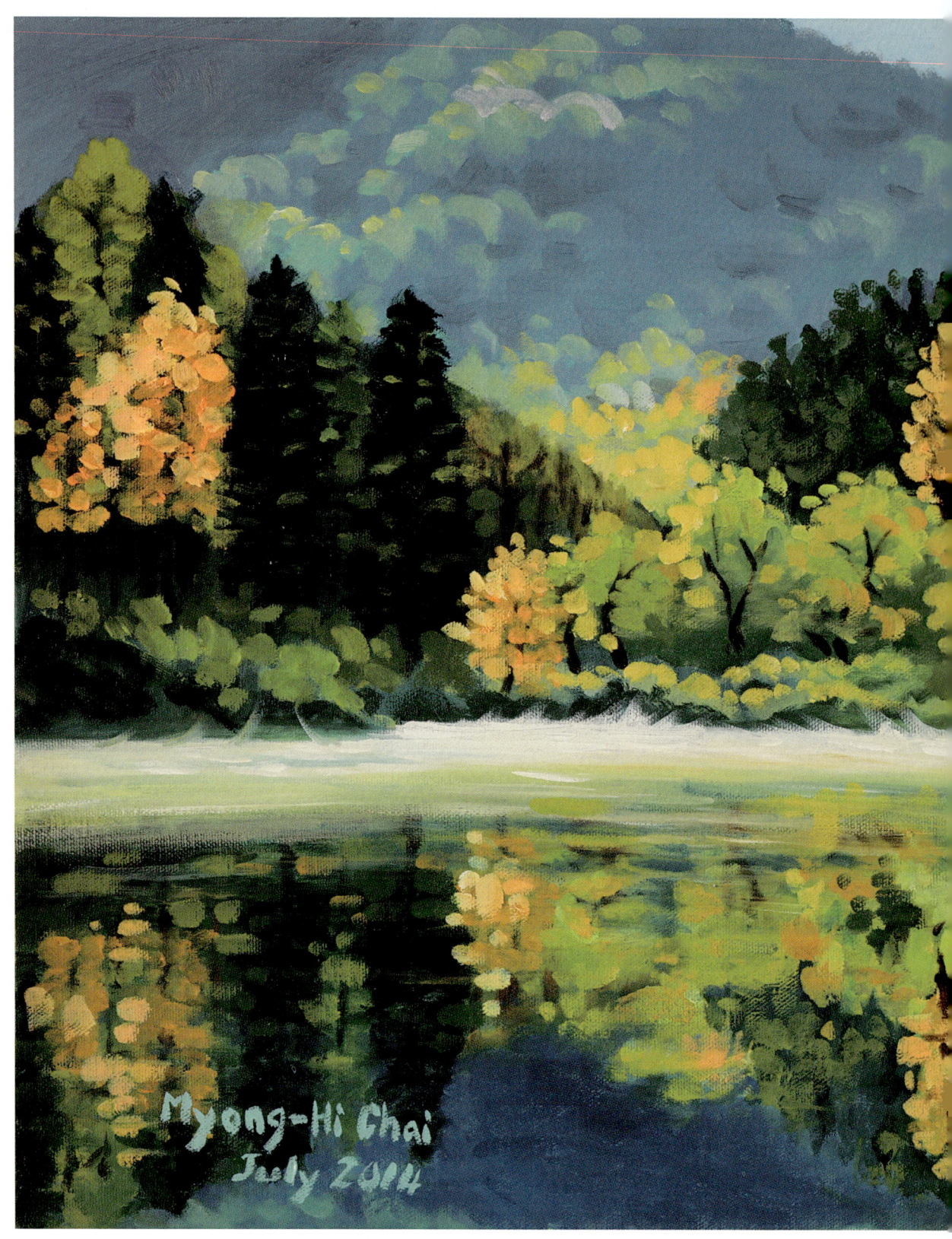

Myong-Hi Chai
July 2014

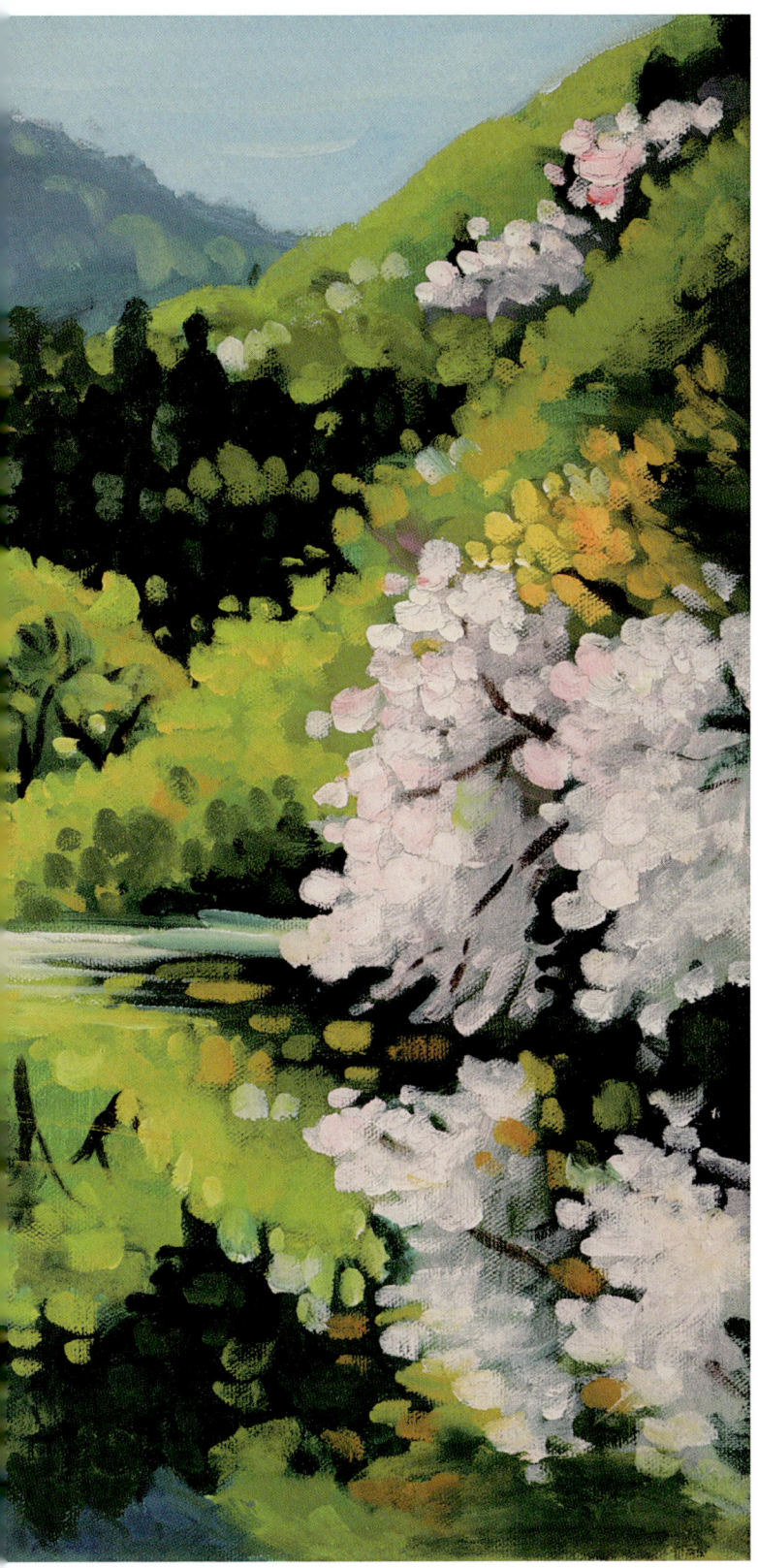

《화순 세량지》 *Seryangji Reservoir in Hwasun*
Oil on canvas, P10(40.9 × 53㎝), 2014

화순 세량지
맑은 호수 위로
풍경이 거꾸로 내려앉는다.

새벽 물안개가 피어오를 때면
마음마저 씻기는 듯하다.

이렇게 가까운 곳에
이런 풍경이 있다는 것,
참 감사한 일이다.

내 마음도 이렇게 비춰주는 곳이 있다면,
돌아보며 후회할 일도
조금은 줄어들 텐데.

Over the clear waters of Seryangji in Hwasun[24],
the landscape is mirrored upside down.

When the morning mist rises
over the mirrored surface,
even the soul feels cleansed.

To have such a place so near—
what a blessing it is.

If only there were a place
that could reflect my heart this clearly,
I might have fewer regrets when looking back.

---

24 Hwasun: a county in Jeollanam-do, Korea, noted for its tranquil scenery and rich cultural heritage.

《소망》 *Wish*
Oil on canvas, P10(40.9 × 53㎝), 2021

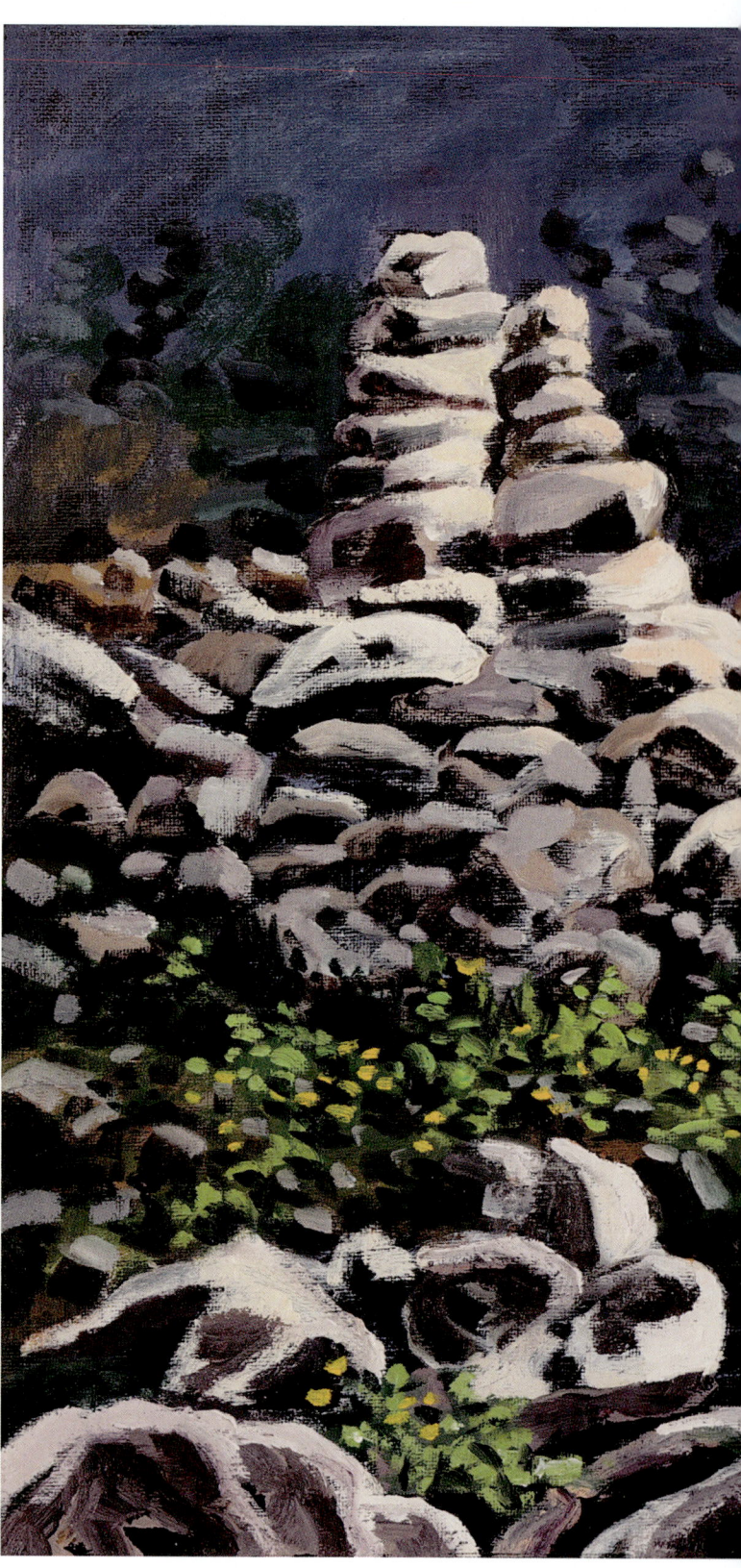

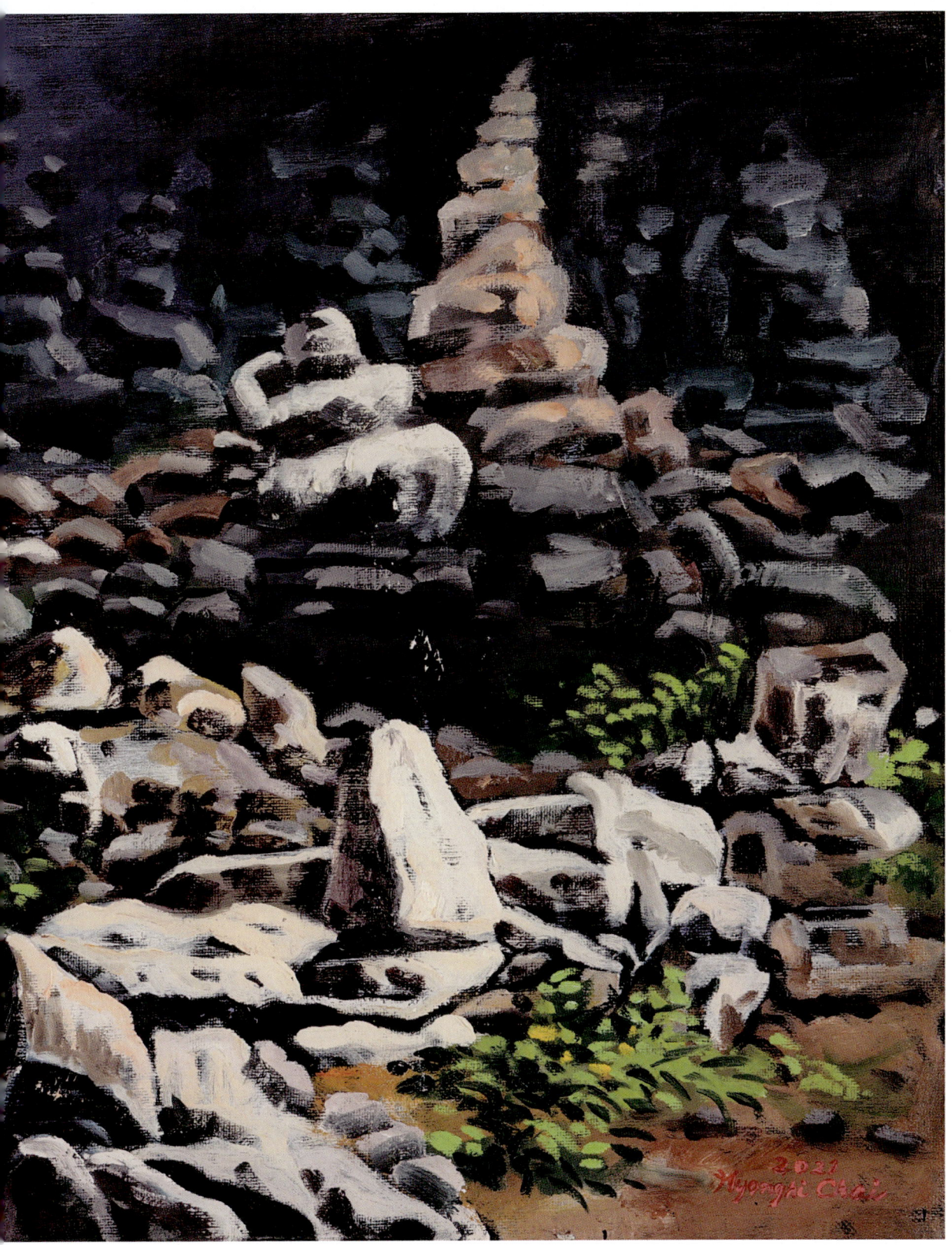

순창 강천사 들어가는 길,
한 모퉁이에서
크고 작은 돌탑들이
방문객을 맞이한다.

돌무더기 속 돌탑엔
가족의 건강과
자녀의 순탄한 앞날을
비는 부모의 마음이
차곡차곡 쌓여 있다.

다른 이의 소망 위에
나의 기도도 하나
조심스레 올려놓는다.

세월의 풍파에
돌탑이 언젠가 무너질지라도,
마음속 소망의 탑은
굳건히 서 있으리라.

Along the path to Gangcheonsa Temple in Sunchang,

large and small stone cairns

stand to greet each passerby.

Amid piles of stones,

parents' prayers—

for their family's health,

for their children's bright path ahead—

are laid carefully, stone by stone.

Upon the wishes left by others,

I gently place

my own.

Though the cairn may collapse

in the wind of time,

the tower of hope within the heart

will stand firm.

아들의 졸업식 날,
앞날이 평탄하길 바라며
스타치스 한 다발을 샀다.

화려한 보랏빛과
차분한 블루 톤으로
기도하듯 그 꽃을 그렸다.

아들아,
네 앞날을 축복한다!

On my son's graduation day,
I bought a bouquet of statice,
wishing him a smooth journey ahead.

In vivid violet and calm blue,
I painted the flowers,
as though in prayer.

My son,
may your future be blessed.

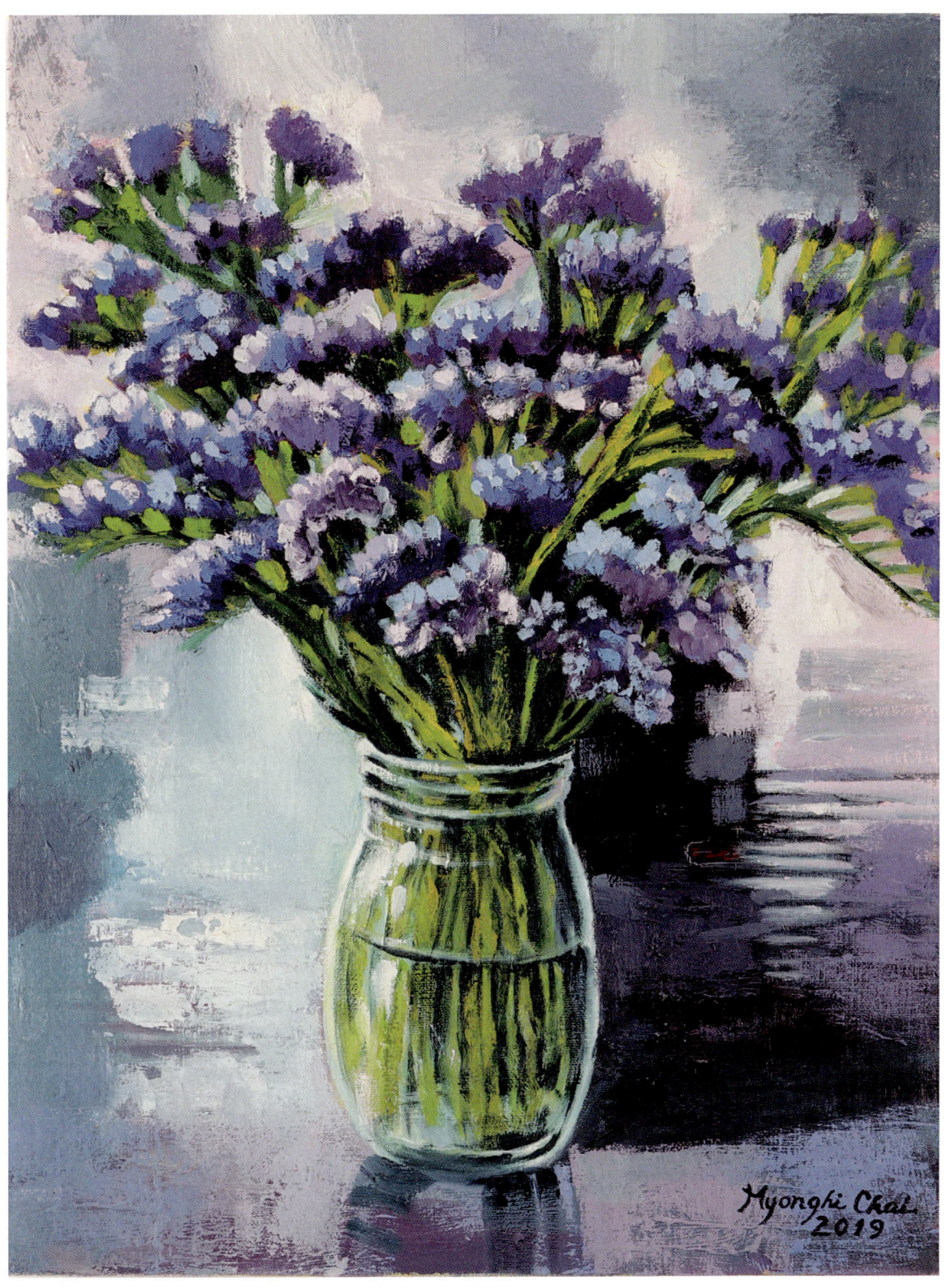

《당신을 축복합니다!》 *God Bless You!*
Oil on canvas, P8 (45.5 × 33.4㎝), 2019

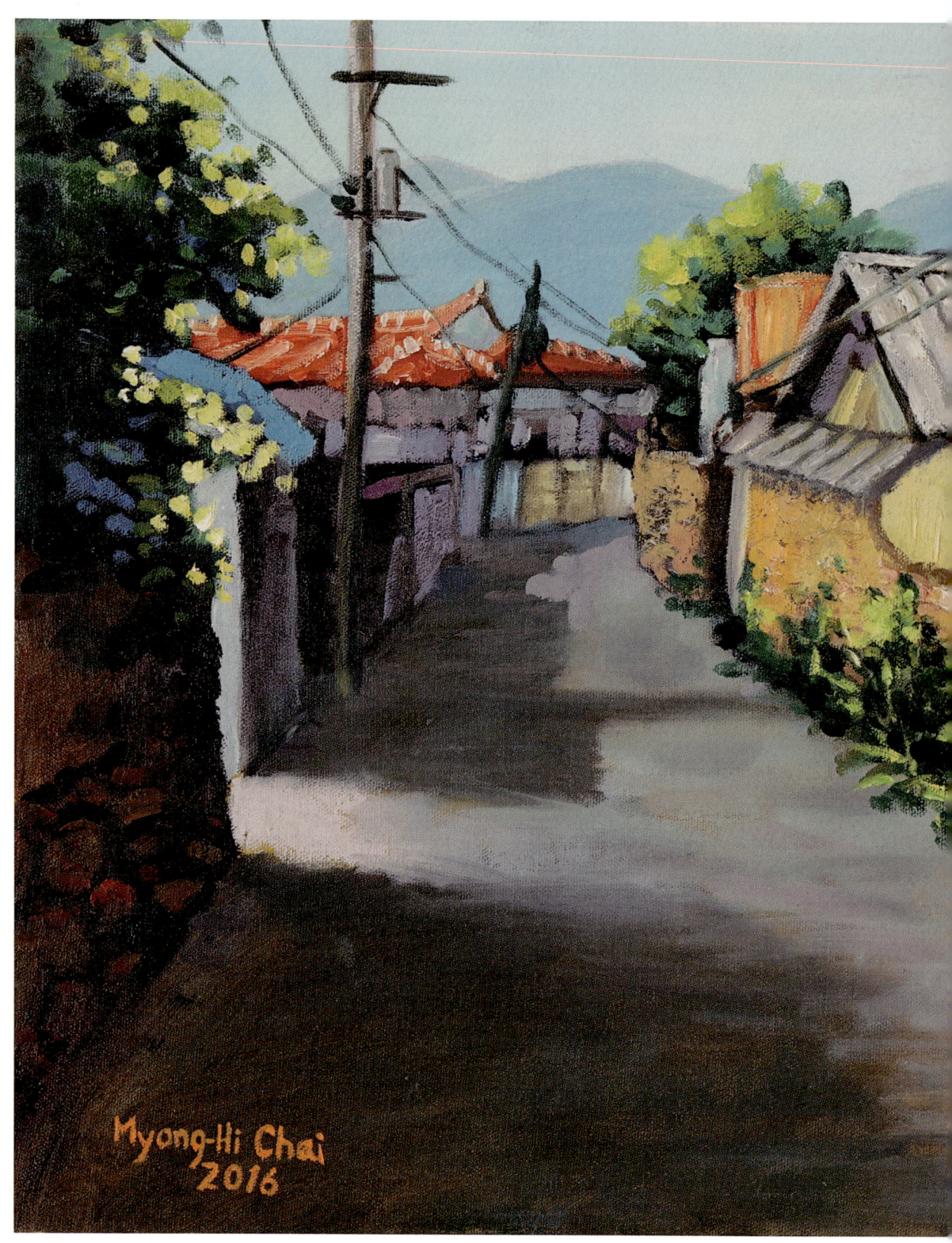

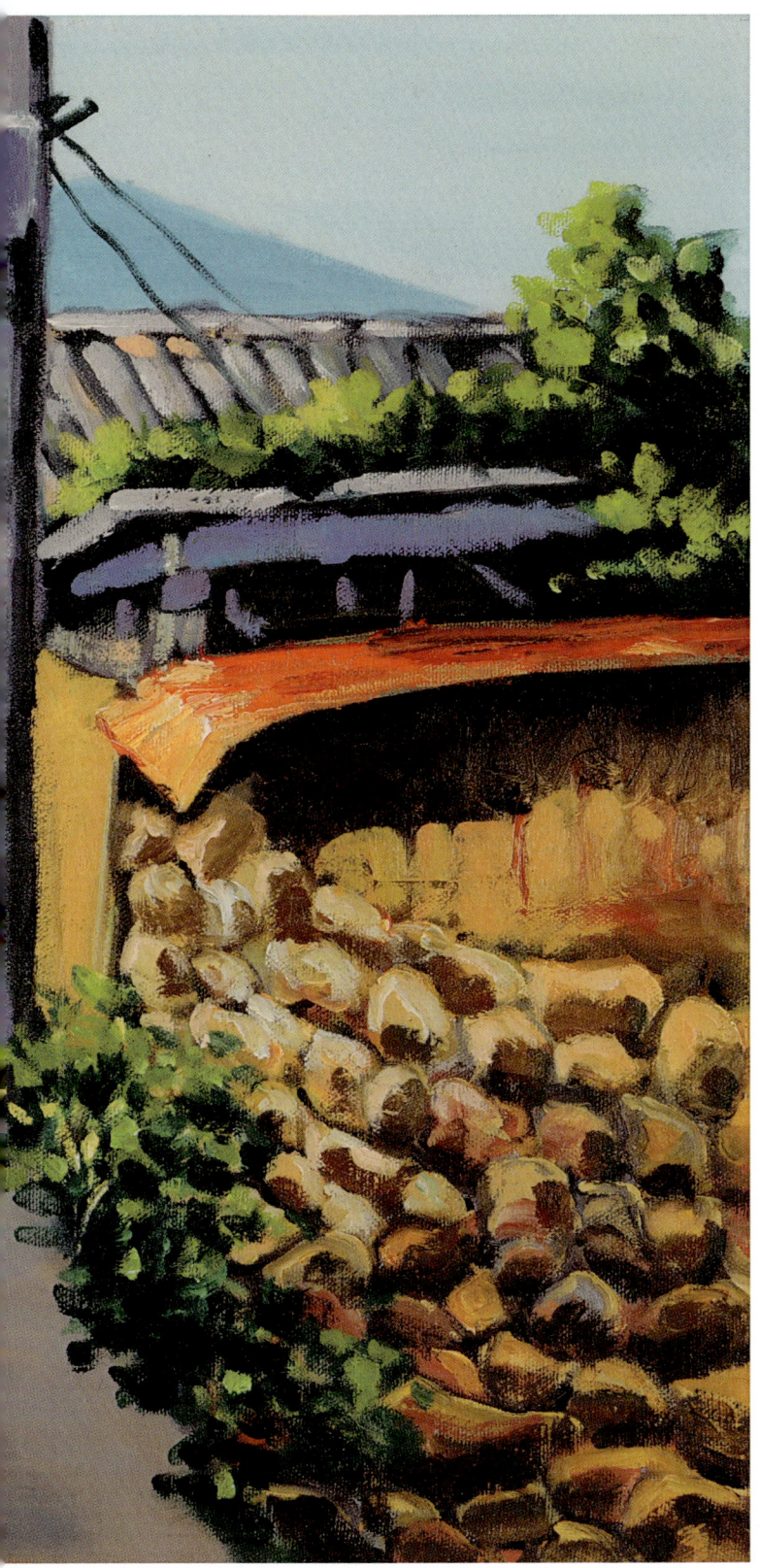

《집으로 가는 길》 *The Road Home*
Oil on canvas, P10(40.9 × 53㎝), 2016

어느 노래 가사처럼,
거친 세상에 홀로 내팽개쳐지지 않고,
지친 하루살이와 고된 살아남기가
무의미한 일이 아닌 것은,[25]

언제나 우리 곁을 지켜주는
사랑하는 이들이 머무는
집이 있기 때문 아닐까.

부디,
모두의 집으로 돌아가는 길이
늘 따뜻하고 행복하기를.

---

25   이적의 「다행이다」에 나오는 가사를 일부 인용.

Just like a line from a song,

we are not left alone to face the rough world.

The weary days,

the struggle simply to keep going—

they are not in vain,[26]

because there is a home

where our loved ones wait for us,

always.

May the road home

always be warm and joyful

for everyone.

26   From the lyrics of Lee Juck's song *"Da-haeng-i-da"("It's Fortunate")*.

《불매향不賣香》 *Never Sells Its Fragrance*
Oil on canvas, P10(40.9 × 53㎝), 2016

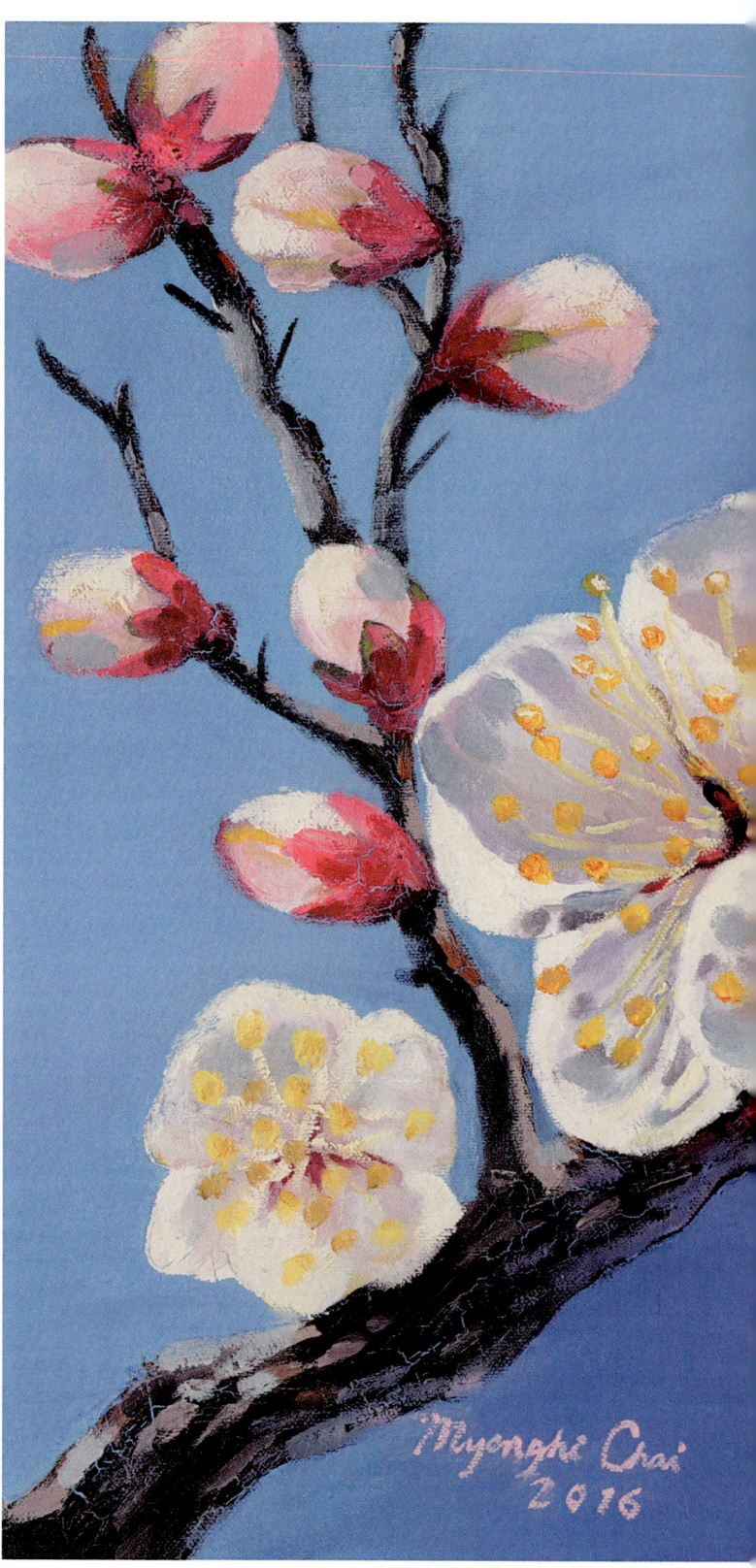

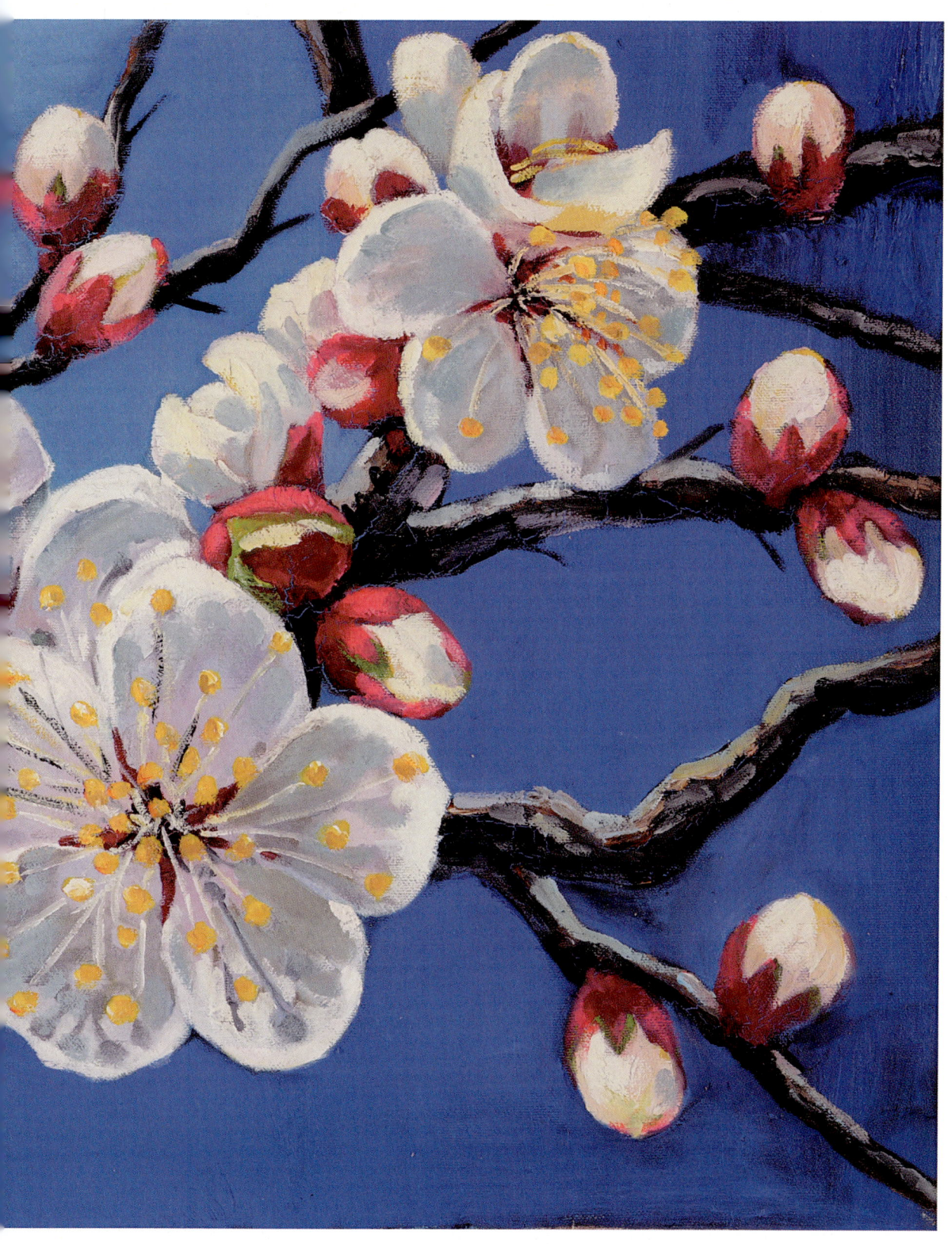

매일생한불매향
梅一生寒不賣香[27]

매화는
일생을 추위에 떨지언정
그 향기를 팔지 않는다.

---

27 梅一生寒不賣香: 조선 중기의 문장가 신흠(申欽, 1566-1628)의 시구로 전해지지만, 작자 미상설도 있다. 선비의 절개를 찬미하는 말로, 오늘날에도 자신의 신념을 지키고자 할 때 자주 인용된다.

The plum blossom—

though it endures the cold for a lifetime,

never sells its fragrance.[28]

---

28 梅一生寒不賣香(mae-ilsaeng-han-bul-mae-hyang): Commonly attributed to Shin Heum(1566-1628) a renowned writer and statesman of the mid-Joseon period, though some sources list the author as unknown. Celebrated as a symbol of steadfast integrity, the phrase is often quoted today by those who seek to remain true to their convictions.

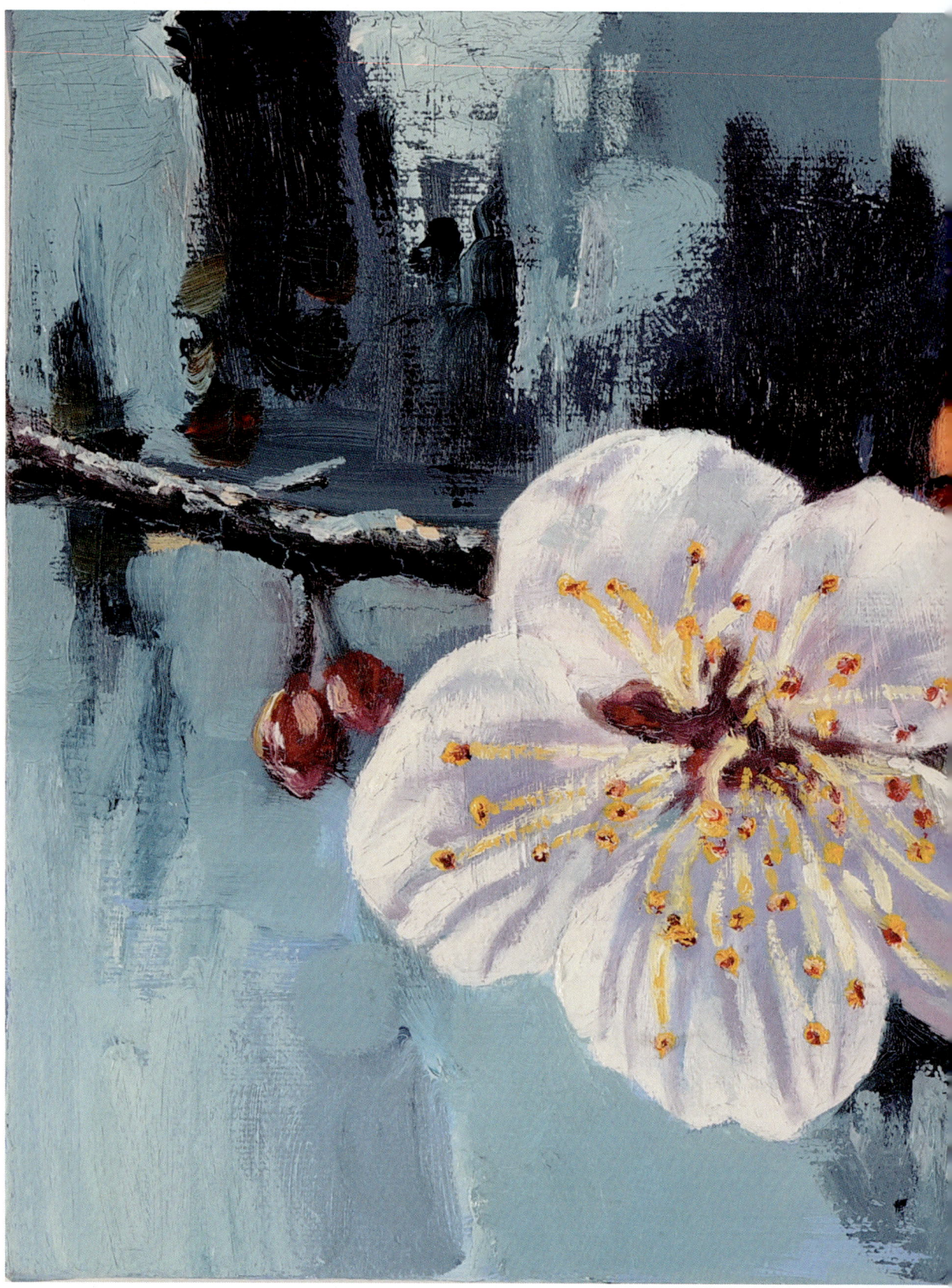

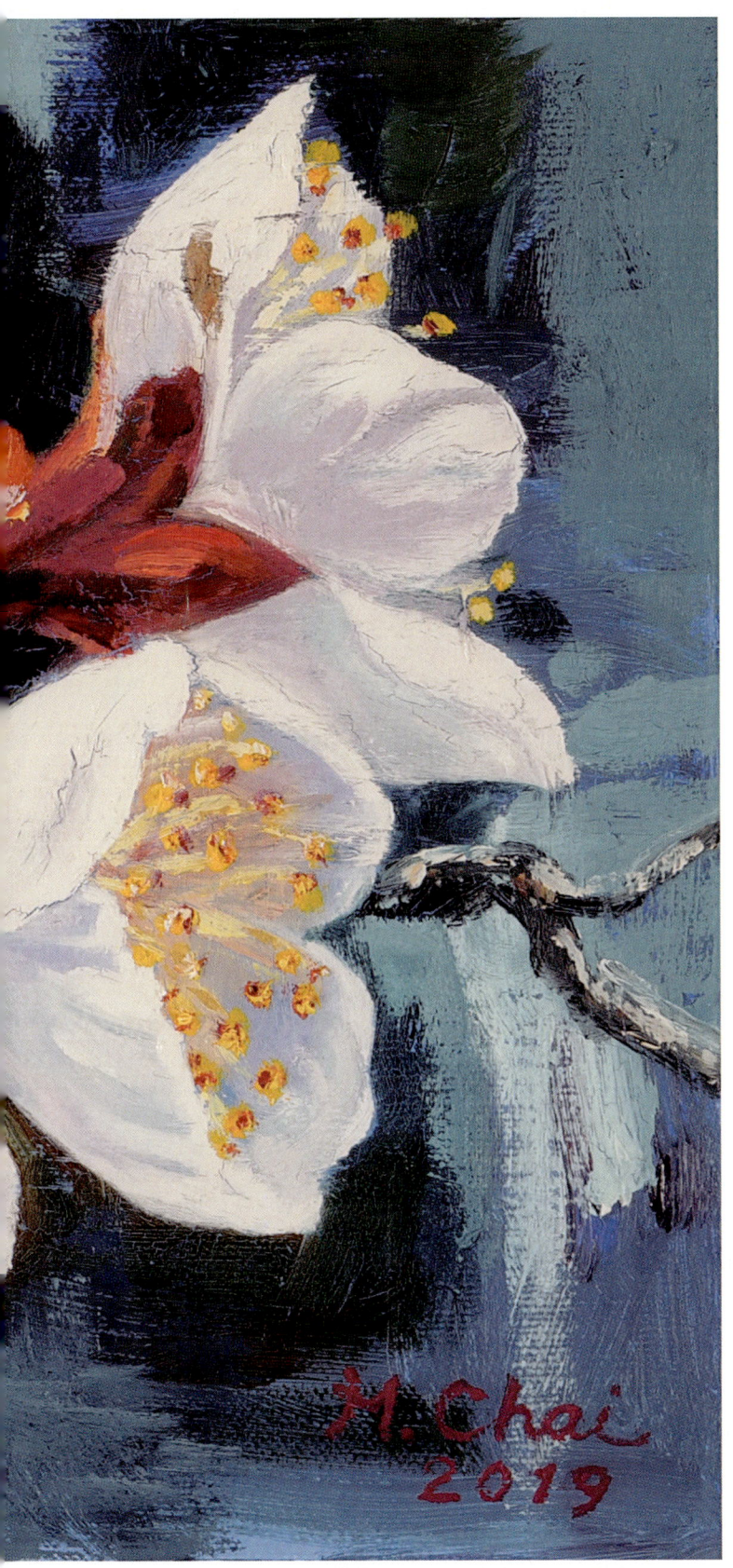

《불매향不賣香 II》 *Never Sells Its Fragrance II*
Oil on canvas, F3(22 × 27.3㎝), 2019

201

매화는
평생을 추위 속에 살아도,
향기를 팔아 안락을 사려 하지 않는다.

The plum blossom,

even as she lives her whole life in the cold,

never barters her scent for comfort.

이렇게 꼿꼿한 매화처럼
지조를 품은 여인이 되는 것은
한낱 꿈인가.

그래도,
꿈꾸어봄 직하지 않은가.

Like the steadfast plum blossom,
to be a woman who holds fast to her principles
may be nothing more than a dream.

And yet,
isn't it a dream worth dreaming.

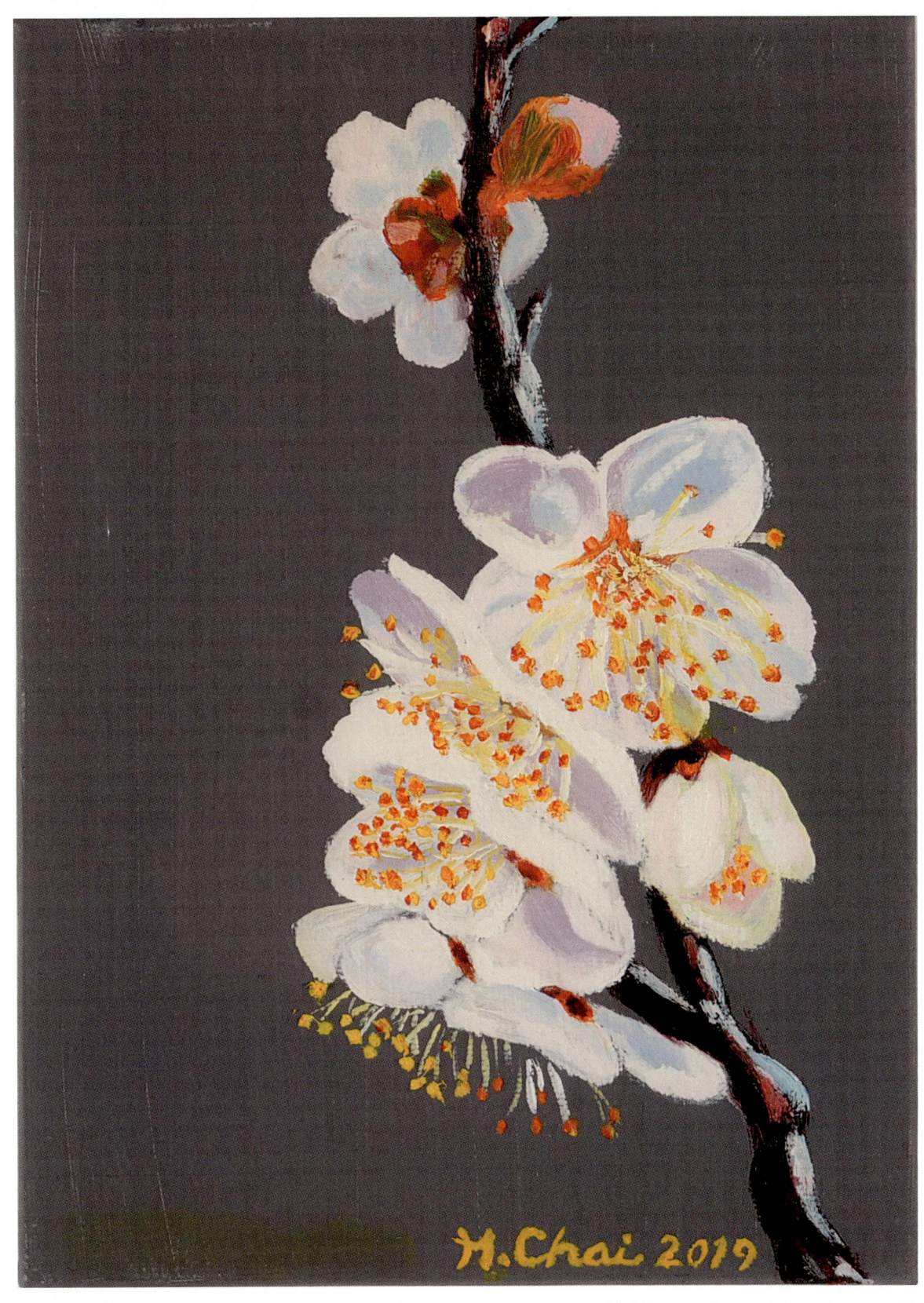

《불매향不賣香 III》 *Never Sells Its Fragrance III*
Oil on canvas, F1(22.7 × 15.8㎝), 2019

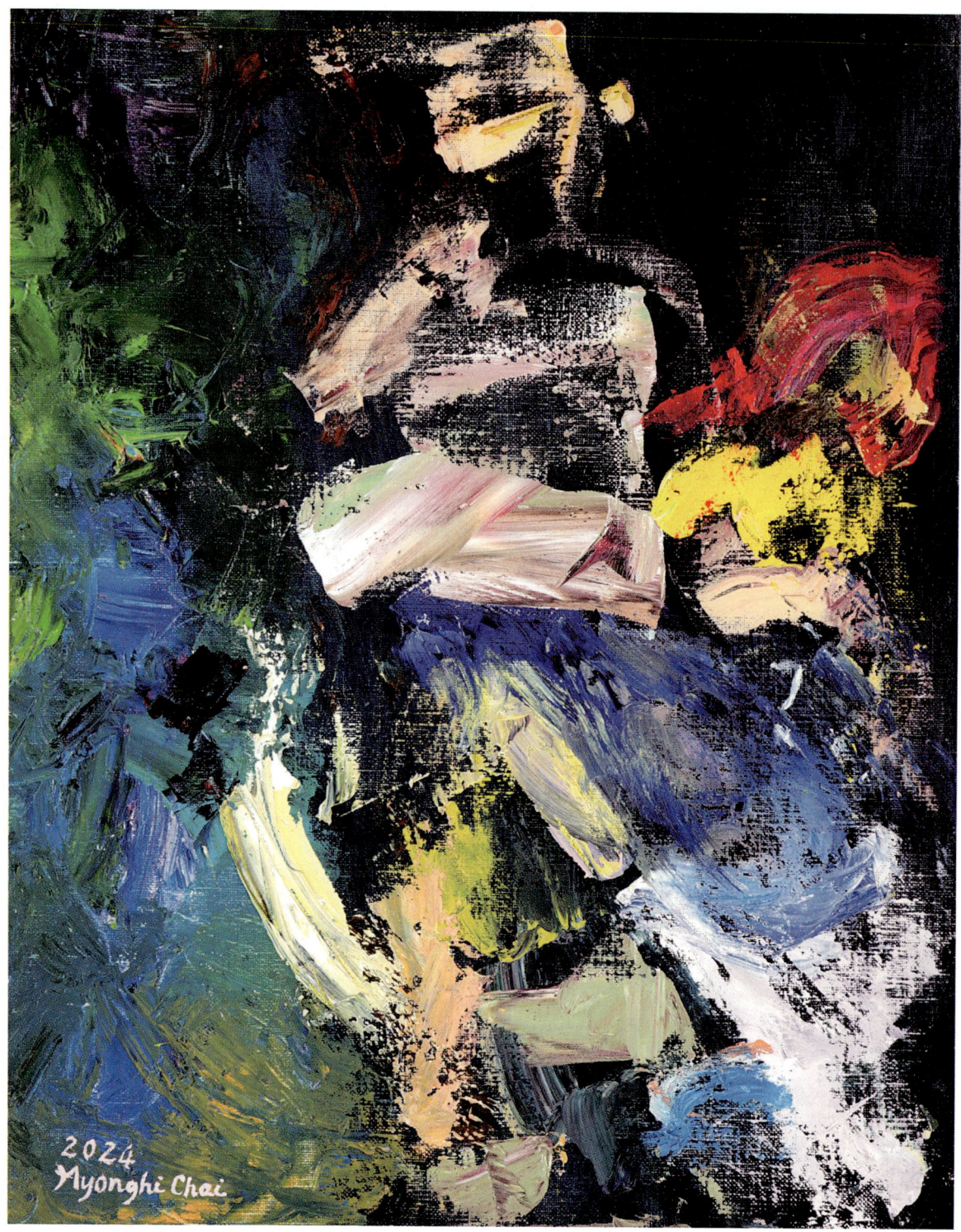

《자유》 *Freedom*
Oil on canvas, P10(53 × 40.9㎝), 2024

야호! 끝냈다!
아니, 이제
그냥 덮어두자.

그래, 이만하면 충분하다.

더는 보지 않겠다.
더 보면
부끄러워질 테니까.

이제,
나는 자유다!

Yay! I've finished it!
Or maybe—
I will just call it done.

Yes,
this is enough.

I won't look again.
If I read it once more,
I might only blush.

Now—
I am free!

꿈꿔온 삶을 살아라

- 헨리 데이비드 소로

참 오랜 시간 한 길만 걸어왔다. 영어영문학을 전공하며 교수의 길을 꿈꾸었고, 마침내 그 꿈을 이루었다. 언어학자로서 규칙을 탐구하고 논리로 가르쳤다. 그래서인지 늘 머리가 앞서고, 가슴이 뒤따랐다.

그러던 어느 날, 우연히 미술의 세계에 발을 들였다. 유화와 연필화, 한국화, 팝아트. 친구 여럿과 함께 한 덕분에 10년이 넘는 시간 동안 이어올 수 있었는지 모른다.

원하는 대로 그림이 그려지지 않아 답답해할 때도 많았지만, 아마추어 화가라고 해서 가볍게 그릴 수는 없었다. 그림은 가슴으로 그려야 하는데, 머리로 그리려는 습관 탓에 지금도 분투 중이다.

돌아보면, 어릴 적부터 그림을 좋아했다. 초등학교 시절 미술대회에 참가해 상을 곧잘 받았고, 중학교 때는 미술부 활동을 했다. 고등학교에서도 미술부에 들어갔지만 "미대에 갈 것이 아니라면 입시 공부나 해라"는 말을 듣고 쫓겨나기도 했다. 그땐 그랬다.

이후 잊고 있었던, 아니 잊고 있었다고 생각했던 그림은 늘 내 곁에 있었다. 일기장과 수첩의 여백에 주변 사물을 스케치했고, 편지지에는 어김없이 튤립과 수선화를 그리거나 난을 치곤 했다. 내 편지를 받아 본 친구들은 기억할 것이다.

그동안 틈틈이 그린 유화 작품들을 모아 이제 한 권의 책으로 엮게 되었다. 처음에는 개인전을 위한 포트폴리오로 시작했는데, 어느새 여기까지 오게 되었다.

작업을 시작하고 나니 부끄러움도 있었지만, 끝내 포기하지 않았다. 이제 영어학자이자 교수로서의 삶을 마무리하며, 그림을 그리는 사람으로서의 새로운 시작을 알리고 싶어서.

이 과정에 많은 분들이 도움을 주셨다. 10여 년 동안 한결같이 유화를 지도해 주신 강남구 화백님, 흔쾌히 국문 원고를 읽고 조언해 주신 김성식 교수님, 멀리 캐나다에서 영문을 꼼꼼히 살펴준 친구 박혜원 목사, 그리고 작업에 몰두한 시간을 묵묵히 지지해 준 남편 류봉진에게 깊이 감사드린다.

비록 부족하지만 이 책이 독자 여러분께 작은 울림이 되기를 소망한다. 부디, "그림 그리는 영어 교수"의 여정을 따뜻하게 응원해 주시길 바란다.

Live the Life You've Imagined

- Henry David Thoreau

For much of my life, I walked a single path. I studied English language and literature, dreamed of becoming a professor, and fulfilled that dream. As a linguist, I sought patterns, taught with logic and reason. Perhaps that is why my mind always led, and my heart followed.

Then one day, quite unexpectedly, I stepped into the world of art— oil, pencil, traditional Korean, and pop art. What began simply as a way to spend time with a few high school friends has lasted more than a decade.

At times, I grew frustrated with the canvas. Even as an amateur, I could never take the work lightly. Art should follow the heart, but my mind often takes the lead—and I still struggle.

Looking back, I realize that I have always loved to draw. In elementary school, I entered art competitions and often won awards. In middle school, I joined the art club; in high school, I joined again— only to be dismissed with the words, "If you're not going to art school, you should focus on your studies." That was how it was back then.

Afterward, my art seemed forgotten. Yet in truth, it never left me. In the margins of diaries, notebooks, and scraps of paper, I would sketch whatever was near at hand. On letters, I drew tulips, daffodils, or orchids. My friends who received them will remember.

Now I have gathered those oil paintings into this book. It began as a portfolio for my first solo exhibition, and somehow it grew into this.

There were moments when I felt unsure—whether my simple paintings deserved to be shared in a book. Yet I never gave up. This book marks both the closing of my life as a scholar and the first step into life as a person who paints.

I owe heartfelt thanks to those who have supported me through this journey—Artist Namgu Kang, who has faithfully guided my oil painting for over a decade; Professor Sungsik Kim, who generously read the Korean manuscript and offered valuable advice; my friend, Pastor Hyewon Park, who carefully reviewed the English text all the way from Canada; and my husband, Bongjin Ryu, who quietly supported me through countless hours devoted to my work.

I hope this humble book offers a quiet resonance to its readers. And I ask that you warmly join me in supporting the journey of an "English professor who paints."